TARA
TAYLOR
QUINN

BEHIND
CLOSED
DOORS

MIRA®

ISBN-13: 978-0-7783-2395-2
ISBN-10:   0-7783-2395-1

BEHIND CLOSED DOORS

Copyright © 2007 by Tara Taylor Quinn.

www.MIRABooks.com

Printed in U.S.A.

Dear Reader,

Last fall I introduced you to Janet McNeil and Simon Green—two regular folks who took up the challenge and went the distance in an attempt to bring to justice a white supremacist group that was infiltrating their neighborhood.

Their lives were torn apart by the things they experienced and learned, and now their lives will be forever different. In the end, they saw justice done. But only on a small scale. Bobby Donahue, leader of the (fictional) Ivory Nation, escaped accountability. His organization continues to thrive.

And now we have a victim. Two of them—Laura and Harry Kendall. An ordinary couple in Tucson, Arizona. She's a botanist. He's a history professor at the University of Arizona. And late one night, while they slept behind closed doors, life changed for them. Irrevocably. Forever.

But they didn't die. So they have a choice: either to give in to fear and become paranoid and unhappy, or to fight back. Not only to fight the outside sources of their fears—an invisible, far-reaching and eminently powerful organization—but to fight their inner demons, as well. Either battle could destroy them.

Laura and Harry didn't ask for what happened to them. Nor could they prevent it. They are middle-class people doing their best to be good to those around them, to love each other, and have a family. They are you and me. And then they aren't...

This is their story.

Tara Taylor Quinn

P.S. I love getting feedback from those who share my books. You can reach me at P.O. Box 13584, Mesa, Arizona 85216 or at www.tarataylorquinn.com.

For all women who have suffered abuse, physical or emotional. May we always find something to hope for, love in our hearts and the strength to fight back.

1

The red LED lights swam, cleared, blurred again. Every muscle tense, Harry lay in bed, listening. Something had awakened him. And it wasn't Laura. Her hand was still half clutched in his under the covers, and she slept on, despite whatever had interrupted his own sleep.

2:04. There it was again. A sort of swishing. Not a footstep. But movement. He recognized it immediately as the sound that had just jerked him abruptly out of a dream—a dream about his botanist wife snipping bits of cactus from a garden that had appeared in the middle of their bedroom…

The sound came again. Was it closer? Harry couldn't tell. And he couldn't identify it. It was like moving air. Not from the vent in the ceiling, but lower. Thinking of the unloaded pistol—inheritance from his uncle—in the back of his closet, Harry slid his hand from Laura's, moving so slowly he almost wasn't.

He wanted to believe he was imagining things, but Harry wasn't prone to an overactive imagination. Someone…or something…was in their house.

Without disturbing Laura, he slipped one bare leg out of the covers. Then the second…

He froze. There was a shadow on Laura's side of the bed, the shape of a man bending down, reaching toward her. Harry's arms shot out to grab the bastard around the neck but he was caught from behind. He bellowed in pain and rage, the sound immediately muffled by a leather-gloved hand against his mouth.

His wife's eyes opened—instantly wide—staring at him in the darkness. He read the fear there, the desperate plea for him to do something. And saw a man gag her.

Infused with frantic strength, Harry alternately yanked his arms, trying to free them from his captor's hold, and hit back against him. A hand grabbed the waistband of his briefs and yanked him backward. He bit and tasted leather, bit again and had a piece of leather on his tongue. He couldn't spit it out. Couldn't swallow.

"Do not move and you won't be injured."

Laura was hauled up, the strap of her pink gown falling down one shoulder. She tried to right it but before she could, her hands were pulled forcibly behind her and restrained. Her whimper sent him over the bounds of sanity.

Harry's foot connected with flesh and bone. His nails scraped leather and denim. The elbow punch he landed resulted in a loud smack in the too-quiet room.

And then, his arms wrenched behind his back, pulling the left one half out of its socket, he felt something thin and hard being twisted around his wrists, cutting into his flesh.

"Unless you want more than a dislocated AC, you'll keep still," the deep voice muttered. He could hear it clearly despite Laura's high, terrified moans.

Tears streamed down her face.

Shoving against his captor with both legs, Harry broke free, kicked again and again, landing some blows. The shadow was doing something to Laura at the bedpost and Harry lashed out like a madman, needing to annihilate his own unseen force so he could get to her.

He couldn't.

Laura's captor joined Harry's and just as Harry realized his wife had been tied to the bedpost, he was attacked by two male bodies at once. He kicked. He bit. He pummeled with the hands tied behind his back, hardly aware of the pain that shot through his shoulder with every wrench. The pain was good; it kept him alive and feeling, aware.

Harry was strong, athletic—a black man who knew how to defend himself—but he was no street fighter.

He landed a kick to one guy's head. The guy fell. And the other was there, smashing his fist into the right side of Harry's face. Stars swam before his eyes at the sudden, excruciating pain in his nose. The fallen man got up. Swung. A crack reverberated inside Harry's head. A second punch made it hard to think. Only the staccato whimpers of his wife's fear kept him conscious. Fighting.

They dragged the antique desk chair to his side of the bed. Harry fought with everything he had, but the two men were bigger, stronger—and less injured. They grabbed his shoulders, numbing his left arm. He felt the edge of the hard wooden chair shove into the backs of his knees.

He continued to fight, to kick and thrash and jerk his body, in spite of the rope securing his hips and then his ankles to the chair. The grunts rising from his throat were unrecognizable—the sounds of a man enduring a nightmare worse than hell.

And knowing it was going to get worse.

Thursday, June 7, 2007. 2:09 a.m.
Flagstaff, Arizona

Luke's cries woke him. Jumping out of bed, Bobby Donahue wiped sleep from his eyes and hurried in to check on his three-year-old son.

"What's up, buddy?" he called as he entered the room lit by the soft glow of the angel night-light above the dresser. He instantly swept the space with sharp, alert eyes. Finding it empty, he switched from automatic defensive mode to compassion for his upset son.

"No boogy man, here, pal," he said, reaching the boy.

Luke stood at the bars of the crib he still slept in, arms outstretched, and Bobby scooped him up.

"You're soaked," he said, holding the toddler against him anyway. "Is that what woke you?"

"Mama!" Luke's wail pierced Bobby's emotions more than his eardrums.

"I know, pal. I miss Mama, too."

Holding the boy until his sobs subsided to hiccups, Bobby drew in the child's warmth. His nearness.

Luke and the world his son would inhabit in the

future were Bobby's reason for being. His son, and all the other pure children. Every breath he took, every decision he made, was for the children of God.

"Your mama loved watching Blue with you, did you know that?"

Changing the diaper the boy wore only at night now and the damp summer-weight pajamas, Bobby snapped Blue's Clues bottoms into a matching short-sleeved top.

"Can you remember how she used to scrunch up her nose just like him?"

Luke shook his head, reaching out to Bobby again.

Taking his son in his arms, Bobby headed back toward the crib, but when the boy's arms clasped his neck, he chose the rocker Amanda had loved.

It had been a year since the car accident from which Amanda—Luke's mother, the love of Bobby's life—had disappeared. A year of grieving, of missing her, of not knowing whether she was dead or alive, but assuming the worst. A year to recover.

Luke still had dreams about her.

And Bobby continued to draw strength from the living warmth of their son. He liked to believe Amanda remained with them. She'd been his angel on earth, and it wasn't such a far cry to think that she was watching over them from the heavenly place she inhabited now.

He rocked Luke for the few minutes it took to get the little boy back to sleep and then, with a gentle kiss on his son's forehead, he laid him in his crib again, checking the monitor to make sure he'd hear any sounds coming from the boy's room during the rest of the night.

Amanda had insisted on the monitor when Luke was

born. And now it gave Bobby great security. He'd die if he lost Luke, too.

Back in his room, Bobby sat propped against the pillows, staring out into the darkness. Some days he was too busy, too filled with the intensity of his work, to think about Amanda much. But on nights like this, the pain of her loss was almost debilitating.

Doing what he'd learned to do at a very young age, Bobby endured as much of the pain as he could, then traveled to other places in his mind, focused on things that felt good. Positive things.

He immediately thought of Tony Littleton. His young college-age friend, a new convert the year before, had left his mother's home the previous summer and moved in with Bobby, helping him care for Luke. He'd also proven to be a loyal and trusted brother of the Ivory Nation.

Tony was in Tucson, at the University of Arizona, where he was being mentored by an influential Ivory Nation brother and studying political science at Bobby's behest, but he still made it home most weekends. Which meant he'd be there by dinnertime the following day.

Bobby couldn't wait that long.

Picking up the phone, he dialed Tony's cell, knowing the boy slept with it right beside him for occasions like this. A true and loyal brother.

The phone rang. And rang. And rang again. Where the hell was Tony at 2:36 in the morning?

For a moment, as Tony's voice mail picked up, Bobby felt the blood drain from his face. *Another car accident.* Could God be so cruel?

And then a conversation he'd had with Tony the weekend before sprang to mind and Bobby smiled. There was a girl on campus Tony had the hots for. A beautiful white daughter of wealthy Republican parents. Replaying the advice he'd given his dedicated recruit, Bobby had no doubt where Tony was tonight.

And he looked forward to the next evening, after Luke was down for the night, when he'd hear all the details.

Please God, let a baby be made tonight. A white baby boy…

Thursday, June 7, 2:37 a.m.
Tucson, Arizona

Jerking his head against the gloved hand at his neck and the other buried in his hair, Harry closed his eyes. They could force him to sit there, to hear, to face the bed where his shy, beautiful wife lay, her gown up around her ribs, but they couldn't force him to watch.

Laura's muffled shriek tore through him and his eyes flew open, quickly adjusting to the dark. To the shadows. The man who'd originally captured Harry was between his wife's knees, pumping frantically in and out. The man's hands were in Laura's long blond hair.

Her face was turned away.

Stay sane, he told himself. Over and over.

Get evidence.

He tried to focus his mind in a way that could help him. But his head hurt so much he couldn't think straight, his entire being consumed by a rage he couldn't control.

There were two dark, mostly indistinguishable

hooded shapes. One with his wife. The other, shorter one, stood behind him, hands hotly gripping the sides of Harry's face.

The man raping Laura was white. His penis was the only flesh showing but even in the shadows, Harry could tell. He couldn't get beyond the vision of what it was doing to his wife.

He hollered, in spite of the gag in his mouth, needing Laura to know he was there, alive, loving her.

With another jerk of his head, he managed to get a gloved finger in his mouth, bit hard. The man behind him didn't even seem to notice.

His original captor slowed and Harry held his breath.

Please God, let them be done. Take them away from my wife, from my home.

Still inside Laura, the man lifted a hand, slid it beneath her gown and grabbed her breast.

Harry saw her body lurch. Laura's injured cry was the only sound in the room—other than the ugly slamming of the rapist's flesh against hers. Harry watched as the man further exposed his wife's glistening white skin and tears pooled in his eyes.

Trying to swallow, he choked. His jailor's grip didn't loosen.

The man on top of his wife shuddered, jerked a couple of times. There was no huge sigh, no taunts or threats or gloats of victory, no sound at all to accompany the dirty releasing of fluid inside Harry's wife.

Sliding away from Laura, leaving her body exposed to the air-conditioned room, the man zipped his fly and Harry got a smidgeon of satisfaction when the bastard bit back a low curse as, with gloved fingers and haste, he caught his still-engorged penis in the zipper.

Harry hoped he'd drawn blood.

Other than his original grunt of pain, the taller intruder hardly seemed to notice what he'd done to himself as he walked behind Harry, placing his hands, like a vice, at the base of Harry's neck and around his jawbone. He was the stronger of the two. And all business.

And when he felt those hands settle on him, Harry knew they weren't finished yet. Laura legs were crossed, her hands tied at the wrists and fastened to one bedpost. Still facing the wall, she was sobbing. He could see the shudders wracking her slim body.

The smaller man approached her slowly. His hands together at the waistband of his pants, the bastard left no doubt about what he was going to do.

A little more tentative than his partner, he pulled down his zipper, his hard white cock falling out. Laura locked her ankles together when he tried to spread her knees. The man hesitated and from behind him Harry heard a whisper. Something about *white*, he thought, but couldn't be certain, not with the roaring in his ears.

That communication changed the smaller man's bearing completely. With more force than the first intruder had used, he pried Laura's legs apart. Not glancing, even for a second, toward her face, he stared at her crotch, touched it with a gloved hand. He seemed to like it when she jerked back as far as her constraints would allow. And then, without further warning, he plunged inside her.

Afraid he was going to have a heart attack before he could get to his wife, Harry sat there, trying to ignore the heavy pounding in his chest, tasting blood and bile on his tongue. And leather. Holding the piece of glove he'd bitten off inside his mouth, Harry promised himself they'd get these guys.

And make them pay for what they were doing to Laura. Make them pay and pay and pay.

Her left breast was exposed, and he focused on that, so vulnerable and so sweet.

The smaller man drew out once and plunged back in, and Harry prayed that Laura could last through another onslaught. Then, before the thought was even coherent, the man had shuddered. And pulled out.

It occurred to Harry that now was the time to fear most. Either they were going to torture Laura or him or…what? Did he really expect them to let him and Laura live?

For what purpose?

The smaller man softly repeated the words Harry's guard had issued earlier. *White stays with white.* Laura didn't show any reaction, any sense that she'd been spoken to.

But then, Harry could only imagine the hell his wife must be occupying.

Maybe it would be better if the rapists simply killed them. At this point death almost seemed a mercy.

He grunted a fierce warning, because he couldn't sit there complacently, just accepting what the bastards had done. The grip on his neck tightened and Harry's head swam with blackness.

Were they going to finish with Laura after they broke his neck? He *couldn't* leave her to them…

Harry's flesh cooled, the red behind his eyes dissipating, before he realized that the gloved fingers around his neck were gone. He opened his eyes.

He and Laura were alone.

She'd twisted herself around until her lower body was under the covers. Her body shook with sobs.

Tears blinding him, pain in his nose and head and shoulder keeping him sane, Harry threw himself upward and over, hopping the chair inch by inch toward the bedpost where they'd tied Laura's hands. And half an hour later, with his back to the post, using the numbed tips of his fingers, he had unfastened the ropes, sickened by the wetness he felt.

Blood? Or sweat?

Laura grunted, a deep, unfeminine sound that he couldn't decipher. But in seconds she was at his wrists, releasing them. He went for his gag next.

"Oh, my love, I'm so sorry," he said even before he'd untied his feet and faced her.

He assumed she'd untied her own gag as well. He couldn't be sure. She didn't say a word. And didn't stick around for anything else he might have said or done.

Before he'd freed one ankle, Harry heard the bathroom door behind him slam.

And lock.

2

She had to get them off her. Now. Away. Off her. Gone.

Hearing nothing except the internal voice hollering for cleanliness, Laura ripped at her gown. Her arms were weak, her hands shaking so badly she couldn't grip. Pinching the fabric between her fingers she pulled, pinched and pulled, but she couldn't get free.

Get this off me!

Her mind wouldn't quiet yet couldn't help.

With tears running off her chin, she stomped her feet, pulling at the garment. Trying to see, to focus on what she was doing.

Pinch and pull. Pinch and pull. And then, almost miraculously, she managed to get a handful of the thin cotton in one fist.

No! Get off me!

Clutching the material, Laura ripped for all she was worth. And stumbling, falling against the counter, she climbed through the tear she'd made down the middle of the gown, leaving the offensive material in a pool on the floor. The blurred image swam before her, blending with the light beige and blue of the tile. It couldn't stay there.

Couldn't stain her space with its filth. And she couldn't touch it again. The disease it carried would crawl through her fingertips, up her arm and, like a spike of poison, slice straight through her heart.

The fuzziness in her mind, the haze surrounding her, enclosing her, allowed only one image at a time to intrude. And her focus was one-hundred percent on that image. The shard of poison—she could see it piercing her heart. Could feel it.

And do nothing.

Then she recognized the gown again. In a heap on the floor. Inches from her bare feet.

Feet that had touched dirt many times. All those summer days she'd walked barefoot as a kid. As she envisioned her toes sliding toward the gown, picking it up, dropping it in the plastic-lined trash can by the toilet, she thought she could do it.

Laura had no idea how long she stood there before she moved. And when she did, she caught a glimpse of her body in the mirror.

She was completely naked. Exposed. Her breast was discolored.

With a shriek, she grabbed a fistful of toilet paper. Using it, she picked up the gown, tossed it in the toilet, flushed and waited. It didn't go all the way down. She flushed again.

And when the toilet water started to rise, she kicked at the handle behind the seat until it shut off, stopping all flow inside the tank.

The gown floated uselessly in the bowl, half down the drain, captive. It was sewage now.

As quickly as she could, Laura slammed the seat down.

Detective Daniel Boyd stared at his computer screen at the Tucson precinct, thinking about the cinnamon twist Danish he was going to get out of the machine just as soon as he'd finished checking the next hundred names and times and phone numbers on his list. He was looking for a call made from a cell phone in Tucson at the same time as one made from a phone booth in Phoenix. He could be home in bed. His shift had long since ended.

But if he didn't get this done tonight, he'd have to do it in the morning. And the work was boring as hell.

It also was going to point him to Sherry O'Connor's rapist—before that vile excuse for a human being struck again. The Phoenix cops had caught his counterpart that afternoon—a wimp who'd blabbed like a baby as soon as they'd brought him in, telling how the two men who'd never met had called a third, the coordinator, who'd arranged it so they'd both be raping teenage girls at the same time. They'd all connected through the Internet, the third man offering to set up time, place and opportunity in exchange for detailed accounts. It got the rapists off, knowing they were both doing it at once.

Sick. Sick. Sick.

Too bad their Phoenix perp hadn't known the name of his Tucson partner in crime. Phoenix police were still trying to trace the coordinator.

And that was for them to handle. Daniel had Sherry O'Connor's rapist to worry about. As soon as he put a name to the number and time, he'd have his man.

"Go home, Boyd, it's three in the morning."

"Yeah, yeah, yeah." Slouched in his chair, he didn't even look up as Robert Miller, a twenty-year veteran officer and Daniel's partner for the past five, walked by. God knew, Miller wouldn't work an extra minute if it was up to him. They'd just come in from a desert crime scene—a young boy whose body had begun to decompose, but luckily for forensic purposes, hadn't been found by coyotes. From an old break in the jawbone, they'd been able to tentatively identify the remains as those of Matthew Frazier, a twelve-year-old who'd gone missing four months earlier on his way home from school. Just hours afterward, they'd found the boy's pants in some bushes about a mile from his home. They were stained with semen from two different men—which made it Daniel and Robert's case.

He'd track down the bastard responsible for the boy's death now that he had a body—concrete evidence. He couldn't save the life.

But this one…

Even after five years in the sex crimes bureau, Daniel couldn't just go home and rest when he was close to solving a case. Taking a break might mean the difference between a young woman living with strength and confidence—and one constantly having to fight fear and panic to recover the slightest hint of peace.

As always, memories of Sheila, or at least an awareness of those memories, kept him awake and working, even if that meant missing a night's sleep. He rarely thought consciously about his older sister. Couldn't allow himself to get that close. But history had taught him that this near the end of a case, he'd miss his sleep one way or another—either working though the long night hours or lying alone in the dark, remembering.

Daniel's phone rang. There'd been another rape. Grabbing his jacket, Daniel called out to his partner who was just leaving, dispatched a forensics team to the crime scene and headed for the hospital.

"Laura! Honey! Open the door!" Harry rattled the doorknob, overwhelmed by helplessness. "Please?"

Wiping dried blood from his nose, which he figured probably wasn't broken, he stared at the door separating him from his wife. "Laura?"

Getting the same response he'd been receiving for the past five minutes—none—Harry slumped his good shoulder against the frame, his swollen face an inch from the jamb.

He could hear movement, the toilet flushing, sniffling.

"Honey?" Shaking with the need to get to her, Harry tried not to feel the throbbing in his face and head.

"Laura? Don't shower. We have to get you to a doctor, baby."

Should he storm the door?

And have her think he was violent, too?

Laura, a botanist who studied the medicinal properties of desert plants, had locked herself in with her closet full of remedies.

Please, God, don't let her be destroying evidence.

"I called the police. They're on their way." They were going to scout the area, as well, in case anyone wearing black leather gloves and a hood happened to be hanging around. That wasn't too damn likely, he supposed, but he wanted them to look.

"They got in through the sliding glass door in the family room," he continued. Talking because it was the only connection he had to her.

"They lifted if off the track, although I have no idea how. It's back on and I've got a broom handle in the track. The officer said that would keep intruders out."

More movement in the bathroom. He listened carefully, hoping, but the sound wasn't coming closer.

"They assured me that the chances of anyone trying to get in again tonight are almost nonexistent."

Didn't make *him* feel any better.

"Laura? Please?" He drew out the last word until his voice broke.

And then he heard the shower.

She hid her nakedness behind the curtain, aware of the water pulsing down around her. Little cold pellets. Striking her skin. She should turn the dial, heat up the water.

But didn't care enough to bend down.

Or have enough strength to do so.

Just then, a warm flood hit her inner thigh, galvanizing her into action. She had to get that vile stuff off her. Out of her. Dripping, she hurried over to the cupboard for a new bar of soap—unable to touch the bar she and

Harry had both used the morning before. She tore off the paper, dropping it on the floor, and started scrubbing her skin before she was even back beneath the spray. She scrubbed until her skin hurt. Scrubbed everywhere. Her arms, her neck and face. Places they'd touched. And places they hadn't.

They'd touched her. They'd left traces of themselves behind.

And she couldn't get rid of them.

Because they weren't just on the outside.

Yerba Mansa.

Out of the shower again, standing in front of the linen closet across from the toilet, Laura snatched the jar of dried, crushed root and the douche bag. She filled the bag with hot water, then opened the jar and inhaled the herb's eucalyptus odor.

Calm. It will make you calm.

Hands shaking, she spilled as much of the precious, healing powder as she managed to pour into the bag's opening, screwed on the applicator lid and listened to her mind repeat pages of botanical facts about the root, let it take care of her as she lay in the bathtub, with the cold water still stinging her skin, and applied the mixture.

Mixture of this root with a cup of hot water, injected vaginally, treats venereal disease, uterine cancer and stops excessive bleeding after childbirth. A sitz bath with yerba mansa will heal tearing....

The muscles in her arm twitched, but she held on to the bag until she'd completed the dose. And then, as if this last effort had taken every ounce of strength and determination left in her, Laura curled into the fetal position, closed her eyes and waited to die.

Harry's entire upper body throbbed. Standing outside the bathroom door he struggled to concentrate, to focus only on the here-and-now.

He realized all movement in the room had stopped. He could still hear the shower but no Laura.

He couldn't wait any longer. Dignity and respect were secondary to more immediate concerns. Like Laura's safety. Her life. His chances of breaking down the door with his injured shoulder weren't great, so Harry hurried out to the garage for an Allen wrench that would be thin enough to let him pick the lock.

Minutes later, the door gave way and Harry stumbled inside.

The police were going to be there soon.

"Laura?"

With one panicked glance, he took in the sight. The floor was soaked. Some kind of powered herb littered the countertop and spilled into the sink.

He couldn't see Laura's shape in the shadows behind the shower curtain. Yanking it open so forcefully he ripped one of the plastic-lined holes holding it in place, Harry spotted Laura immediately.

Oh, God. "No!"

Down on his knees, completely uncaring about the cold water that was spitting on them, he hauled his beautiful wife out of the tub and onto his lap on the floor.

"Laura?" he cried softly, hating the weakness in his voice, his limbs, his heart.

She was breathing. And conscious if the tears were any indication.

"Oh sweet baby, we'll take care of you, I promise," he said, conviction behind every word. "We're going to make this better. We'll get them."

He didn't know how, but he knew, in that second, that he'd keep this promise to her.

Harder sobs were Laura's only response to his vow—to his presence in general. Tears streamed from beneath her closed lids. She wouldn't even look at him.

Harry prayed to God she was still in there. Laura was a peacemaker, always had been. A gentle, loving person.

Had they wreaked irrevocable damage on that precious spirit he loved so completely? Broken her?

"Come on, sweetie," he said. He pulled a blanket from the bottom shelf of the still-open linen closet, wrapped it around her shivering, limp body and hugged her to his chest. The pain in his shoulder was growing more noticeable, yet he welcomed it—needed the immediate feeling to focus on. He had to get away from the horror, the fear of what this night had done to Laura, if he was going to get them through these next hours.

"It's okay now, love," he crooned, his bruised face close to her neck. "I'm here, I have you. You're safe."

He didn't know if her shiver was from the cold or in reaction to him. God, he needed her to talk. To yell at him, to whisper her fear or blame him for not being man enough to protect her. In their own home, their own bed.

"You're strong, Laura." He had no idea where the words came from, but he couldn't stop them. "You know that. Anytime a fight's been necessary in your life, you were ready for it. You stood up to your parents when you fell in love with me, fought like crazy to be a black man's wife."

"Y-y-y-our....wife..."

Tears prickled his eyes again as he heard that soft voice. The love of his life was still here with him.

With a silent oath, Harry once again dedicated himself to finding out who'd done this to Laura—and to making sure they were locked up and put away forever. If all he could give her was peace of mind from knowing that they'd never be able to get her again, then he'd risk whatever it cost to see that she had it.

And anything else she needed.

By the time the two forensics officers from the investigative services bureau, sex crimes division, were at their door, Laura was calm and dressed in sweatpants, T-shirt and a jacket zipped up to her chin—in spite of Tucson's June heat. Clinging to Harry's arm, she went with him to the door. He wouldn't have it any other way. He couldn't seem to let go of her, either.

"Can you describe what happened?" Jim Mendoza, the older of the two officers, asked before they were even in the door.

As succinctly as possible, Harry did as they asked, somehow getting words past the emotion.

"Did you recognize either one of them?" The speaker barely glanced at Laura, though his question was clearly directed at her.

She shook her head.

"Can you describe them?"

"One was taller than the other," Harry said, the vision imprinted on his brain. He named approximate heights and weights. "They were dressed identically in black jeans, leather jackets that came to just above their hips and black hoods made out of some kind of cotton. The hoods tucked into the jackets. They both wore black leather gloves." Harry handed over the scrap of leather he'd bitten off.

The younger cop, Bill Warren, got on his cell phone, relaying the information to others in the field.

"We'll need to get more information from both of you." Mendoza was moving slowly into the house. "But first, we need to get her to the hospital." Once again, he barely glanced at Laura.

Or at Harry, either, for that matter. Warren clicked off his cell phone, eyeing them both, his face lined with compassion.

"An ambulance is waiting outside for you, ma'am," he said to Laura. "An officer will accompany you to the hospital."

She squeezed Harry's arm and he looked down to see the fresh tension tightening her upper lip, panic in her eyes.

"I'll drive her," he said. The grip on his arm loosened to a more comfortable pressure—notwithstanding the sharp pain shooting from his shoulder to his fingers.

"We'd rather your wife didn't leave the custody of a police officer," Warren began. "That's so—"

"There's less chance of any claim of evidence tampering that way," Mendoza inserted.

Laura's weight fell against him, her shaking intensifying. "Listen, gentlemen," Harry heard himself saying the words without conscious thought. "We appreciate your position, but right now, my only concern is my wife. She doesn't want to ride in an ambulance and as she's not in major physical distress, I'm not going to ask her to do so."

Mendoza looked at Laura fully for the first time, staring at her hair, still damp from the shower. "You didn't bathe, did you?" he asked, his voice urgent.

"She did," Harry told him.

"They didn't tell you not to?"

Not wanting to waste another second on something that couldn't be changed, Harry shook his head. "The dispatcher mentioned it, but Laura's comfort seemed more important." he said.

Not that those instructions would have mattered. Based on Laura's somewhat incoherent behavior, he didn't think he would've been able to prevent her from getting in that shower, even if he'd thought of the Allen wrench earlier.

"They'll still be able to use a rape kit," Warren said. "You two go on ahead and we'll talk to the detectives in charge."

Harry nodded.

"We need to look around here first, though."

"Fine." Harry opened the door wider, moving so that his good arm was around Laura as he led her through their house to the garage and saw her safely buckled into the front seat of his car.

He wanted her as far away as he could get her before the police turned their bedroom into a crime scene.

* * *

"Did either of you get a glimpse of their faces?"

In a private office at the hospital, Laura tried to concentrate. She had no idea how long it'd been since she and Harry had been whisked through emergency-room protocol and ushered into separate treatment rooms. She'd not only lost track of time, but all sense of herself.

Her body ached everywhere, as though she'd been rolled down a twenty-mile hill of rocks wrapped in burlap. Her wrists were raw and burning in spite of the salve they'd put on them. And she had what felt like menstrual cramps.

The policemen, Detective Boyd and his partner, Robert Miller, were looking at her. So was Harry.

The last she'd heard, Harry had been describing the dark hoods and black leather gloves again.

"Do you have anything to add to what your husband said?" Miller asked, pen poised above a pad of paper.

"That's all I saw, too," she said, relieved that she sounded so…human. Sane.

Capable.

She didn't feel any of those things.

"What about voices?" Boyd asked, his gaze intent as it moved between her and Harry. She liked the way he looked at her, as though she was someone he really cared about. Someone he had faith would be able to help him.

She *wanted* to help him.

Except that she needed to go. As far and as fast from this night as she could get. And never, ever, *ever* think about it again.

"Did you notice any identifying features?"

She shook her head. "The smaller one never spoke."

With a raised eyebrow, Daniel Boyd turned to Harry. "Not a word?"

"He whispered something at the end, but never actually spoke—not so we could identify a voice." The sight of Harry's misshapen, swollen face almost made her start to cry again. His shoulder was in a sling.

"What about the other one?"

"He didn't say much, either," Harry said. "A warning not to move if I didn't want to get hurt any worse."

"Was his voice low or high? Gravelly? Did he have any kind of accent?"

Laura couldn't even remember hearing the man speak.

"Deep. No accent." Harry wasn't as calm as he'd appeared before they'd arrived at the hospital. But he might've been putting on an act for her sake. "He said I'd have more than an AC injury if I didn't keep still."

"An AC injury?" Miller asked.

Harry nodded. And Laura just felt lost. It was like they were talking about two different incidents in two different rooms. She'd had no idea.

"Some type of medical background?" Miller said to Boyd

"Yeah. AC refers to acromioclavincular," Harry offered. "I've just been told it's a medical term for shoulder joint. Whether he has medical training or not, the bastard was articulate."

Miller and Boyd both wrote in their notebooks.

"Harry's a professor at U of A," Laura blurted, in case the detectives failed to take him seriously.

Boyd watched her for a long moment.

"And neither of them spoke again?" he finally asked, his forehead creased as he glanced from one to the other.

She shook her head. And held her breath to stave off her immediate dizziness.

"They each said one more thing," Harry muttered. "The same thing…"

Blocking out the rest of her husband's sentence, Laura watched him as though from far away.

"I wasn't sure about the first time, but afterward, when I heard it again…"

Harry swallowed, and Laura couldn't look at him anymore.

"Tell me about the first time," Boyd said, his voice softer.

"When the smaller guy was approaching Laura, he paused, like maybe he wasn't going to do it…."

Cold as ice, Laura read Boyd's name tag again, wondering why only the *Y* had faded.

"…and the guy behind me says 'white stays with white.'"

What? Laura raised her head, shaking inside all over again. What was Harry saying?

"You're sure about that?" Detective Boyd asked, writing some more on his little pad.

"Yeah."

"Did you hear it?" the other detective piped up.

Laura could hardly breathe as Miller looked her right in the eye.

"No," she said as quickly as she could. She'd already answered his questions once.

"And the second instance?" Detective Boyd asked.

"When he'd finished with Laura, the smaller guy whispered the same thing."

No. Laura didn't want to talk about this anymore. She didn't want to see the pointed glance the detectives exchanged, or think about what it all meant.

"We were targeted because I'm black," Harry's words were both a challenge and a cry of pain and tore at Laura's already raw insides.

"Or it was a random attack by bigoted jerks who, when they found a white woman with a black man, used that to fuel their hunger for violence," Miller said.

"You don't think they picked us out ahead of time?" Laura asked him. Please, God, let that be so.

Shrugging, Miller said, "Chances are good they didn't, but we'll have a better idea after we go over what we've got here, along with whatever our team found at the scene."

It wasn't the absolute affirmative answer she'd wanted, but Miller's words comforted Laura.

Boyd took over then, asking more questions, and she was able to answer him without losing her breath. He was kind, like the doctors and the counselor she'd already seen. Compassionate. Guiding her through the interview as unobtrusively and gently as possible— which was saying something, since he—and the doctors before him—had to intrude in the most intimate ways.

"You're sure neither one of you noticed anything familiar about either one of them? Think of everyone you've seen in the past month. Maybe a gas station cashier? Grocery clerk? Anyone?"

As they shook their heads, Miller asked permission to access their credit card and cell phone records to follow up—just in case they'd missed something.

He really seemed to want to rule out the possibility that the men who'd violated them had known them.

Laura wanted that ruled out, too. Random violence was hard enough to deal with. If she had to fear every single person she smiled at through her day, how could she go on?

Harry got pretty agitated when Boyd reported that so far, they had a disappointing lack of evidence. Desert ground was hard and there were no obvious footprints, although they'd be investigating again in the light of day. The gloves precluded fingerprints. They were checking for similar crimes in the state, but the detectives didn't expect much there. They'd already know if there'd been any. And since neither Harry nor Laura had noticed any telling characteristics about their attackers, other than approximate height and weight, which could describe thousands of men in the city, they had nothing.

Except a piece of leather glove with Harry's saliva all over it.

"When you find them," Harry interrupted and Laura stared at him, wondering if her husband had heard the near-hopelessness of their situation, "look at the larger one's penis. He got it caught in his zipper and I'm betting he'll have either a cut or a bruise."

Eyes narrowed, Boyd studied Harry while Miller wrote. Laura squeezed Harry's hand. God, she loved this man.

"This won't help us find him, of course," Boyd

said. "But it could certainly help with a post-arrest identification."

"Which we'll need," Miller said, pushing pen and pad into his shirt pocket. "Our chances of a clear rape kit reading are slim."

Her holistic healing had destroyed the evidence.

Maybe, if they were lucky, there'd be a hair on the bedclothes, but while that could give them some identifiers—if there was a root—it wouldn't point to an exact individual.

"We got fibers from under Harry's fingernails," Boyd continued. "But no skin. We can only hope there's semen on the bedclothes that can be processed for a DNA sample."

Harry's face blanched at that last piece of information; his hands clenched into fists.

Watching her husband, Laura wanted to tell him it was okay. To let the attackers go and never see or hear of them again. She just wanted to know that she and Harry had been a random pick.

She most certainly didn't want the intruders to have any reason to seek revenge.

3

The sun had risen. Driving home from the hospital, Harry could barely tolerate the brightness. There was no new day for him this morning. Only a spotlight shining in the darkness that had overshadowed everything else.

Snuggled up against him in the car, Laura sighed, but didn't speak. She was awake, just not talking.

Harry didn't have much to say at the moment, either. What could possibly make a difference?

Detective Boyd had said he'd call as soon as they had news.

He prayed that would be today.

Not that catching the bastards was going to allow Harry a night's rest. He doubted that he'd ever be able to go to bed and sleep again.

"You sure you're okay driving?"

Her words held only a hint of Laura's spirit.

"Of course." He was perfectly capable of seeing them safely home.

The doctors had said his left shoulder had only been

partially dislocated, but the agonizing jolt they'd administered to move it back into place had nearly knocked him unconscious. Hours later, immobilized by a sling, it still ached. The rest of him was pretty numb.

"I'm going in to shower," Laura said the minute they were in the house. Harry nodded. He had things to do and he'd be happier if she wasn't watching.

Following, Harry almost ran into her as she stopped abruptly outside the guest bathroom door. Without so much as a look back, she went in and shut the door. Seconds later he heard the shower running.

And understood. She couldn't face their bedroom yet.

Gathering underwear from her drawer, a light summer dress from her closet, her favorite pair of flip-flops, and toiletries, Harry once again stood outside a closed bathroom door with his wife on the other side. When he turned the knob, the door opened.

He'd half feared she'd locked him out again.

"It's just me," he said, staring at the shower curtain. "I brought your things."

"Thank you."

Turning to leave, Harry reminded himself of what the counselor at the hospital had told him. He was going to have to give her time, a lot of it, as much as she needed.

He'd give her forever.

And in the meanwhile, he'd see those men in hell for doing this to her.

The curtain rustled as he grabbed the door. "Harry?"

He turned back to see her soaked blond hair plastered to her head and face as she held the curtain up to her chin.

"Yeah?"

Her gaze met his. "Thank you."

Choked up, all he could do was nod. But he stood there, letting his love for her shine through his eyes, until she slipped back behind the curtain.

They needed to recaulk the tub. Grayish green shadows of mold showed through the clear plastic that lined the surface. Laura didn't know a lot about mold. It reproduced from spores that were in the air and landed anyplace there was moisture, where they would feed off whatever was there.

It caused respiratory problems in people who were susceptible.

It could grow anywhere. There wasn't a part of the world that didn't have mold.

A species of mold, *Penicillium notatum,* had been discovered by accident on dirty dishes in a laboratory sink after World War I. Penicillin was later born from that and saved millions of lives.

When her back started to feel raw from the pounding water, Laura turned. There was soap scum on the tile just beneath the built-in ceramic dish on the wall. She'd obviously missed that spot when she'd cleaned.

Sometimes it took effort, but she could get it off. She'd do it before hard water stains made it impossible.

Was there salt in the water softener? She couldn't remember if Harry had recently put some in.

She'd never worried about it before. He always took care of that.

She didn't have to worry about it now, did she?

Frowning at the soap scum, she made a mental note to look in the softener the next time she was out in the garage. That would have to be soon. Her truck was there.

Except… The garage was dark.

Laura turned again.

The bed had been stripped. Boyd had warned them. Everything, including the gown the forensics officers had pulled out of the toilet, had been taken down to the police lab.

Staring at the bare mattress, Harry considered spray disinfectant. He considered slashing the damned thing with a knife.

Instead he hauled it up with his good hand, flipped it on its side and dragged it out to the trash. He'd call someone to take the mattress away.

They had a bed in the guest bedroom they could use if they couldn't get a new mattress today.

At eight o'clock, fifteen minutes after he and Laura had returned home, he called his office at the university and left a message for the History department secretary telling her he wouldn't be in that day.

Next he called the Botanical Garden where Laura worked, and spoke with her assistant and friend, Kelly Holbrook, saying only that Laura was under the weather and wouldn't be in. His wife, who had a federal grant to study the medicinal qualities of desert plants, was her own boss. The garden where she did her research was city-owned and had even become something of a tourist attraction.

He cancelled their appointment at the fertility clinic, then arranged to have the sliding glass door barred and pin-locked until he could get a wrought iron dead-bolted security door placed on the outside.

And when he rang off, he was standing in front of his closet door. The pistol was right where he'd stashed it years ago. Uncle Clement had owned a cleaning business in Manhattan; he'd believed that a black man always had to protect himself. He'd insisted, when Harry spent a summer with them as a teenager, that his nephew learn to shoot.

There were bullets under the sweaters he never wore in the bottom drawer of his dresser. He wasn't sure he'd remember how to load it, but surprised himself when the bullets slipped in easily. He was competent even with a swollen face and one arm tied to his body.

"What are you doing?"

Laura's shocked voice jolted him. He hadn't expected her to be out so soon.

She was standing there dripping wet, a seldom-used guest towel wrapped around her. He didn't see any visible signs of the trauma she'd been through.

"I just loaded this."

"Why?"

"I would think that's obvious."

"Not to me it isn't."

Her gaze was resolute, harder than he was used to seeing, her chin raised.

"Laura, I was caught once. I will not be unprepared again."

"You've never used that thing. You know what the

statistics say about civilians with guns, Harry. They're often turned against you."

"This one won't be."

"Harry—"

"Laura." His voice was sharper than he'd intended, but didn't soften much as he continued. "I am not going to back down on this. From now on, I will be able to protect you. Period."

Frowning, her lips a straight line, she stared at him. Her eyes welled with tears. But eventually she nodded.

"Harry?"

Lying in bed that night, Laura gave up trying to sleep. Her husband, his sling off now, was sitting up, his swollen face turned toward the door of the spare bedroom. It stood open, and the hallway light was on.

"Yeah?"

"I need you."

"I know, love, I need you, too." Though his voice quivered with emotion, his eyes didn't move from the door.

"No, I mean, I *need* you."

He'd understand what she was saying.

"Please?" she whispered when he remained silent.

"Laura, I don't—"

"Please," she interrupted, infusing more strength into the one word. He had to do this for her. He just had to.

And…she believed that he needed her to do it for him, too.

"I can't relax, can't go to sleep," she told him.

"Did you take one of the sleeping pills they gave you at the hospital?"

"Of course not." He should know better than that. She rarely even took aspirin. But she *had* taken the morning-after pill the doctor had given her.

"Maybe you should, just this once."

Laura lay there looking up at him. He was still talking to the open door.

"Harry, it's killing me, knowing they were the last ones… I need to feel *you* inside me. I need you to fill me up. To wipe them out."

Her voice rose with an intensity that was foreign to her. "Please, Harry. Please do this, for me? I want you there, only you…"

Laura hadn't even realized she'd started to cry until Harry wiped a tear from her cheek with the pad of his thumb.

"Sshh. It's okay, baby. I'm right here." He took her into his arms and Laura rubbed his chest with desperation and a kind of frenzied passion, teasing his nipples. That always worked for him.

"Laura…"

"Please, Harry…"

"The doctor said—"

"That I'm perfectly fine."

"She also said you can expect a period of frigidity."

Following her finger with her tongue, flicking across the wiry, sparse curls on his chest to his nipple, Laura said, "I'm not frigid."

Groaning, Harry pulled her face up to his. Kissing her softly, gently, not in the least passionately.

Laura slipped her tongue inside his mouth.

"Laura…"

She slid her hand down his belly and beyond, fondling him into the beginning of an erection. "Please, Harry." She wouldn't have to beg much longer. Harry could never resist her seductions.

With one more groan he said, "If you're *sure* this is what you want…"

"I am," she said, her voice quavering, but not with doubt. "Completely sure."

He kissed her then, fully, passionately, his lips hardly swollen compared to the right side of his face and nose, and she opened her mouth eagerly. The warm possession of his lips always made her lose sight of everything and everyone around her. From Harry's very first kiss—outside her embryonic plant life class at the University of Arizona—she'd felt that peculiar magic talked about in storybooks and scoffed at by pragmatists. She kissed him back, remembering how it used to feel. Trying to find that feeling again.

"Mmmm," she moaned against him, her arms clutching his neck, holding him to her with a fervor that scared her.

And then he moved, lying half on top of her, straddling one of her legs with both of his—his weight resting on one elbow. She recognized the position, his touch, told herself how badly she needed his warmth. More from habit than sexual drive, she moved her leg to tease the hardness that should be there.

It wasn't.

And all her motivating self-talk vanished, Laura froze.

Harry pulled back immediately.

"I was afraid it was too soon," he said softly, his fingers pushing strands of hair behind her ear. "It's okay. And understandable. It's just going to take a little while…"

"It's not me," Laura said, although she knew she wasn't being completely honest about that. Her head welcomed Harry. Her heart did. Her body felt dead. "It's you," she told him, rubbing a hand over his crotch. "You don't want me. I'm dirty now. Used. You saw what they did to me and—"

"Laura!" It was the second time that day Harry had spoken so firmly. The first had been that morning, when she'd caught him loading his gun—a gun that now lay beside them between the bed frame and the mattress.

He slid over, fully covering her, moving his body against hers. In only a moment, he was fully hard.

"Don't you ever," he started, his breath coming in spurts as he continued to move, "*ever* think I don't want you." His mouth was an inch from hers and he kissed her hungrily, his tongue leaving her lips wet. "You are the most desirable woman in the world to me," he said. "Tonight even more so, not because of what I did or did not see, but because you are you—a woman who's soft and gentle, a peacemaker who's also a survivor. No matter what. I can't get enough of you, Laura. If we live to be a hundred and fifty, I will never have enough of you."

His eyes glistened in the dim light as he stared down at her. She loved him so much. Needed so badly for things to be okay between them.

"Please make love to me," she whispered, spreading her legs to accommodate him. They were both still dressed, her in shorty pajamas she hadn't worn in years but had put on because she'd felt too vulnerable in the light cotton gowns she preferred, and him in a pair of cotton pajama bottoms she'd forgotten he owned.

"I want to so badly, Laura," he said, frowning as he drew back, his face a few inches from hers. "But I'm not sure it's right. I'm not sure we should…."

Feeling a fire inside her that she'd only known once before, when her parents had tried to forbid her from seeing Harry because he was black, Laura stared into his eyes.

"You are my husband," she said emphatically. "How could it possibly *not* be right?"

"I know the doctor said you weren't physically damaged, but—"

"I'm no more affected, physically, than if *you'd* had sex with me." She didn't think it was her body he was worried about. "Please trust me on this, Harry." She softened her voice. "I'm not going to fall apart on you, I promise. Not unless you refuse to do this. I feel as if the whole world's been down there in the past twenty-four hours and you're the only person I want there."

"Oh, God, Laura, I want to be there. So much…"

He kissed her again. And slowly, as gently as he had the very first time, many years before, he made long lingering love to her, hardly missing a beat despite his sore shoulder. She seemed to be watching it all from above, noting every move he made, recognizing them from years of Harry's lovemaking.

There was one bad moment—when she was naked and he saw the ugly bruise on her breast—but she pulled his head down to her nipple, and the moment passed.

And when he entered her, Laura was so desperate to have him replace what had been before that she pushed upward, giving him no chance to change his mind. She rode with him, thanking God for every thrust of her husband's body, telling herself over and over that Harry was healing her.

And hating every second of his touch. It didn't feel in the least exciting. It felt like a man invading her. Taking from her. Using her. And when he climaxed, he reached that particular summit alone.

Half an hour later—hall light off and Laura settled for the night—Harry sat propped up against the pillows, Laura's head just below his rib cage, and watched. His eyes were fully adjusted to the dark, and so much as a speck of dust moved through the air he was going to know about it.

And if it posed a threat, he'd annihilate it.

The new alarm system was already installed—thanks to a friend of a friend—and the windows had double locks.

Harry stayed quiet and still, his hand in the middle of Laura's back where it had lain for the past half hour as he did another mental check of their surroundings. Laura wasn't asleep yet, he could tell by her breathing. She hadn't spoken a word since her fervently whispered *thank you* as she'd pulled her pajamas back on before snuggling up against his stomach.

It was only 10:30. And it was going to be a long night.

The first bit of wetness didn't register as tears. He'd figured, with her skin against his, that they were both sweating. But when Laura's next breath, more of a sob, jostled his hand on her back, he knew better.

"Come here," he said, pulling her up to rest her head against his good shoulder. And then, not caring about the ache in his other shoulder, he held her in both arms, rubbing her back, her hair, whispering to her as she released such wrenching sobs he felt his own eyes fill with tears.

Nothing he said seemed to get through to her—exactly like the night before, when she'd locked herself in the bathroom. She let him hold her but hardly seemed aware that he was there, didn't nuzzle into him—didn't relax at all. He could've been an inanimate piece of furniture for all she seemed to notice him.

His offer of sustenance, of comfort and strength, seemed to go unheeded.

More than an hour later, she settled down on her side of the bed, her head on the pillow, her back to him and, with a shudder, went to sleep. By sheer force of will, Harry stayed there in bed, watching her.

What the hell did he do now?

What *could* he do?

He couldn't fix this for her. Couldn't wipe out the violence. Or the fear.

He couldn't erase the pain, the violation—or her memory of him being overtaken, bound and beaten, unable to help, while two men took turns raping her.

She hiccupped in her sleep and Harry's entire body

deflated. What kind of man allowed such atrocities to his wife without giving up his own life to protect her? Replaying the scene in his mind for the hundredth time, Harry tried to figure out where he'd gone wrong. What he could've done differently.

How he could have prevented the attack.

He should've put a better security lock on the sliding glass door. He should've invested in an alarm system, although their neighborhood was considered safe. He should've insisted on a guard dog, in spite of Laura's allergy to pet dander.

He should have heeded her father's warning and kept his black ass away from the white man's daughter.

Harry reached for the pistol. The touch of cold metal against his skin didn't take away the rage. It didn't diminish the anguish coursing through him. It didn't make him feel any less emasculated.

As he sat there, calling on every ounce of self-control he had, Harry knew one thing. His love for Laura was not weak, faithless or changeable. Somehow he was going to make this right.

Even if that meant keeping his black ass far away from her.

The thought filled him with despair.

Still resolute, he sat beside her, eyes wide open, offering protection through the long hot night.

4

"Mr. Moss, if you're elected to a seat in the U.S. senate, what will you do about our growing border-control issues that our current politicians haven't already tried?"

George Moss stepped away from the microphone, assessing the young man standing halfway back in the audience at the Tucson elementary-school cafeteria Saturday morning. He was twenty-something and well-dressed, his tie slightly loosened at the neck. Blond hair cut short and chin held high enough to command respect but not so high as to appear egotistical.

Returning to the podium, making eye contact with his questioner, Moss said, "I have the two things you need to make anything happen. Drive and energy."

At the young man's nod, he could've stopped.

"The number of illegal immigrants in Arizona is rising dramatically," he continued, speaking for the brotherhood that had given his campaign the financial support that was taking him to victory. "Because there's no record of these individuals, there's no way to trace them, to account for them, and if they break the law, there's no way to identify or find them."

Sitting now, the young man didn't smile but seemed satisfied with the response.

The questions went on, all of the current "hot button issues" being raised, just as he'd been coached to expect.

But the answers were less difficult than his advisors had warned him they'd be. He didn't have to refer to his prewritten responses. He only had to say what he knew to be true.

"We need a renewal of family values if we're to rescue this great country," he told the audience at large, engaging with as many of them as would meet his gaze. "Women are successful members of the workforce, but they have another talent, a far more valuable talent, that most men will never be blessed with. A talent this country so desperately needs. They are the keepers of the heart, ladies and gentlemen. The nurturers. It is they who, day by day, moment by moment, instill values in our children."

As the room erupted in applause, George Moss's determination to win at any cost solidified. Someone had to save America.

Detective Daniel Boyd finally got a few hours sleep and woke Saturday morning with his mind still in gear.

Sean Williams. The name popped up in his first second of consciousness. The name he'd been looking for in the early hours of Friday morning, just before the Kendall call came in. Sean Williams. A forty-year-old schoolteacher who'd been apprehended late Friday afternoon and charged with the rape and murder of two fourteen-year-old girls—one of them Sherry O'Connor. The crimes had been committed five years apart. God only knew how many more there were that they hadn't pinned on the bastard yet.

With the DNA sample they'd taken yesterday after the man's arrest, they had enough to put him away for 150 years.

With a grunt and a sigh Boyd rolled out of bed, shuffled across the hard wooden floors of the bedroom that had belonged to his mother all through his growing-up years and into the bathroom that could also be accessed from the hallway.

He'd had new tile, vanity, toilet and tub put in the previous year, which still gave him pause on days like today when he was coming off a hard case—or starting a new one—disoriented, waking from a deep sleep.

And too little sleep.

He'd get up, somehow expecting to find the room just as it'd been during his childhood.

Williams was off the streets, but the two men who'd beaten Harry Kendall and raped his wife were free. Which led Daniel to the realization he'd accepted years before.

Only one thing in life was guaranteed.

There was always another case.

Harry stayed in bed until nine. He'd finally dozed off just before five. Throughout the long night Laura moaned in her sleep several times. Whimpered once.

And slept on. Understandably. The events of the past thirty-one hours had exhausted her mentally, emotionally, physically.

And perhaps sleep was her mind's way of protecting her from the memories that would surface immediately upon waking. The time spent asleep was a respite, an escape, that she needed.

When he could no longer stay still, Harry slid from the bed, careful not to disturb his wife. Moving barefoot across the carpet in the guest room to the hall, he glanced at the closed master-bedroom door before walking into the great room with its walls of windows and vaulted ceilings. Laura had painted it in off-whites with beige trim. Light and tranquil, he'd always thought. Just like her.

Today tranquility eluded him.

Harry stared out the window. Saturday. A sunny day with brilliant blue skies—not a cloud to be seen. Perfection. But things were rarely what they seemed. Beneath the surface hid an evil that cut so deeply hearts would be forever marred.

Out there, among all the moms and dads and kids enjoying a day off on that cheerful-looking Saturday morning, two heinous men existed.

Were they close? Maybe on the next street? Sleeping in? Or having coffee?

Did they have jobs? What kind of jobs? Would they go to work today, mingling with coworkers who thought they were normal guys—who trusted them?

Maybe they were married. At home in bed with their wives—women who hadn't been emotionally damaged.

Women who had no idea that the men they took into their beds, their bodies, had forced themselves on an innocent woman, leaving her stricken and lost.

Did they have children? Trusting little people who looked up to them? Who relied on them for all of life's necessities—both emotional and physical?

Could they strip a stranger of her emotional safety, possibly forever, and at the same time provide it for their kids?

No! He couldn't accept that. Couldn't accept any of it.

Rubbing the back of his neck, Harry wondered if the tension would ever disappear. He needed aspirin. Lots of it.

So where did scum of the earth go on a Saturday morning? What did they do? Eat eggs in a dirty diner while assaulting the tired waitress with inappropriate innuendos? Wake up in old beds with stained sheets, suffering from hangovers that would be gone as soon as they stumbled to the kitchen for a beer?

Did they live together? Brothers, maybe?

Or did they live completely separate lives—except for those occasions when they got together to destroy the lives of people who'd never knowingly hurt anyone?

Eyes watering from all the brightness outside, Harry fell to the couch and, in an attempt to escape thoughts that were a slow torture, grabbed the phone.

He listened to the dial tone for several seconds, allowing it to soothe him with its monotony. And then he hit the third speed-dial button—for his parents in Oregon, where his father owned an accounting firm.

"Hi, son, how are you?"

The calm voice made him feel more tense because of what his father didn't know.

"Not good, Dad."

"What's up? Laura's not sick is she? Or you?"

No, but… What did you call what they were? Sure, they were sick, but their disease wasn't something that could be detected in a lab. It wouldn't show up on a microscope slide or respond to antibiotics. It couldn't be healed with holistic remedies.

"No, we're…not," he said, after a failed attempt to say they were fine.

"What's going on?" He could hear his mother in the background. "Kaleb? Is something wrong with Harry or Laura?"

"I don't know, Alicia," Kaleb's voice held no impatience as he answered his wife. "Harry, what's wrong? Did one of you lose your job? Was there bad news from the fertility clinic?"

What Harry would give to be a boy again, safe under his father's care, always knowing that no matter what befell him, his father could fix it.

"Laura was raped."

"What?"

Harry couldn't repeat it.

"Oh my God." Kaleb Kendall's voice dropped—and filled with a horror Harry had never heard before. Not even when his father had first shown him a documentary about Martin Luther King's assassination and told his young son about his black heritage. "When? Is she all right?"

"What happened to Laura? Where is she?" Alicia's voice, closer now, brought tears to Harry's eyes. If ever a woman personified the word *mother,* it was his mom.

"It happened the night before last—at home. Laura's here now. Asleep. Other than…they…she wasn't… there were…"

When the words just wouldn't come, Harry stopped, stared at the grain of the polished wood floor. "Other than rope burns on her wrists, she's physically uninjured."

"He broke into your home? Were you there?" Kaleb's tone rose only slightly, but Harry knew that his father was seconds away from rage.

A rage he would contain—and use in any way he could to right a wrong.

"Who did? Kaleb! What's going on!"

"I was here." The sun shining in the window seemed to mock the darkness inside him.

"In the room?"

"Yes." He bit out the word, his self-loathing and anger clouding every thought, every feeling.

"I see."

What did his father see? A broken woman? A man to be pitied?

"Did he have a gun?"

"A *gun?* Kaleb, you talk to me right now. Put him on speakerphone. Tell me!"

"No gun," Harry closed his eyes. "Just rope. There were two of them."

"Good God in Heaven! Did they both—"

"Yes." Harry interrupted before his father could verbalize the image still persecuting him.

Kaleb's sigh said more than any words could.

"Just a second, Alicia," he heard his father say a moment later. "It's bad and I need to help Harry first."

Help him. And how did his father propose to do that? This wasn't a lost position on a Little League team, or a failing grade. Could his father travel back in time, wipe out the grueling events? Could he clear away the sense of violation Laura would feel for the rest of her life?

Kaleb asked the same questions Harry would've asked, questions the detectives had asked. Alicia was strangely silent and Harry knew she'd pieced together enough to guess what had happened.

In his mind's eye he saw the tears streaming down her face.

"It was because of me, Dad." He said aloud what he'd known since those whispered words had struck his heart.

"Don't you even start thinking like that, boy." The sternness in Kaleb's voice contrasted sharply with the compassionate outrage he'd shown Harry thus far. "Two against one? There's nothing you could've done—except get yourself killed."

Yeah, well, if they'd killed him, maybe they wouldn't have gone after Laura. Without him in the picture there'd been no need.

"It was a hate crime—because I'm black and she's white."

Silence fell on the line. And then… "Times have changed, son. The world today is different from the one your mother and I grew up in. You know that. You've always known that. Look at us—two black people living in a white neighborhood and your mother's president of the homeowners' association. We live in a society of freedom and acceptance. At least as far as the color of our skin is concerned."

Kaleb didn't really believe that. And he knew Harry didn't either. But it was the edict by which they lived.

And they'd found acceptance by doing exactly that.

"The guy with his hands around my throat spoke just as his buddy was approaching Laura." The words stuck in his throat.

"What did he say?"

"White should stay with white."

"Donahue."

"Daniel Boyd here, Mr. Donahue."

"Detective. It's been months. Do you have any news on my wife? Is that why you're calling?"

"You weren't married to Amanda Blake," Daniel said. For a brief time the previous year, he'd believed the missing Flagstaff woman had been kidnapped and was being held by a man at a motel in Tuscon, but she'd disappeared again before he had any real proof. A frantic Donahue had called him half a dozen times a day for two weeks, and while Daniel could have diverted the calls, he'd taken every one of them.

"She wore my ring. Bore my son." Bobby Donahue's words were softly spoken, his voice subdued.

His grief was real, which was why, in spite of what he and much of Arizona's law enforcement believed about Donahue's "business," his "church," Daniel had taken the time to speak with him.

"As far as I'm concerned, your wife's case is closed,"

he said now, before the younger man got himself worked up with hope again. "The woman who was seen at the Desert Stop motel fitting her description gave false identification and left no forwarding address. She is untraceable. She could be anywhere—or she could be dead. Unless she shows up again, there's nothing more I can do."

"Oh." The deflation evident in that one word struck Daniel, despite his cynicism about Bobby Donahue. "So why am I getting a call from the Tucson police?" Donahue asked.

"Tell me you didn't order a rape in Tucson. A white woman married to a black man." The intricate and seemingly foolproof disguises Donahue used to cover his white supremacist activities didn't fool Daniel for a second.

"What? Of course I didn't."

"You're sure?"

"As God is my witness."

"If I find out you're lying to me, I'm going to hunt you down, my friend, and just like you, I don't feel any particular need to play by the rules."

"I understand, Detective. You helped me with Amanda. I owe you and I'm a man of honor."

And that, Daniel knew to be true. In his own twisted way, Bobby Donahue was a trustworthy, loyal and God-fearing man.

"If I ever ordered a rape, which I would never, of course, do, I simply wouldn't answer your question."

Satisfied, Daniel Boyd nodded. And silently disconnected the call.

* * *

At first Laura didn't recognize the despair that accompanied her waking to a bright new day. She stretched. And her entire body ached. She felt a chafing between her legs.

"Hi." Harry, dressed in shorts and a T-shirt, his hair still wet from the shower, sat up against the pillows beside her, smiling down at her.

At least, his lips smiled. His eyes searched hers, sending love—and seeking it. Seeking reassurance.

It was something she couldn't give.

"Hi." Breaking eye contact, she sat up, pulling the covers over her chest.

"You should probably call your folks. Your mother will be starting to wonder why she hasn't heard from you."

Glancing at the small LED screen on the guest-room night table, Laura was shocked to see that it was almost eleven. Unless she was away she called her mother every Saturday morning. It was a kind of unwritten rule. Her mother didn't meddle in Laura's affairs—and Laura checked in regularly.

"I'm not ready to talk to them yet." She thought about it. Tried to push herself. And felt tears choking her throat.

Her mother would take it hard—reacting to the attack as strongly as if it had happened to her. Laura couldn't experience those feelings again right now. Couldn't live through the commiseration and compassion that would allow her to fall apart completely.

If she did that, she'd never be able to pull herself back together.

"I called Dad."

Thoughts of Kaleb and Alicia Kendall brought a tiny hint of warmth. Until she envisioned their reaction to—

"They want to see you, but will wait to visit until we're ready. They asked if you want to go to Oregon and stay with them for a bit. And Mom says she'll have her cell with her at all times if you need to talk."

"Could you call them for me, please?" Laura asked. Harry's parents had always been a safe place for her, for both of them. Not only accepting their love, but rejoicing in it. Welcoming her, a white woman, into their family. "Let them know I can't answer any questions yet, if that's okay, but I'd like to hear their voices."

Harry had the phone to his ear before she'd finished the last sentence.

Daniel Boyd had worked easier cases than the Kendall rape. And harder ones. He was going over the scant information he had as he pulled up in front of their home late Saturday afternoon, then started up the walk to their door. He straightened his shoulders. Experience had taught him that there was no way to be prepared for whatever scene would take place inside that house. He was familiar with the range of emotions that might be released—anger, pain, grief, guilt—and could never predict which ones he'd face. Experience had also taught him that the sooner he uncovered more evidence, the higher his chances of finding the perpetrators of this particular nightmare.

Robert Miller was home with his wife and kids—certainly his right, since they were off duty. But Daniel couldn't sit at home when a crime scene was getting colder by the second. And he didn't have a wife or kids.

Cops relied on crime scenes for evidence. And in this case, Laura Kendall's body—and to a lesser degree, her husband's—was the crime scene. Her memory—and her husband's—were about the only way he had to uncover any missing pieces....

He hated this part of the job. Nailing the bastards gave him a high unparalleled by anything else in his life. But looking a raped woman in the eye, having to imagine what she was feeling, figuring out how to get into her brain and find the information he needed, gnawed at his gut every time.

Forcing her to relive the worst night of her life was even worse.

He knocked on the door with two quick raps, praying to the god of cops that something he had to say, or ask, would trigger the inconspicuous clue that would let him do his job. If it came, he'd recognize it. Of that he was sure.

Harry could tell that Laura was doing better since speaking to his parents. She'd not only accepted his offer to make chicken parmesan for dinner, but she'd wanted to help. She was rolling boneless chicken breasts in his secret mixture on the counter while he broke spaghetti in half and dropped it in boiling water when they heard the knock on the door.

Her sudden tension seemed to bounce off the walls around them.

"Who could that be?" Her tone seemed to blame

him, as though he'd invited guests without informing her. Something he'd never done. And never would.

"I don't know," he said, trying to hide his own concern.

Harry's spirits sank back to that morning's depths as he saw the detective on his doorstep. They'd been about to have the first normal moments since their ordeal had begun.

"Dr. Kendall, may I come in? I have a few things I need to discuss with you and your wife."

"Of course. And please call me Mr. Or Harry. The title is just to impress my students." Harry held open the door, motioned Daniel Boyd inside and invited him to have a seat on the couch while he waited to see if Laura would come in of her own accord.

He was relieved when she did.

Harry resented the reminder Boyd's presence brought into their home, resented the intrusion on what might've been a return to ordinary life for him and Laura—a nice meal prepared and eaten together. But even more than he wanted that normalcy, he wanted the bastards who'd invaded his home to be caught.

And punished.

He needed them to pay for what they'd done.

And to know they wouldn't be back. Not to his home—and not to the homes of any other innocent, un-suspecting couple.

5

"We found a size eleven shoe print in the dust at the back of your yard."

The detective had taken a seat on her favorite couch. Laura faced him, sitting in the relatively isolated armchair across from it.

"What kind of shoe?" Harry's question bothered her, although she appreciated his physical nearness. He'd settled on the arm of her chair, his arm lying on the back, just above her head.

Why did he have to care what *kind* of shoe one of those jerks wore? Laura wanted as little information as possible about the men who'd broken into their home—into their lives. The less she had, the less she'd have to picture…

"There wasn't enough of an imprint to be sure, but the tread was thick. Probably a work shoe or boot." His eyes narrowed, Detective Boyd looked at Harry. "You're sure you didn't see what they had on their feet?"

Laura was getting used to the way her mind blocked

out incoming stimuli at will. Harry would've seen their feet. Because they'd have been attached to the legs that were on their bed in front of him…

"I didn't." Harry's frustration was evident in his reply. "They were black, I'm positive of that. Soles and all. But whether they were shoes or boots, I couldn't tell you."

"What about the toes? Were they rounded? Did they seem steel-encased?"

"I don't remember seeing them."

They would've been upside down, making the toes nearly impossible to see. Laura chose to let the two of them figure that out on their own.

The detective's gaze was kind as he directed his next questions to her. "Did you feel any footwear?"

"No."

"You don't remember any sensation of rubber or hard leather against your skin, maybe brushing against your ankle?"

"No."

A lot of questions about shoes. Until this moment, she hadn't given them a thought. Shoes didn't seem to have much to do with the crime that had been committed here.

"Did they learn anything from the samples they took at the hospital?" That was what she wanted to know. Did they have the guys' identities yet? Not what shoes they were wearing.

"Nothing conclusive. The fibers we got from under Harry's nails were standard denim—used by most clothing manufacturers in the United States and beyond. There was no semen on the bedding. We did pull off several hair follicles and will check every one of them."

"Probably mine and Harry's," she said, closing her mind to the thought of the attackers' hairs mingling with hers and Harry's in their bed.

There was much to run from here. And yet, since speaking with Kaleb and Alicia, she felt more *there*. More like herself. Or at least like someone she recognized. They'd treated her as they always did—like a beloved daughter—assuring her that they were a family and would get through this together. Would go on together. And laugh together again.

As impossible as that was to grasp, she believed them. Harry's parents had a way of finding the best smelling roses in the middle of a thorn patch.

"The most conclusive piece of evidence we have so far is point of entry," Detective Boyd was saying.

"They didn't use the sliding glass door?" Harry asked, sounding confused.

Boyd nodded. "But they used a tool that, while common in the window-installation world, isn't something most guys carry around in their trunks. From the marks on the window, it appears that two four and three-quarter inch double suction cups were used to pull the glass up and the door off the tracks."

Made sense. What goes up must come down. What goes in also comes out. The door that's installed can be uninstalled.

They were going to have to call a construction company on Monday morning and have the thing replaced. With a heavy wood door that had triple dead bolts. Their wrought iron idea wasn't good enough.

Harry had already taken care of the windows, but maybe they could get an extra set of locks on each one. Just in case.

Because even if they managed to catch these guys, they weren't the only rapists in the world. There were more of them out there. In Tucson and anyplace else she might decide to move. Rapists were a part of life.

There was no escaping them.

Tony Littleton had been home for twenty-four hours before Bobby Donahue had a chance to spend any private time with him. They'd attended a political rally for senatorial candidate George Moss the night before—Tony's college class assignment—and then Tony had spent the morning with Luke so Bobby could work uninterrupted. The toddler was finally down for his Saturday-afternoon nap and everyone who'd had business with Bobby was gone as well. Bobby and Tony had dinner plans—a small group of like-minded people getting together—but for now it was just the two of them in the living room of the modest house Bobby owned outside Flagstaff.

Bobby could hardly wait to hear about Tony's week.

"So…tell me what's going on." he said, hands dangling between his knees as he sat on the edge of the couch, facing Tony.

Tony's blush gave him away.

"So it worked?" Bobby asked with a grin. "The advice I gave you?"

Tony met his eyes briefly, then looked down, but his smile was unmistakable. Bobby had never been as innocent as this young man, but he could still recognize the signs.

"I called you Thursday night," Bobby said, helping his young friend.

Tony's blush deepened.

"You were with her, weren't you?"

Tony nodded. Suddenly, he started rambling in a way Bobby would never have done—but found endearing, just the same.

"You have to see this girl, Bobby," he said. "When I look at her all I can think about is kissing her. Touching her. Her skin's so white—like she's never been out in the sun. And her smile…"

"You were good to her?" The statement was also a question. Sometimes good men, especially young ones in the throes of about-to-be consummated sexual desire, forgot themselves.

"Of course!" Tony said, meeting his eyes. "She wanted it worse than I did. She really liked it. She made these noises and squirmed so much I could hardly hold out long enough to pleasure her. It's like you told me, come together or not at all, and I was determined to do that, but man, it was hard. The night was incredible. It's all I've been able to think about…"

Bobby considered deferring his next comment— hated to put any kind of a damper on the young man's joy—but he wasn't willing to take the risk. "That has to stop."

"What?" Tony's brow furrowed.

"Obsessing over anything other than our service to God and our cause. Practice the mind exercises I taught you last summer. Put your thoughts on things outside yourself. A man who obsesses over sex goes down a dark and dangerous path."

"There was nothing dark or dangerous about this, Bobby, I swear. She's so sweet and giving and eager. We made each other...*happy,* you know? Like it felt totally right."

"And that's as it should be," Bobby said, grinning again. "God gave you the ability to experience those pleasures. But you must never let any earthly pleasures consume you. Too much consumption leads to ruin. Whether it be sex, alcohol, drugs—whatever—you become no more than an addict. You give up control of your mind that way."

Opening his mouth, Tony seemed about to argue and then, as Bobby watched, understanding dawned on the young man's face. He saw the light of peace once again enter Tony's eyes. "I'd lose sight of what matters most," he said slowly, meeting Bobby's gaze with the open intelligence that had first drawn Bobby to him.

"Right."

"Obsession with her might lead me to make wrong choices."

"Correct."

Tony was silent for a while. Sitting back, Bobby was content to let the young man's mind wander. Tony's meanderings often led to thought-provoking conversations that energized Bobby.

"Did you ever feel that way about Amanda?"

Bobby's eagerness diminished, especially in light of the call he'd had from Tucson earlier that day, which had given him hope, then dashed it almost immediately. But because this was Tony and Bobby understood that their friendship was rare and true, he answered.

"Briefly. When I first met her, I couldn't get her out of my head." He chose his words carefully. "But unlike you, I'd been with other women before. And I was older."

Frowning, Tony asked, "And then you just told yourself to stop feeling like that and it ended?"

Bobby held back a laugh. Tony had been a picked-on geek in high school and was particularly sensitive to being a target for humor—even well-meant shared humor.

"Of course not," Bobby admitted. "But I knew I had to control my emotions or they'd control me. Whenever I'd get them at inappropriate times, I'd immediately start thinking about something else. At first I had a topic I went to whenever it happened."

"The cause."

"Yes.

"And later, I could simply think about anything outside myself and the obsession with Amanda would stop. Don't misunderstand," Bobby added, "the feelings never lessened. I adore her as much today as I ever did. I just learned to control the amount I thought about her."

Tony shook his head. "I'm not nearly at that level."

"Then count colors."

"What does that mean?"

"Wherever you are, pick a color and start counting how many times, on how many different things, you see it in your everyday surroundings. That'll take your mind off whatever you're obsessing about and give it back to you."

Tony's expression lightened. "I can do that."

"Of course you can." Bobby almost stopped right there. But this was Tony, and his goal was to be completely honest with the man he trusted like no other.

"One other thing," he said slowly. "When you're with her and the time is right and proper for that kind of *communication,* choose to give yourself up to the feelings. Only in those sacred moments can you allow them to control you. You'll find that as long as you give them rein sometimes, it's much easier to turn your back on sexual urges at other times."

"You've really got a gift, you know?" Tony said after several seconds had passed.

Bobby nodded.

"Thank you."

"Anytime," Bobby said, meaning it. "To you my door is always open, my phone is never off."

Tony's heartfelt nod met an answering emotion in Bobby. Having someone in his life he could say that to almost made up for the pain of having lost Amanda.

Tony glanced over at him, his head half bowed. "That woman we were talking to last night, the one asking about Moss's campaign, kept looking at you."

Bobby didn't even feign interest. "Forget it, Tony."

"Why? You—"

"I said forget it," Bobby interrupted, something he

rarely did to Tony. "I've made the decision to remain celibate for the rest of my life. It's my tribute to Amanda."

Tony paled. "The rest of your *life?*"

"Yes."

"You really think you can do it?"

"I know I can."

"You loved her that much."

"Yes."

Shaking his head, Tony said, "I've never known anyone as strong as you are."

"Yes, you have." Bobby's reply was immediate and filled with conviction. "You're sitting inside his skin right now."

"I know this is going to sound pie-in-the-sky, but I honestly do not believe you need to have any immediate fears." Detective Boyd's voice had lowered, thickened with emotion as he took Laura's hand at the door.

He was so convincing, so sincere, she almost believed him. Except that she couldn't seem to get past the solid black wall in her mind.

Harry's hand on her back was nice, comforting, but it couldn't scale the blockade, either.

"I've been working these cases for five years and I was on the streets for fifteen years before that. In my experience, victims who don't know their attackers are rarely, if ever, attacked a second time. I follow the statistics, and while the percentages aren't entirely accurate because of the number of non-reported cases, I can tell you that the danger of repeat rapes on the same victim generally occurs only in instances of spousal abuse, acquaintance rape and date rape."

Laura nodded, wishing he'd just keep on talking, filling her mind with his experience and reassurance.

Talking was good. She didn't have to think if she could concentrate on his words—

"What a minute." Stricken, she stared up at the detective, squeezing his fingers. "I just remembered something."

Boyd's gaze changed from compassionate to focused as he bent toward her. "What's that?"

"When the…second one…you know…" She knew the word *orgasm,* but she couldn't make herself say it. Not in the context of rape. *Her* rape. "Just now, when you were talking about how they probably won't come back, I had a flash of them here and it was like Harry said. There…at the…end, he did whisper. Why wouldn't I remember that and then suddenly have it come to me?"

"It happens that way," Boyd said. His touch on her fingers felt like her hold on reality. Harry's hand rubbing her back kept her upright. "Memories filter down slowly, when you're ready for them."

She frowned, closing her eyes as she struggled to forget and remember accurately at the same time.

"What did he say?" Boyd's intensity wasn't lost on her.

"White stays with white, just like Harry said. And maybe another word, too. I didn't get it. Baby?" Harry's hand froze on her back. Laura opened her eyes as her voice broke, hating her weakness. "I'm sorry I can't remember exactly."

"Don't worry about it," Detective Boyd said. "It'll probably come to you later."

His understanding felt a lot like approval. It helped so much.

She held on to his hand, not wanting him to go. And at the same time wishing he'd disappear and she'd forget she'd ever met him. Or his partner, Robert Miller. They represented safety. And they represented the fact that she'd been violated, damaged, irrevocably changed.

Harry walked Boyd out to his unmarked sedan, keeping Laura in sight as he did.

"Is there anything else you know about this case but didn't want to say in front of Laura?" Harry asked.

There had to be. And Harry had to find out what it was. He couldn't wait around for people to do their jobs. The attackers were on the loose twenty-four hours a day, meaning Laura was in danger twenty-four hours a day.

"I've told you everything I can at this point," Boyd said.

"What about the fact that this is a hate crime?" Harry reined in his frustration with difficulty. This problem wasn't Boyd's fault. "Doesn't that narrow down the suspects? Or at least give you a place to start looking for them?"

"We haven't determined that it *is* a hate crime," Boyd said, unlocking his car but not getting in. "Miller thought it was at first, too, but the more we talked, the more we aren't sure. Haters usually leave some kind of calling card. They're proud of their work and want to take credit for it."

"The man whispered 'white stays with white,'" Harry said, despising the emotion suffusing his words, raising his tone in spite of his effort to remain calm and controlled. "What else do you need?"

"You aren't sure that's what you heard," Boyd said. "And Laura's not sure she heard anything."

"She just said she heard the same thing I did."

Daniel Boyd stared him in the eye and Harry had a feeling the detective was trying to tell him something—communicating man to man. A personal message, one he'd be out of line actually putting into words.

"She heard you say the word 'white' in connection with that second incident." Boyd's tone was soft. "Right now your wife's so busy trying to forget what happened, she's probably confused about what she really remembers."

"Just do me a favor and look into it, will you?" Harry asked, feeling more like a schoolkid than the college professor he was as he stood there sweating in the hot night air with his hands in his pockets.

"I already have."

6

Double suction cups. What did they look like? How expensive were they? Where did you get them?

Laura stirred beside him and Harry smoothed a hand over her head, hoping she'd settle back into sleep. She'd finally given in and taken one of the sleeping pills the counselor at the hospital had recommended and the doctor had prescribed.

That had happened, after a difficult phone call to her parents. Harry cringed even now, reliving the moment Laura had told her mother she'd been raped.

From several feet away, he'd heard Sharon Clark's *Oh, my God, oh, my God* coming over the line.

His in-laws had tried to insist on coming over, disregarding Laura's pleas that she was too tired. Only when Harry had spoken to Len had the man seen that there'd be no benefit to Laura from another replay of the tragedy. The Clarks had relented when Harry and Laura accepted their invitation to dine with them after church the next afternoon.

Harry was dreading it.

More suited to Laura's frame of mind would be dinner at their favorite neighborhood restaurant with Jim and Elaine, friends of theirs from college.

Harry's hand stilled on his wife's head as he considered telling their friends what had happened.

Was it necessary?

Better for Laura to have everyone know? Or to be able to regain her footing in the life she'd lived before Thursday night, without all the questions and concern?

The joint counseling session the hospital had scheduled for the following Tuesday couldn't come too soon as far as Harry was concerned. He had far more questions than answers—about everything.

She lay inert, a twenty-six-year-old college graduate with boyishly short black hair and a body that she'd given away years before.

"God, that's good," David Jefferson said, his face inches from hers as he pumped his penis inside her. A penis she refused to look at—as though, if she didn't see it, she could maintain some kind of distance. "So good." His words were getting more breathless and she waited, knowing it was only a matter of seconds before he gave that final grunt and emptied his seed into her belly, intending to impregnate her.

Only seconds before his naked body would slide off hers and she could turn over and go to sleep.

To dream about her little boy, her son, the heart of her heart. The child she hadn't seen in a year. He was three now, and as David slid in and out of her, she tried to picture that little face, to remind herself that while she owed David Jefferson her life, owed him *this,* she existed for an entirely different purpose.

One day soon she'd have her son back.

"Have you told Kelly?" Sharon Clark asked her daughter as they put the finishing touches on the vegetable salad they'd be having with their roast for dinner.

"No." Laura took the dressings out of the refrigerator. Thousand Island for her folks. Honey mustard for her. Italian for Harry.

She was doing better today. Or maybe she was just more relaxed because she was with her parents, in the home where she'd grown up. The home where she'd been innocent and at peace.

"Isn't she going to wonder why you haven't been at work?"

Sharon had yet to look at her without obvious concern in her eyes, as though, if she just looked hard enough, she'd see the marks those men had left on her daughter's soul.

"Harry told them I wasn't feeling well. That's enough."

"But you and Kelly are so close…"

"I know, Mom." Laura wasn't sure she was making the right choices, only that she was doing what she had to. She was living her life solely on that level right now. She was protecting herself from the past—and the future.

Miller had done his research well. Two companies had installed windows within a five-mile radius of the Kendall home in the past two weeks. All the installers except one had an alibi for the previous Thursday night.

The remaining one was female.

Daniel felt the tension building within him, starting at his neck and traveling in both directions. If there wasn't a break in this case soon, he'd be popping pills for a migraine—and sleeping flat on the floor in an attempt to ease the soreness in his back.

Staring at a list of suction-cup suppliers, preparing to get a warrant for all records of sales in Tucson over the past six months, Daniel heard his cell phone ring. He unclipped it from his hip.

"Boyd."

"I did some reading last night," Harry Kendall said after introducing himself. "I'm pretty certain that as far as the smaller guy goes, we're dealing with a power-reassurance rapist. Enough of the profile fits. Non-violent attack in the middle of the night. Breaking into the victim's home. No weapon. Lack of athleticism."

Taking the phone away from his ear only long enough to switch sides, Boyd remembered how it felt to be powerless.

"It's the other one I can't place, and he was the one in charge," Harry was saying. "My best guess is the power-assertive rapist. He definitely fit the athletic, macho image and was physically aggressive without being overtly sadistic.

"Neither of them appeared to feel any animosity toward Laura. The first one treated her more like a…machine. And the other acted as though he wasn't quite sure what to do with her."

Daniel murmured something noncommittal. He and Miller had already been through the profiles—various

FBI standard descriptions of rapists that were used not only by law enforcement agencies throughout the country, but also by university psychology classes, women's self-defense programs and so on.

Apparently by victims' husbands, as well.

They'd been through them and more or less dismissed them. The profiles described single rapists—not teams.

"It's eleven o'clock on Monday morning, Mr. Kendall. Have you been to bed yet?"

"Yes. I'm getting in four or so hours, from dawn until about nine."

"Is your wife there with you?"

"No." The man didn't seem at all pleased by that. "She insisted on going to work, so I did, too."

"You're at the university?"

"In my office, yes. I'm teaching summer sessions."

"Do you have any classes today?"

"Three. I specialize in American history, which is the most popular history elective, so I tend to have a full schedule. I just finished class. I've got two more this afternoon but I can cancel them if you need me."

Tapping a pencil against the edge of his desk, Boyd stared at the list of stores for which he had to prepare paperwork to subpoena suction cup sales records. He sighed, considering the hours he'd have to spend pouring over those records.

"What I need, Mr. Kendall, is for you to take care of your wife and let me do my job."

The silence was almost painful.

"Look, I know what you're going through," he said,

stepping away from his desk to the deserted hallway beyond. "I understand the rage, the feeling of being emasculated, the need to take back the power that was stolen for you—to prove to your wife and yourself that you're man enough…."

He paused, giving Kendall a chance to deny any of the assertions.

And when he didn't, Daniel said, "I also know that for me to say that you did everything you could, that what happened is no reflection on you, won't do any good at this point. But what I need you to understand is that I'm highly trained to find these guys. I've been at this a long time. If they're out there, I will get them."

Kendall still said nothing. Daniel took that as a good sign.

"Don't let these guys take any more than they already have, Mr. Kendall," he said slowly. "Don't let them rob your wife of the man you used to be."

Still nothing.

"Okay?"

"Yes."

Daniel half smiled. "Okay."

He'd said goodbye and his phone was halfway from his ear when he heard, "Wait."

"Yes?"

"One more thing."

"Sure. What?"

"Do you think we're dealing with a power-reassurance here?"

Daniel shook his head. The man wasn't letting this go, wouldn't stop tormenting himself.

"I just need to know that much," Kendall said. "I need to know what I'm dealing with. In case they come back."

"They aren't coming back."

"Please."

"Yes," Daniel heard himself say, regretting the answer even as he gave it. "One of them fits the power-reassurance profile." He was only distorting an emotionally upset man's equilibrium that much more.

Because if Kendall had done his research, as Daniel was sure he had, he'd realize that the power-reassurance rapist was—sometimes—known to repeat on the same victim.

On Tuesday, Laura was late getting home from work. She'd been harvesting pads of a variety of prickly pear that she and Kelly had spent the past six months cultivating for an experimental diabetes treatment. Harry was standing in the driveway as she pulled in.

Her stomach dropped. "What's wrong?"

Following her into the garage, he opened her truck door, his expression intent. "Just worried about you."

"Oh." Laura reached up to touch his cheek. "I'm sorry. I should've called."

She'd been preoccupied with getting out to her truck while there was still someone to walk with her, locking herself in and spending every second she was stopped at every light watching, ready to gun the gas if anyone approached her vehicle.

"I was testing for levels of Opuntia Streptacantha sap, but had to wait until midafternoon to harvest because of the acid levels in the pads…."

Nodding, grinning, the lines on his face smoothing, Harry pulled her out of her little Ford Ranger and into his arms.

"I love you, sweetie." His words were muffled against her neck.

Only a few days ago Laura would have fallen naturally into Harry's embrace; now she had to force herself to lean against him. And couldn't stay there long.

Releasing her immediately, Harry didn't seem to notice.

She wasn't afforded the same luxury. For the rest of the evening, Laura struggled with unwelcome thoughts—bizarre notions about Harry's hands being dirty. About his touch being abhorrent.

Feeling trapped.

Fighting the need to run away and the fear of facing reality.

And making herself sick with guilt.

Someone was out back.

"Get in the other room," Harry commanded, jumping up from his seat at the table Wednesday evening.

Hearing her leave, Harry flattened himself against the wall next to the sliding glass door so he could see out without being seen.

"Harry? What is it?"

He didn't answer. Didn't know how many there were. Or how close one of them might be.

So far, he couldn't see anything other than the pool, deck chairs, grill and bougainvillea growing up the privacy wall enclosing the yard.

There. He saw it again. Leaves moving along the back wall.

Was that how they'd gotten in the last time? From the neighbor's yard behind them?

What if the rape had only been their first warning? What if someone was out to get Laura away from him, to make them an example for other couples who might be considering mixed race marriages? To make a statement like those the Ku Klux Klan had been making for decades?

Hooded extremists attacking homes in the dark of night.

"Harry?" Laura came out.

"Get back!" He hadn't meant to shout, but he'd do it again if he had to. "Call 911."

He heard her pick up the phone in the living room.

And quietly unlocked the door leading from the kitchen to the garage. He could lock it from the outside—and gain access to the backyard from a side door.

He needed a weapon. Didn't have time to get the gun.

Grabbing a screwdriver from his workbench, Harry moved quickly, stealthily, toward the garage access door. Thank God he'd oiled the damn thing a couple of weeks before. He made it out to the yard with almost no sound.

Perusing around the corner of the house, he could see the entire expanse of the backyard. At first glance, he couldn't see anyone. Had he scared them off?

Harry hoped not. He was going to get these bastards, and if they were lucky, hold them until the cops arrived.

He'd like to annihilate them.

There! It came again. The rustle in the leaves. Someone was in the bushes at the back of the yard.

Crossing quickly to the wall, Harry crept along the bushes until he was only a few yards away.

And then he saw the shoes. One pair. Tennis. Male. Not quite as big as Harry's ten and a half.

The smaller guy, then.

Searching the rest of the wall, he determined, to the best of his ability that the intruder was alone.

Spying?

Planning the next invasion?

Harry thought, very briefly, of waiting for the cops. But what if the guy decided to leave before they showed up? What if he knew Harry was standing there? Maybe the intruder planned to jump him....

Harry lunged. Ignoring last week's injuries, he hurled himself under the bush like a baseball player sliding into home base. He grabbed the man around the ankles and yanked, pulling him off-balance.

"What the—"

Dragging the body out by the feet, he dove on top of it, planning to hold the man down until the cops arrived.

He had one of them.

And because of that they'd damn well catch the other.

"Get off me!"

It took Harry a full thirty seconds to realize that the voice was female, and so was the body beneath his.

Careful to hold on to the intruder's wrists, he rolled off her.

"Who are you?"

"Maggie Boucher. I live on the other side of the wall. I moved in a couple of weeks ago."

The woman was about his age with short brown hair and a plain face that showed quite clearly the myriad emotions she was feeling, from consternation and concern to a healthy dose of fear.

Harry wanted to believe her. But…

"What were doing sliding around behind my bushes?" he asked as she sat up, her wrists still in his grasp.

"I was trying to coax my cat to come home," she said, holding out a slab of fish. "He's declawed and it's not safe for him to be outside. He followed me out with the trash and got scared and took off over here."

As the woman spoke, a light-colored, long-haired funny-faced feline came slinking out from behind the bushes, gaze intent on the piece of fish in his owner's hand.

It had grown completely dark, but he could see the woman's face in the light shining from his patio. Laura must have turned the light on.

Which probably meant she was watching them.

"Would you like to come in for a cup of coffee?" he asked, sitting on the grass in the slacks he'd worn to work.

"No, thanks," Maggie said, cat in her arms as she stood. "I…need to take a shower." She looked down at the stains and scrapes she'd sustained at his hands.

"I'm really sorry. Let me at least see you home."

"That's all right. I'm not afraid. I take a walk around the neighborhood every evening. I'm sorry I trespassed."

For the first time in his life, a woman appeared to be afraid of him. Harry felt dirty.

And helpless to do anything to change what he was becoming. Because if he had the evening to do over again, he'd make exactly the same choices.

This time, it had been Maggie. The week before it hadn't. Tomorrow it might not be.

"You shouldn't do that," he said now, as the woman started across his backyard to the gate she wouldn't be able to open. He'd put a dead bolt on it over the weekend.

"What?"

"Walk alone at night."

She hugged her cat. "I've been doing it for years."

"My wife was raped last week," Harry blurted, as though that explained everything. His actions. His words. His warning.

Maggie stopped in her tracks, eyes wide, mouth open.

"In this neighborhood?"

"In our house." He was scaring her. But that was good. Necessary. If a little fear could prevent what Laura had suffered…

"Oh, my God. I'm so sorry." Horror had replaced the disbelief. Maggie looked up, focusing on something over Harry's shoulder, and he saw Laura standing on the inside of the sliding glass door.

He waved. Smiled. She waved back, eyeing the woman with the cat.

"Please let me walk you around the block to your house," Harry said. "We'll just have to wait until the police get here, so we can explain that this was a false alarm."

With one last glance at Laura, the woman nodded.

On Thursday night, Harry's foot touched Laura's leg in bed—waking her instantly. Heart pumping, Laura tried to go back to sleep before full consciousness took hold. And counted her heartbeats instead, her nerves like shards of glass beneath her skin.

Slowly, gently, she moved over to the edge of the bed. Harry hadn't been sleeping much and she didn't want to wake him. He didn't have to get up for an hour and a half.

But she couldn't lie there being touched, either.

Tonight made it a week since *it* had happened.

Hugging the side of the guest bed, she kept still, eyes wide open, and stared at the carpet, looking for comfort.

There was none to be found. Not in the carpet that she'd chosen after weeks of studying books filled with options. Not in her mother's voice.

Or her husband's touch.

"Why aren't you getting pregnant?"

Catching a glimpse of herself in the mirror on the bedroom ceiling, hardly recognizing the short dark hair that was once long and amber, she slid her hand down to cover David's groin.

"You said you thought it was the stress." In truth, it was the two abortions she'd had in the twelve months she'd been living with this man. Those were the only two times she'd left the apartment without his approval or knowledge. Free clinics were easy to find near college campuses and the staff asked no questions. David's lust for her, combined with her proven ability to give birth, was keeping her alive. Birthing another child for the brotherhood would kill her.

She was going to die anyway. She knew that. Had known it since she'd gambled on the cops' ability to take down the Ivory Nation and lost. Since her ex-lover had ordered this man—her captor—to kill her because of that betrayal. But she had a job to do first, before she died. An innocent little boy to rescue.

"I want you to come into the clinic for testing."

"Okay." Anything to keep him happy with her.

She'd already been submitting to ovulation monitoring, his vaginal exams to determine the position of her uterus, anything he could manage to do at home, undetected by the fertility clinic where he worked or the third-year medical program he was in.

His hand squeezed her naked breast. Her body was always naked in his bed. That was one of his rules.

"You are a beautiful woman, you know that?" The huskiness was back in his voice. Meaning tonight was going to be a two-timer.

She didn't much care. The more she pleased him, the longer he'd keep her around—the more chance he'd help her get her son back. She'd have to convince him that he'd be a much better father to Luke. Or maybe she could persuade him to give her access to Luke through his connection with Bobby—offer to babysit or something. She'd had to lie low for the first several months, for David's sake as well as hers. Discovery was sure

death. Bobby did not tolerate disobedience or dis-
sension.

But she'd been to the mall and to the university a few
times in the past month, even walked by a group of
cops, and no one seemed to care about the slender,
black-haired woman who moved so quietly among
them. Making it harder and harder to lie low—to wait.

Urgency filling her, she climbed on David's shaft,
pushing herself down on him without foreplay. He liked
it when he had to force her vagina to accept him.

Teasing his nipples with her tongue, she contracted
her muscles, pulling an orgasm out of him.

"Oh, God, yes," he groaned.

"You're more of a man than Bobby Donahue ever
was," she whispered breathlessly, pretending to be as
ready to come as he was. He liked it when he made her
lose control—or thought he did.

His hands on her hips, he stopped pumping into her,
his eyes piercing as he studied her. "You've never said
that before."

"Couldn't you tell?"

"I thought you were in love with him."

"I did too, once. But that was before I got to know
you." She lowered her voice, thinking only of her young
son—a boy who'd be brainwashed before he was five
if she didn't save him. "This year with you, David, everything you've done for me, it's like I've finally met
the man I was made to be with. You've brought magic
into my life for the first time."

"Really." He was frowning.

"Really." Bending down, she covered his mouth with

hers, thrusting her tongue inside, moaning as she spilled her urgency into the caress, making it good for him.

He kissed her with equal fervor. And then he pulled back, although he was still inside her.

"What are you saying?"

The hope in his eyes was exactly what she'd prayed for. Months of being his whore was finally paying off. The man had a soft spot. And he was looking at it. At her.

"I love you, David," she said, saying it with just the right amount of embarrassment, vulnerability and awe. A perfect act. "So much." She kissed him again. "I believe in you. You are definitely one of God's chosen."

And when he rolled over on top of her, pumping into her with a new and frenzied vigor, she met him thrust for thrust. The plan was working.

7

Harry noticed the filmy smear on the back window of his car when he came out from work Friday afternoon. How something could have smashed against the glass without also getting on the paint, he wasn't sure, but went over to wipe it off, regardless.

Until he got close. And stopped in his tracks.

It wasn't a smear. There were four very clear words there, carefully traced in block lettering with a bar of soap.

Say hello to Laura. They knew who he was. Where he worked.

They were taunting him.

Shaking—with anger and fear—Harry pulled out his phone. Called Laura and told her to stay at work until she heard from him.

Then he called Daniel Boyd.

And got Robert Miller.

"I'll send someone to escort your wife home," the detective said urgently. Then, getting specific directions from Harry, he said, "Stay right where you are. Don't touch anything, and I'll meet you there."

* * *

The soap was a common brand, one of billions of bars that could be purchased anywhere in the country. The words were written in block letters with no clear identifiers.

"I'll canvas the campus tomorrow and again on Monday," Miller told Harry on the phone late Friday evening. "Someone has to have seen this guy."

Laura was sitting across from him, *The Truman Show* playing on the large-screen television she'd bought him for Christmas.

"And in the meantime?" Harry asked Miller, frustrated, helplessness making him sick to his stomach. He moved out to the kitchen so he could talk. "Should I get Laura out of town?"

"Your wife is fine." Miller sounded so sure Harry almost believed him. "There was no warning, no threat. This was simply a case of a perp getting arrogant. Rubbing salt in a wound."

"He's after me because my wife is white."

"Again, Mr. Kendall, I understand how you'd think so, but nothing about this case is consistent with a typical hate-crime attack. There was no torture. And no actual threat to you or your wife in today's incident."

Harry swallowed the rage building inside him. "Torture comes in many forms, Detective," he said, resenting Miller as much as he'd found himself resenting Boyd over the past week. Not because of anything they were or weren't doing. But because Harry felt so damned powerless to do anything at all. "If the attack had been random, one of a kind, why taunt me?"

"Perps often pump themselves up reliving the crime. My guess is we got us a first-time offender here. He's feeling his power. Not yet desensitized enough to take things in stride."

And *that* was supposed to make Harry feel better?

"He knows where I work."

"Easy enough to find out. He knows where you live. All he'd have to do is follow you."

The bastard was hanging around his house? Around Laura? Hand to his head, he dropped down to the table. "She's not safe here."

"Listen, Mr. Kendall, we're doing all we can. We've got feelers out with the known white supremacist organizations operating in Tucson. We haven't ruled out the possibility that this was a hate crime. But in all honesty, it doesn't look that way. If we spend too much energy in that area, we might miss the real culprits and all information leading to them will be cold. In the meantime, we've got extra surveillance around the Botanical Garden and in your neighborhood, as well."

Harry had seen patrol cars driving by recently. Something he hadn't noticed in five years of living on the quiet residential street. They weren't close to any of their neighbors, but there'd never been any problems in the neighbourhood. They waved when they saw each other, said hello at the grocery store. Watched each other's houses during vacations or absences. And as far as Harry knew, no one had ever had reason to call the cops.

"If I'm being targeted," he said, unable to let this go, "maybe he's someone from school." He *was* being targeted. It was the one thing Harry knew. Without doubt. And he'd keep harping on it, keep riding the detectives' tails until they figured it out, too.

There was too much at stake here.

"They could both be on campus," Miller's voice was noncommittal. "Could even turn out that this was some kind of fraternity initiation. If so, they've tipped their hands. If they're there, we'll find them."

Harry didn't want to wait. He was tired of waiting. Tired of not being able to hug or kiss his wife. Tired, period.

A hit.

Daniel Boyd sat up straight, his gaze glued to the computer screen in front of him. In between working on other cases, he'd spent nine days staring at credit-card receipts, following up with visits to every establishment Laura and Harry Kendall had visited in the past month, searching out every human being they might've had contact with. And he'd spent his nights studying cell-phone records, paying particular attention to incoming calls. Meanwhile, his partner had pursued the physical leads, interviewing everyone the Kendalls had associated with in recent weeks, from the personnel at the fertility clinic to students in Harry's classroom. After all that, something as innocuous as a bitten-off piece of leather had scored.

He picked up the phone.

"Hello?" Jess Robbins's voice sounded huskier than usual.

"You asleep?"

"Daniel? It's almost midnight! Yes, I'm sleeping—or I was. I have to be at work in the morning, catching up on things I didn't get done during the week, and unlike you, I do require regular rest."

Midnight. Shit. "Sorry."

His apology was met with a yawn. "It's okay." Her voice gained momentum. "If I had your energy, I'd probably work as much as you do. There's never enough time to catch them all, you know?"

He did know. So did she. Jess was the best when it came to forensics. That was why she was going in to work on Sunday morning.

"What's up?"

They hadn't gone out in months—in spite of her not-so-subtle hints. As soon as he solved this one, he'd remedy that.

"That black leather glove you did the work-up on for me—"

"The one I could've lost my job over, using the county's lab—and my time—for an unauthorized report, you mean?" she interrupted with her usual dry sarcasm.

Which Boyd completely ignored.

"There's only one place in the state that imports that type of leather—in the form of premade clothing, including outerwear."

"Congratulations."

"Unfortunately, the company supplies retail stores all over Arizona."

"A small inconvenience to someone with your tenacity. And energy." Sarcasm gave way to a softer, warmer note in her voice.

Daniel melted a bit. "You want to have dinner next week?"

"You just trying to get out of the doghouse for waking me up?"

More like feeling guilty for how readily he'd asked for her help. "No."

"Call me when you break this one, big guy, and I'll grill you a nice juicy steak."

He could taste it already.

It was two in the morning. Laura had been asleep since eleven. And apparently still was. No lights had come on.

A national news channel popped up on the large-screen TV as Sunday night, and Harry's sleeplessness, wore on.

He stared at the screen, remembering back to those halcyon days of ignorance. The kind of days most people lived, doing daily tasks and chores, unaware that living right beside them was a violence that could destroy the spirit, mar the soul, change everything forever…

The face of an Arizona politician flashed onto the screen and with a shaking hand, Harry pushed the volume up a notch, distracting himself from unproductive thoughts.

"Mr. Moss, you're campaigning for one of Arizona's senatorial seats in Washington on a platform that calls for strengthening the family…."

"That's right." Moss, his thick graying hair kept short, nodded.

The man expostulated in his soft-spoken voice about anti-abortion and anti-gay statutes that he supported. Closed minds, Harry thought. Closed doors.

How much did Moss pay for that suit? Harry wondered. The fabric moved fluidly with every gesture the politician made. There wasn't a wrinkle to be seen.

He'd never seen George Moss in newspaper photos or on television in anything other than a perfectly pressed and expensive suit.

Did Moss ever get dirty? Had he ever been in love with someone society told him he couldn't have?

Did he have a daughter who'd been raped?

Or a wife?

"What about border patrol?" the interviewer asked.

Harry half listened. An Arizona politician didn't get interviewed these days without that particular question being posed. There were no easy answers. And no politically safe ones, either. Which was why no one really gave them.

"The number of illegal immigrants is rising." Moss launched into the pat reply—something everyone knew. "The public is at risk."

But not just from illegals, Harry wanted to tell him. Young white men put the public at risk, too. Bigots put society at risk.

Moss sat forward, uncrossing his feet. Studio lights glared off the shine on his shoes. Staring straight at the camera—straight into Harry's eyes—Moss said, "It's estimated that approximately forty-four-hundred Americans are murdered annually by illegal aliens." Estimated by whom? Harry wondered.

"That's approximately 21,900 Americans murdered by illegal aliens since September 11, 2001," Moss continued. Was he fear-mongering? Of course he was. But was there any truth to any of these assertions?

If so, maybe closed doors weren't all bad. Harry turned to see what Laura thought of that. Her parents supported Moss—and all conservative candidates. Had she heard these statistics before?

He turned—and felt the knife in his gut again as he realized she wasn't there beside him. She was in bed. Alone. Without him.

Luke whimpered, his body stiffening in Bobby's arms, before settling back down to sleep with a hiccupped sigh. Two in the morning, and Sunday night's Ivory Nation worship service was still going on, with six more members yet to stand. This promised to be the longest weekly spiritual meeting ever.

Tony, seated next to him in the meeting room in the basement of Brother Jones's downtown Flagstaff antique store, was one of those who'd asked to stand in front of his fellow brothers and cleanse himself. Tony had confessed to Bobby that he'd accepted the assistance of a minority teaching assistant the week before. The young man's bag was already packed and in his car; he'd be driving back to Tucson for his eight o'clock Monday morning political science class, but he refused to leave until he'd been made pure once again.

Adrenaline rushed through Bobby's veins, singeing him beneath the skin, as he anticipated Tony's turn.

"I am a bad man seeking to be good." Roger Wilcox, a local news reporter, faced the group of one hundred and fifty men and boys, ranging in age from two to sixty-one, who regularly traveled from around the state to attend these sacred meetings. Few women were members of the Ivory Nation, but those who were held their own meetings on Wednesday mornings in this very same place. Always with Bobby in attendance.

"I know that Cain is the direct result of Eve's fornication with Satan," Roger continued. "That the End is near and that we white men, are the chosen people of God. That we alone will survive the cataclysm that is soon to come."

Hearing the words gave Bobby a thrill that wiped away any feeling of sleepiness. Forty-two times tonight he'd heard them. And each time was as good as the first.

Roger took off his shirt. "I do not deserve the shirt on my back," he said, as had many of his brothers before him that night. "This week I gave up my seat in a waiting area to a minority woman who was pregnant." Roger choked up, shaking his head. "She was spawning the devil's child and because others were staring at me I bowed to social pressure."

Roger turned his back to the group and, without a wince, received the slap of a leather strap on his bare skin.

Yes. Bobby almost spoke the chant aloud, envisioning the welts that he'd worn on his own back over the years. Roger would be a better man, a better servant of God for tonight's obedience.

The serene smile on Roger's face as he again faced the brethren stirred envy in Bobby's soul. There was nothing like the high of a good cleansing. Smiling nods from the men around him confirmed what Bobby knew to the very core of his being. They weren't mere mortals.

They were God's chosen people.

Roger dropped his pants.

Bobby's own garments grew a bit tight as his body reacted to the extreme levels of emotion. There was nothing even remotely sexual about his slightly enlarged penis.

"I am an extremely bad man," Roger told the group, as he stood humiliated before them. "I deserve to be lashed for my sins. The unclean woman smiled at me—" he started to tear up and Bobby held his breath, immediately fearful "—and I smiled back."

Saying nothing else, accepting the verbal slurs that flew at him from the members of his Ivory Nation family, Roger spun to face the wall behind him. He jerked a time or two as the backs of his thighs took the whipping he deserved. Five of them for a second infraction. Each one harder than the last.

And when Roger again faced the righteous men seated before him, dressed in nothing but briefs and white-laced boots, his face was glowing.

And his penis enlarged.

Yes.

They needed milk. Exhausted when he got home from work Monday night, the last thing Harry wanted to do was go to the grocery store. But he sure as hell wasn't sending Laura alone.

Boyd had found nothing.

Miller had found nothing.

The predators were still out there. Still hating him.

And Laura, because of him.

Every hour, they got closer to the rapists repeating themselves. His research told him that the power-reassurance profile predicted a seven-to-fifteen day cycle.

Every hour, they got closer to a hater's adrenaline building to the explosion point again.

"If you want to wait here, I'll run in," Laura said, opening the door of his Lexus as he pulled into the store parking lot a couple of blocks from their home.

He considered the offer. Glanced at the brightly lit parking lot between the car and the door. Twenty five yards of blacktop. At night.

"I'll come in with you."

"I can go, Harry. I'll be fine."

She probably would be.

"I said I'm coming."

"Harry." The unusual firmness in her tone took him aback. "We have to stop this. I'm a grown woman. I can go to the store by myself."

Under different circumstances, of course she could.

"You are the victim of a hate crime, Laura. And the perpetrators are still out there. Could be following us everywhere for all we know. They could've seen us leave the house and come here and—"

"That's enough! Harry, listen to yourself."

He did. Day in and day out. Nights, too. And he knew he was right.

"I'm not backing down on this, Laura. I can't. They got by me once. It won't happen a second time."

The softening of her expression as she stared at him—and then nodded—didn't make Harry feel any better.

She felt sorry for *him*.

They were in the frozen-food aisle when Harry noticed the medium-height, college-age man watching Laura. There was nothing particularly threatening about the kid. He wasn't muscular. Didn't have tattoos all over his body or spiked hair. He wasn't wearing chains or bullets through his ears. As a matter of fact, he had on painter shorts, a U of A T-shirt, and an expensive and popular brand of tennis shoe.

So why were Harry's instinct's screaming at him to pay attention? Why did it feel as though something was crawling on the back of his neck?

He moved between the kid and Laura, blocking his view. And he stayed that way as his wife completed their shopping. When she asked him what kind of cereal he wanted, he picked one.

He didn't care what it was. He'd eat whatever was there when he got up in the morning. Another aisle over, he saw the kid again.

Looking at Laura. Harry was sure of it. Laura didn't seem to notice.

And wasn't that part of the problem? Her refusal to see the dangers that still lurked? To realize that the rape had merely been a warning?

Hands in the pockets of his shorts, every muscle tense as he prepared to protect his wife, Harry stood in the checkout line, slid his debit card through the pay slot, loaded bagged groceries back into the cart, most of his attention on the area around them. He'd lost sight of the kid, but didn't allow himself to relax.

Predators lurked.

Outside, he resisted the urge to roll the cart quickly to the car, pacing himself so that he stayed behind Laura. Chances were, nothing was going to come at them from the front.

And there, leaning against the lamp post—almost brazenly, as though challenging them—was the kid.

Harry stared at him.

He stared right back.

And Harry *knew*. This kid was one of the rapists. The smaller one.

"Get in the car," he said softly but with intensity, passing Laura the keys.

He waited until she did so. And then he was finished with waiting.

Pushing the basket against the tire of his car, lodging it there as a barrier to prevent the guy from getting around him, Harry lunged. He grabbed the kid and spun him around in one motion, locking his arm around the bastard's neck.

"Where's your partner?" he practically spat in the younger man's face. "Is he nearby?" Harry took a quick glance around. "Maybe waiting for your signal?"

"Harry?" Laura was there.

"Get back in the car, dammit," he said, tightening his hold around the kid, mostly to make a point. So far, the other man wasn't struggling so much as trying to pull Harry's arm from around his throat.

"Where is he?" he demanded with another jerk of his arm.

The kid looked at him—and Harry faltered for a second. Pure fear stared back at him.

"I don't know what you're talking about, man," the kid choked out. "Take my wallet. My keys. I don't care. Take whatever you want." His voice was getting higher, fainter, his face crumpled like he was going to cry.

"Harry! Let him go! You're hurting him."

"Josh!" The young man started when the female scream reverberated in the parking lot. Harry had barely been aware that people were beginning to crowd around, but now he became fully conscious of them.

A young girl ran up, swinging her purse at Harry's head. "Let him go!" she screamed.

And with a very sudden and sickening image of himself, of what he'd just done, Harry released his grip.

"Someone call the cops," the girl shouted.

"No!" This time it was Laura's voice raised in alarm. "Please, he didn't mean anything."

As Harry stood there, dazed, Laura moved next to him, pressing her side against his, holding his arm with both of hers.

"I'm really sorry." She spoke to the young couple as a crowd continued to gather behind them. "I…I was raped last week. Right around the corner from here. My… husband…saw the…them…and thought he was…"

"Oh, my God!" The girl's entire demeanor changed. "In this neighborhood?"

As Laura nodded, the kid frowned at Harry. And someone behind them said the police were on their way.

"I saw you looking at her in the store," was all Harry could offer. He'd just assaulted a man. He was going to jail.

And yet he couldn't tell himself he'd have done anything differently.

"She reminded me of someone I knew," the kid responded, still frowning as he rubbed his neck but speaking with more compassion than hostility.

Harry nodded.

And waited for the cops to arrive.

Wednesday evening, with a quick glance around the popular Mexican restaurant, Laura slid into the side of the booth that was against the back wall.

Kelly Holbrook, fellow botanist, assistant and closest friend, threw her denim purse on the orange padded bench opposite her and sat down.

"It's great having dinner after work. Much better than a one-hour lunch," she said, shoving her long auburn hair over her shoulder as she grinned. "We can actually have a drink."

"A margarita." Laura agreed, keeping her eye on an athletic-looking white man eating alone a few tables over. He was the right height. The right weight.

And one of about twenty men in the room who fit the bill.

She needed that margarita.

Two weeks ago, it would've been lemonade.

"Where's Harry tonight?" A streak of dirt marked the front of Kelly's light-green regulation tank top. Though she couldn't see them, Laura knew there were similar marks on the tan shorts of her friend's work uniform.

And on her own, as well. After a morning spent tending to plants, measuring growth and taking soil samples, the two of them had spent the afternoon comparing lab reports on six different cultures of prickly-pear pectin in Laura's office behind the greenhouse at the Tucson Botanical Gardens. The space had been given to them as part of a grant to study medicinal plants indigenous to southern Arizona.

The man was still there. Looking around.

"Tae kwon do," she said now, anxious for a waitress to take their drink order.

"Harry's doing martial arts?" Kelly's eyes grew wide. "Since when?"

"Tonight." The man looked right at her.

"Why?"

She didn't want to think about that. Or the man eating a few yards away. His fingers were long, lean.

Would they bruise a woman's breast?

Did he recognize her? Unlike him—if it was him—she'd been in plain sight.

Did he know what her breast felt like?

"Laura?"

Kelly's voice brought her back with a start. Laura focused on her friend's remarkably creamy complexion, the kindness in her eyes, refusing to allow her gaze to wander again.

"I asked you why Harry's suddenly into martial arts."

"He says he's beginning to feel like an old man sitting in his office all day every day."

The response was lame. The truth, too painful to share. The other night, during that scene at the grocery store, Harry had been one-on-one. He was determined to be able to take down two men. He was going to protect her at any cost.

And that scared her, too.

"I thought he played tennis."

"He does." But tennis, while keeping a man fit, didn't teach him self-defense moves that could maim or kill an aggressor.

"He felt like trying something a little more physical, huh?" Kelly filled in the blanks that Laura was leaving.

"I guess." She didn't want to think about Harry tonight. "Someone from the university was talking to him about it and…"

That much was true. It had been a student of his the year before; they'd been talking about art history and the student had claimed that tae kwon do was art of the body. He'd cajoled Harry into agreeing to try it someday.

It'd been one of those "somedays" she'd thought would never come.

Harry was a lover, not a fighter.

Or he had been.

Now he'd only been spared a felony assault charge thanks to the good hearts of a young college couple who refused to press charges—and a D. A. who agreed with them. But not until Harry had spent a couple of hours in jail the other night. While the milk they'd gone to purchase had soured in the car.

The man rose. Glanced her way. Dropped some bills on the table. Turned.

And left the restaurant.

"Didn't you say that Duane and Lateisha are expecting?" Kelly asked shortly after dinner arrived, giving Laura's chaotic thoughts a place to land once more.

"Yeah." Laura scooped rice onto her fork. "She's six months along. They just found out it's a boy."

Kelly had met the couple several times at gatherings and cook-outs at Laura and Harry's house over the past few years.

"What about you?"

Laura choked on a bite of cheese enchilada as Kelly's question sailed innocuously over the table.

She wasn't going to talk about herself. There was nothing to talk about. Nothing anyone needed to know about her. Ever again.

Fork in midair, Kelly perused her. "The fertility clinic," she reminded her, head slightly tilted. "You were talking about it nonstop and then a couple of weeks ago, right after the appointment for the procedure, you just quit mentioning it. I thought that meant you might be pregnant. I've been waiting for you to tell me it worked."

"We didn't have the procedure."

"But you had the appointment…."

"That was the day I had the flu," Laura said quickly, unable to meet her friend's gaze. "We had to reschedule."

"So when is it?"

When was it? Laura could hardly comprehend the question.

Keeping a hold on reality and just getting through each day was about all she could manage. Thoughts of putting her body through medical procedures, or actually bringing an innocent child into such an ugly world, were inconceivable.

She might change her mind.

The counselor she'd been seeing twice a week since the rape had assured her that would be the case.

Laura didn't believe her.

8

In gym shorts and a T-shirt, Harry lay back in one corner of the couch on Thursday evening, Laura curled up at the other end.

She'd changed into pajama shorts and a T-shirt.

It was a few hours short of the two-week mark.

"Marsha Gainsboro came to see me on Monday."

The sixty-year-old head of the History department, who'd been at the university almost forty years, intimidated just about everyone who came into contact with her. She'd taken a liking to Harry the first day they met—back in his undergraduate days.

"What'd she want? To move your office again? Make you take on more class hours? Or change the textbook you're using?"

She'd done all of that during the five years he'd been on the U of A faculty.

"I'm not really sure what she wanted," Harry said slowly, filtering his thoughts—something he'd never done with Laura until two weeks ago.

Something he did all the time now.

"She talked about getting semester grades in, but I'm always on time and the due date was set long ago. She mentioned fall semester, but there again, that schedule was finalized months ago."

"Maybe she just wanted to make sure you were still okay with everything."

Maybe. He didn't think so.

"She also asked me if I'd rather team-teach the fall seminar with Sanderson instead of Bartles."

"Sanderson's younger—and more interested in social history, like you are."

"Sanderson's black."

"So?"

"Bartles is white."

Laura's foot moved, almost imperceptibly, but Harry could've been convinced there'd been a mini-earthquake tremor all the way from the California coast, he felt the motion so clearly. She was no longer touching him.

"Harry, you can't possibly believe that Professor Gainsboro has any prejudice against you…"

Pouring the rest of his glass of wine down his throat, Harry scrutinized his wife.

"Can't I?"

"No! She's been your mentor for more than ten years."

"People change."

"Not that much."

"Maybe I just wasn't looking before. Maybe she knows something I don't. Maybe she heard that we were trying to have a baby and was appalled by the thought that white wasn't staying with white."

The acid was back, eating away at his stomach. Laura's horror-stricken expression didn't help.

"Don't talk like that!"

"Someone out there thinks it, Laura," he said, unable to dispel the intensity of his tone. "I hear that guy every single day, whispering insidiously inside my head. *White stays with white,*" he whispered. And then again.

"Detective Boyd said—"

"I don't care what he said," Harry said now, leaning closer to Laura. She *had* to believe him. To realize what they were up against. He couldn't be with her twenty-four hours a day. Couldn't protect her all the time. "You heard the other one mention white, too, Laura. That was no co-incidence. *We're* the ones who stand to be hurt by ignoring this. *We're* the ones who have to do something about it."

"No, Harry." Laura stood, backed away from him. "No."

Emotion choked him as he watched Laura stride to the hallway leading to the guest bedroom.

Hope rose through the darkness for a second as she stopped and looked at him, her face shadowed in the hall light.

"I want peace, Harry. Can you understand that?" Her words were half whisper, half impassioned plea. "I don't want to do anything about this except recover. I don't want to challenge these guys or risk inciting them in any way. I don't want them even to remember me. Nor do I want to remember them." Her voice grew stronger as she continued. "I don't want to hear about them or think about them again. I have to move on."

"Move on to what? This was a direct attack against

you and me, Laura. Last Friday's incident at school just confirms that! If we don't stop these guys, who knows what they'll do next? Run me off the road? Burn down the house? Get you alone?"

She shook her head. "It was a random incident," she told him, fear lacing her words. "It happened. It's done. Nothing can undo it, but nothing says I have to dwell on it, either."

Sweat started at the back of Harry's neck. Standing, he came slowly down the hall, stopping several feet away.

"And what if these guys break into another house, Laura? What if we do nothing and that allows them to attack another couple as they did us? An attack we could've helped prevent? Can you live with that?"

Lips trembling, Laura stared at him for a long minute. The tears welling in her eyes cut clear through him.

"I will do whatever I can to help the police," she said quietly. "I want them to do their jobs and will cooperate fully in whatever way they deem necessary. Other than that, I have to get on with my life."

She was in the guest room, with the door shut in his face before he could reply.

Her words were like flames, burning him long into the night.

She'd said she was getting on with *her* life.

As though it was something completely separate from his.

Lifting his suit coat from the back of his chair, Daniel Boyd slid his arms into the sleeves as he headed for the hall.

"Meeting the Kendalls?" Miller asked, looking up from the mass of folders he'd been frowning over at his desk. Laura and Harry Kendall were coming in to identify a suspect.

"Yep."

"Reception'll show them back."

"They know us," he said, frowning at his partner. "They'll feel more comfortable this way. You could come, too."

"You go ahead. I'll be there."

Daniel shook his head. Robert Miller was a man he'd trust with his life but would never understand. Miller was a good father. A family man. Yet sometimes Daniel found him strangely lacking in compassion.

Turning, he picked up his step. If all went well, he'd be eating Jess's grilled steak by sundown. Not a bad way to spend Friday night.

The Kendalls went in separately. Laura first. Daniel wasn't taking any chances on a defense attorney having the identification suppressed in court due to victims influencing each other.

Dressed in tan shorts, a light-green polo shirt and tennis shoes, Laura looked about sixteen as she stood in front of the two-way mirror, her long blond hair pulled into a pony tail.

"No." Laura said slowly, drawing out the word, and Daniel felt a far-too-familiar surge of impotence. She frowned, scrutinizing each of the five six-feet-tall men standing in a row on the other side.

"Look again," Miller urged, his face tense—reminding Daniel once again that while Robert was different from him, he cared, too.

"I don't recognize any of them. But then, how could I be expected to?" she continued, glancing from Boyd to Miller. "I didn't see their faces."

He'd known that, of course. "I was just hoping there'd be *something* you'd recognize—something you hadn't realized you'd seen."

"If…" She licked her lips, her gaze darting to the door that led to the hall where her husband waited. "If you could get them to whisper, maybe…"

Boyd nodded to Miller, who picked up a phone.

Each of the five men whispered in turn. Laura Kendall showed no response whatsoever. Boyd nodded to have the exercise repeated. A whisper, by its nature, didn't transfer well through a microphone and speakers.

Stiffly, Laura turned. Shook her head.

"Look one more time, Mrs. Kendall." Daniel was convinced the second guy on the right was their man. "You sure there's nothing familiar about any of them?"

Shoes maybe? The shape of a hand? As tempting as it was to lead her into the identification, he knew better. It would be thrown out of court right along with the case he'd built.

"Nothing. I'm sorry." Avoiding his gaze, she let herself out.

"I don't recognize any of the voices," Harry, still staring at the men lined up with their hands crossed in front of them, looked as disappointed as Daniel felt.

"And how could I recognize his features? He was hooded and covered up and all in black."

Daniel was hoping the county attorney would take that into account and charge the man anyway.

Mike Goodall, the hit Daniel had come up with during his search of sales records, had purchased two pairs of black leather gloves, made from the same material as that taken from Harry Kendall's mouth, two days before the rape. Upon further investigation, Daniel and Robert had discovered that Goodall had priors for assault and attempted rape and, when questioned, had lied about his alibi for the night of the rape. He'd purchased a pair of 60-pound-capacity hand-held suction cups off the Internet the month before. They'd searched his place and found a pair of size eleven boots that matched the tread pattern taken from outside the Kendall home.

"Did someone check his penis?" Harry Kendall asked, his voice rising with obvious frustration.

Daniel needed something to give this man. Needed to do his damned job and get the guys who'd irreparably violated this small family.

"We already got the judge to sign an order for a photo lineup," he said.

Miller stepped up to the window. "We need this done in a medical setting, but I know a doctor who'll work us in. I'll see if we can make this happen today."

They had to do it today. Otherwise, without a charge, they'd have to let Mike Goodall go.

Two hours later, Daniel and Robert stared at the photos lined up on the table in an interrogation room at the station.

Miller shook his head.

"Not a single mark. On any of them," Daniel said. "Could be it healed and didn't leave a scar but…"

"No scar, no proof," Robert Miller finished with a heavy sigh. "Shit. Two young guys break into a home, terrorize a happy, successful couple and we can't find one iota of evidence. You'd think they were professionals."

"Except for the message on the windshield," Daniel said. "That was sheer stupidity."

"Still turned up nothing."

Daniel let out a string of words his navy father would not have been proud of. "So we're back to square one—except the trail's colder." He snapped at his partner, as though this was somehow Miller's fault. Just because the man went home to his wife and kid every night. "Get back out there, find anyone who'll talk to you about any gang activity in the city—let's look again at the hate-crime angle."

Miller nodded. "I'm already on it. But in the past five years we've gone from one to five-hundred supremacist groups on the Internet. Hitting the streets isn't going to do it for us. And how in hell do we infiltrate five hundred of them?"

"I don't know," Daniel said, annoyed. Tired. Angry that the answers were eluding him. "But we'd better figure that out."

In the meantime, there went his steak dinner.

As she left the station, Laura watched her rearview mirror all the way back to work. No one was following her. She knew that.

Her nerves weren't convinced.

Detective Boyd believed one of the men in that room had been her rapist. And because she'd been unable to identify him, that man might soon be free.

Bette Midler's "Wind Beneath My Wings" came on the radio. Laura turned it up, thinking of Harry and how meeting him had helped her escape the shell she'd been encased within since birth. He'd helped her fly.

And now he thought *he* was the reason she'd crashed and burned.

He couldn't be. The incident had been random, not aimed at them. Not a hate crime. They hadn't beaten her up or done any of the other horrible things people like that generally did. There'd been no threats. Then or since.

She couldn't get up every day if she had to fear that she was the target of hate simply because she'd fallen in love with a man who had darker skin than she did. The world wasn't so closed-minded. Not anymore.

Harry was just wrong.

Slightly sick to her stomach, Laura went straight for the ladies' room instead of the lunchroom when she got back to work. Emotional stress was taking its toll on her system. Upsetting her stomach.

There was no other reason. She'd taken a morning-after pill. She had nothing to worry about.

When the bathroom visit didn't totally dispel the nausea, Laura took her sandwich out to her favorite flowering garden to sit with the plants and the birds and remember what life was really about.

Some of her best memories were of times alone in the gardens in her parent's backyard, where she could focus on the magic of life, the inexplicable beauty of natural colors and shapes and scents that took her breath away—the strength of a seemingly fragile stem and leaf pushing up through the earth to reach for the sun.

Today—as she had every day during the past two weeks—Laura glanced over her shoulder as she bypassed her usual seat in the middle of the garden, to choose a cement bench at the back of the fenced enclosure. She could see everything—and no one could see her. She had her pepper spray in her lap, her phone open beside her with the Botanical Garden's security programmed into her speed dial.

Inhaling the sweet combination of Jasminium Sambac, Damianita shrubs and creosote, she opened her mind and heart to the beauty around her, allowing powers stronger than anything human to work on her and through her. To heal her.

And still she was afraid.

"Hey! Whatcha doing?"

Laura screamed, accidentally flinging her lunch into the middle of a Damianita shrub a couple of yards in front of her.

"Laura?"

She recognized Kelly, saw the concern on her friend's face as she came closer. Clasping her hands, Laura tried look normal, calm, while painfully aware that her sandwich sat atop Daminaita foliage.

She wanted to retrieve it. Her knees were too shaky.

"What's up?" Kelly asked. Sitting beside her, she took Laura's hand. "What's wrong?"

"Nothing." Feeling sick, Laura tried to grin. "You just surprised me, that's all… I was meditating. Guess I went too deep…." Breathless, heart still pounding, she forced out the words.

"Laura." She'd heard Kelly say her name countless times. Yet this time it was different. Commanding. And yet compassionate.

"Tell me what's going on."

Frantic to ease Kelly's mind, Laura looked right at her. "Nothing. I'm fine."

"Okay, you're fine." Kelly continued to hold both of Laura's hands. "But something's not right. You've been acting strange ever since you were sick," Kelly said. "You're not seriously ill, are you? Some scary diagnosis and you're just not telling me?"

"No. Really. I—"

The shake of Kelly's head stopped Laura's words. "Your sense of joy is missing," she said. "The way you have of bringing calm and serenity wherever you go. It's not working."

How did one bring serenity into a dark room where two men were ripping off your underwear and forcing themselves…inside you.

"I—" Her throat was so dry.

"Did you get bad news from the clinic?" Kelly's gaze was as warm as the squeeze she gave Laura's cold fingers. "Are you or Harry infertile?"

"No, of course not. I'd tell you that."

"So what *wouldn't* you tell me?"

The gentle, loving way Kelly was looking at her almost made Laura cry. She tried to speak, but couldn't.

"Does Harry know?" Kelly's frown was a sure indicator that she wasn't going to back down.

"What do you mean?"

"Does he understand what's bothering you?"

"I tell Harry everything. You know that."

Relief replacing her frown, Kelly nodded again, this time more easily. Kelly knew Harry well. Because of time spent with Laura, but also because Kelly was getting her doctorate at the university and had taken an evening class the previous year on the same nights Harry had been assigned to teach one. He'd walked her to her car during the dark winter months.

"I need you to tell me what it is, Laura." Kelly's voice dropped. "Please. I'm driving myself crazy worrying about you and trying to guess what's wrong. Is it me?"

Laura shook her head quickly, but before she could speak Kelly went on. "I've gone over every conversation we've had, tried to figure out if there's something I did or didn't do that might've upset you."

Each word was a weight on Laura's heart—and a catalyst to movement. She was trying to get on with her life in the aftermath of horror. She'd never considered that her strategies for survival were hurting Kelly.

Watching the expressions cross her friend's face, seeing the moisture in her eyes, Laura *wanted* to speak. But she wasn't sure how…

Her counselor had told her that speaking about the

incident was the way to find healing. That she had no
reason to feel ashamed, or in any way to blame.

And still, thinking of marring Kelly's day with this
ugliness did make her feel guilty.

But if she kept it to herself...

Kelly stood. "Okay," she said, glancing down at
Laura. "If you won't tell me, you won't, but I hope you
know that if you need a friend, you can trust me to—"

"I was raped." With the sun in her eyes as she looked
up, Laura couldn't see Kelly's expression. But she felt
the air gush from Kelly's lungs. And her heart sickened
as her friend sat down.

9

On Monday, two weeks and four days after the attack, Harry sat in his office, watching the nine-inch television on one corner of his desk.

He used to listen to the news if he was in his office over the lunch hour. Lately, the TV was on whenever he was there. He needed the noise. The diversion.

And in the meantime, he studied the facts. Considered theories. He was a scholar. He could figure this out. He *had* to figure it out. It was becoming far too clear that the Tucson police department wasn't going to get the job done. Which meant Harry had to handle this on his own.

He'd been reading—FBI and other law enforcement abstracts—and had learned that understanding the psychology of the attacker was crucial to finding him. Only by getting into his head could the investigator predict his next moves. And be ready for him.

Harry turned to his computer screen.

Those who hate gather together to feed each other's need for bolstering, to validate beliefs that make them feel powerful. For the same reasons, they isolate themselves from people who don't believe as they do.

Haters are insecure and need to constantly hear the rhetoric to avoid the introspection that could lead to self-doubt and feelings of impotence, vulnerability, ineffectiveness and weakness.

Almost rabid for information now, Harry continued to read.

Time spent away from the cohort, away from the communal rhetoric, allows hot tempers to cool and hate to dissipate. Haters must avoid that. Cool tempers lead to introspection, which leads straight back to a sense of inferiority. To prevent this, haters must constantly turn up the intensity in teaching and action to keep their hate burning—keep the feelings of power alive...

Turn up the intensity. Meaning the next attack would be worse? Would it target the same victim? Or just support the same cause?

"Dr. Kendall?"

Turning, Harry quickly minimized his screen as he saw the grad student hesitating on the threshold of his office.

"Denise, come in."

"I wasn't sure you'd be here, since this isn't your office hour. I don't want to interrupt if you're busy...."

"No." He tried for an easy smile. And busied himself turning off the television. "I'm ready for a break. What's up?"

"I wanted to talk to you about yesterday's lecture on the War of Independence."

Pulling an old wooden chair closer to his desk, Harry motioned for Denise to sit, welcoming the brief respite.

"I've got twenty minutes before class," he said. "Will that be enough time?"

Denise nodded and, to his surprise, completely engaged Harry's brain in a fifteen-minute conversation about a particular black commander's position in the war. Denise, like Harry, believed the man, though burdened by second-class status, had actually been one of George Washington's most trusted compatriots.

He gave Denise an article to read, one he'd come across years ago, when he'd been a grad student. An article that had led him to primary sources that, in his opinion, proved the theory they'd been discussing.

The ensuing paper he'd written, and then turned into his doctoral thesis, had been published in a prestigious journal of eighteenth-century American history.

It had also, he was certain, earned him his current position as the youngest full professor at the university.

"That's his door."

The softly spoken words from out in the hall froze Harry's blood. His entire body instantly chilled, and he stiffened, gripping the arms of his chair.

Instinctively listening for a response, for validation that he'd really heard something, Harry wasted precious seconds. Then, with a glance at Denise, whose head was still bent over the paper, he rushed for the door, only half aware of his chair falling over behind him.

The hallway was empty. Harry ran to the closest

exit. No one was out there, either. And by the time he got to the other end, nothing.

"Dr. Kendall?" Eyes glistening brightly in her dark face, Denise stood in the opening to his office. "Are you okay?"

"Fine."

"What's wrong? What happened?"

Frowning, Harry surveyed the empty hallway once more. "I wanted to find out who was speaking outside my door."

"Someone spoke?"

"You didn't hear it?"

Denise shook her head, hitching her backpack up higher on her shoulders. "But I was pretty focused on what I was reading. That's powerful stuff."

Harry's nod was preoccupied at best. Denise stayed in the doorway as he passed by. He righted his chair before he fell into it.

"What did the person say?" she asked with concern.

Waving off the question, Harry concentrated on calming breaths. Composure. "I'm not sure," he lied. "I probably just imagined it."

He feared that was closer to the truth than he wanted to believe.

"Boyd."

Daniel Boyd glanced wearily around the large room at the desks surrounding his. Most had people behind them, it was Monday afternoon and weekends always brought a new surge of crime.

"Detective? This is Harry Kendall."

Daniel issued a silent swearword. It didn't help.

"Mr. Kendall. What can I do for you?" *That I'm not already doing?*

"It's been eighteen days, Detective."

"I'm aware of that." Daniel dropped his pen, leaned further back in his chair than was wise, and tried not to let the tension get to him. He'd almost fallen asleep last night when Laura Kendall's face swam before his vision, sending his mind on another wild-goose chase after two men he couldn't picture and hadn't found. He'd gone from there to Connie Frank, a young woman who'd been raped in a ditch at the side of Ina Road on Saturday. She'd been walking alone in the middle of the night—an easy target for any crazy driving by.

He had semen this time, though. She hadn't bathed before another driver had come by and taken her to the hospital.

Thank God for semen.

And for the fact that there was only one perp this time. One bastard to hunt down and haul off the streets.

"Power-reassurance rapists repeat on a fifteen-day cycle," Kendall was saying. Daniel took a deep breath.

"Power assertives are on a twenty-day cycle, Detective."

The man had been reading criminology journals again—gaining enough information to drive himself crazy, but not enough to do Daniel's job for him. Harry Kendall needed a psychologist, not a middle-aged detective who was doing everything he possibly could and then some.

"We've got extra patrols in your area, Mr. Kendall."

"So *you* do think there's a chance they'll be back."

"There's always a chance. But it's slim."

"Then why the patrol?"

Because I can't forget what they did to your wife—and I've got to sleep some time.

"Just a precaution."

"Do you do this for every rape case?"

He needed a shot of whiskey. "No."

"Then why ours?"

He considered lying. Disconnecting the call. "Because I don't like unanswered questions," Daniel told the truth, kicking himself as he did. It was time to see Jess. Steak dinner or not.

"Because of what I heard."

Kendall's obsession with racism was going to be the man's undoing.

"Because there were two of them and that doesn't fit the profile for a rape crime." And because they hadn't taken anything, damaged anything, harmed either of their victims other than in the obvious ways.

"I have to know, Detective. How worried are you that they'll be back?"

➤ He should've hung up. If he weren't so damned tired, he would have.

Bullshit. He was a slave to Harry Kendall's feelings. He couldn't separate work from his personal reactions.

But he would, by God.

"In my opinion, your chances are slim to none," he said slowly. "You were an easier target two weeks ago. You have no dog, you had no alarm system and a door that was easy to break into without making a sound. You've taken care of the latter two."

"You think they're still in the area."

Harry Kendall was a smart man. Too smart for his own good, Daniel feared.

"Considering the message written on your car, I think it's possible. Now really, Mr. Kendall, would you rather I spent my time on the phone with you, or out there finding the guys who hurt your wife?"

"Just one more thing," Kendall was rubbing Daniel's nerves raw, past the point of deep breaths. "Something happened today."

Weariness forgotten, Daniel straightened, picking up his pen. He looked for Miller and saw that his partner's chair was still empty. Robert was out canvassing the area around Ina Road—hoping someone in the neighborhood had been out partying late Saturday night, coming home in the wee hours, noticing a vehicle parked on the side of the road while the driver raped a young woman named Connie.

"Did you see someone hanging around?" Daniel asked Harry, eyes narrowed as he focused on his notepad. "Or get a phone call? Have they threatened you?"

An actual threat could give them an angle. Maybe prove that it really was a hate crime. And perhaps make some sense of this particular recurring nightmare that was Harry and Laura Kendall.

"I heard the voice."

"Where?"

"Outside my office door. I had a student with me,

but she was reading and didn't catch it. He said, 'That's his door.'"

"Did you go out and look to see who was there?" Daniel asked urgently.

"Of course, but he was gone."

"Did you hear footsteps?"

"I—I think so."

"How many sets?"

"I don't know."

"You're not sure you heard them at all, are you?"

"No."

"Mr. Kendall, have you seen the counselor the hospital referred you to? Because if not, there's someone I can recommend."

"I go twice a week. Once with Laura and once by myself."

Kendall's voice tightened. "I *heard* this voice, Detective. Not just a voice, *the* voice. The rapist is on campus."

Daniel was through with talking. He wasn't trained to see to the emotional well-being of the victims who came through this precinct.

He sighed. "I'll look into it, Mr. Kendall."

And he would. As soon as he'd finished following all the real leads lying in piles on his desk. The first of which would, he hoped, take him to the man who'd raped Connie Frank.

Those leads were still fresh. He was waiting on the DNA reports. And there was the schoolboy, young Matthew. They had a good suspect—a known pedophile currently out on parole.

Laura Kendall would have to wait.

His gut filled with acid at the thought.

Her short black hair was gelled into the spikes he found sexy and she had dinner waiting when he came in from school Monday evening.

"God, woman, have I died and gone to heaven?" David Jefferson asked, barely noticing the food on the table as his gaze roved over her barely covered breasts down to the tight black bikini panties, which was all she had on with the lacy red tank top.

Woman. That was all he ever called her. The only name she'd had for the past year.

"I want to be your heaven, David." She licked her lips, giving him the wide-eyed look that let him see a little bit of fear. He liked it when she was afraid.

She'd been a good girl once. Long ago.

Now she was merely a woman not long for this world—a woman with one final mission. And this man was her only way to achieve it.

Harry called to say he was working late on Tuesday.

"You have papers to grade?" Laura asked. She pictured him sitting at his desk, tall and slim and smart.

"No."

"What then?" At a planting table at the Garden, she touched the velvety leaves that were beginning to appear on the shoot she was transplanting.

"Just some research."

Harry was a history professor. He did a lot of research. Mostly at home.

"You need your reference books, huh?"

His pause gave her a moment of concern.

"Harry?"

"I have a few things to look into."

Dread seeped through her veins. "What things?"

"Just…things."

Was he seeing someone else? Their relationship had deteriorated so far lately…

"Harry?" She'd never doubted him before. She could hardly breathe as her world started to tilt again.

"I'll be home by seven, Laura, long before it gets dark, I promise."

In spite of her inner assertions that she'd be fine either way, Laura was relieved to hear that. Still…

"Why won't you tell me what you're doing?"

"Because you don't want to know."

"Yes, I do."

He paused again, and Laura waited, trying to clear her mind, disarm the panic, concentrate on the tender buds in front of her.

"I'm going to the university food court over the dinner hour."

A dinner date? Her eyes began to water.

"Why?"

"Because I heard the voice on campus yesterday and I have to find it. I'm going to check out student gathering and eating places to start."

Hands shaking, Laura stood up and walked to a corner of the roofed but unwalled area, deserted except for her. "Did you call Detective Boyd?"

"Yes."

"Why not let him handle it?"

"He's had twenty-four hours. And I'm not sure he believed me."

"Why wouldn't he?"

Harry told her about the speaker being gone when he got to the door. About the student who hadn't heard it.

And she wondered if Harry was losing his grasp on reality.

Laura's parents called just as she was leaving work. They were in her part of town for a planning meeting—a bi-monthly gathering of the higher-ranked leaders of their church—and wanted to know if she could meet them for dinner.

Secretly glad not to be heading home to an empty house, she readily accepted.

And then wished she hadn't.

"It's been two weeks. Have you heard back from the doctor about…you know?" her mother asked almost as soon as they sat down at the restaurant.

Laura nodded, and said, "I'm completely clean," wondering if everything in her life from now on was going to be about the night she was raped.

Dinner came. Her parents ate. Laura nibbled. She hadn't had much of an appetite since the attack. And hadn't started her period, either.

Would her body ever get back on track?

"How's Harry?" Sharon asked as she slowly cut her way through an entire plate of lasagna.

It had taken forty-five minutes for them to ask.

"Fine." Her conscience, conditioned by years of being an only child raised in a church where family hierarchy was everything, gave her a gentle nudge. "Considering."

"He's being good to you, isn't he?" Len's tone was sharp.

"Of course," she quickly said. "The best. It's just that he won't let go of the idea that the attack wasn't random."

"I thought the police said it was."

"They did. And still do."

"Then why…"

"Harry thinks it happened because I'm white…and he isn't."

Taking out his credit card, Len laid it on the table and leaned in toward the burning candle in the center. "He might be right," he said, his glance moving from his wife to his daughter.

"Daddy!" Laura tried to chuckle. "Of course he isn't. The world isn't like that anymore."

"To some people it is," he said.

She wasn't going to let him scare her. She just wasn't.

"Harry and I have been married for years, and we were going together for a long time before that—and we've never had a single episode that would indicate anyone harboring hate toward us," she said, leaning forward so her parents could hear her lowered voice.

Her father's silence was comforting at that moment; it meant he didn't have a valid argument. And then his words fell like a bomb on the table between them. "I think you should move back home."

"What?" It was a good thing she hadn't eaten much. Her stomach was turning inside out.

"For a little while at least," her mother added with a quick look at her husband.

And that was when Laura knew she'd been set up. This dinner, this edict—and she had no doubt it was one—had been planned all along.

"Does Harry know about this?"

This time, she took no comfort at all when her father remained silent.

10

"You called my dad, didn't you?"

Harry hadn't even closed the garage door when his wife's venom hit him. In a strange, sad way, he rejoiced.

There was life in her.

"He called me," he replied.

"When?"

Dropping his briefcase by the door, he left the tie he wanted to take off around his neck and helped himself to a cold bottle of water from the refrigerator. He was hot. Tired. Hungry. And he'd wasted an entire evening chasing a phantom voice.

"Yesterday." He'd been ripe for the suggestion. But he would've agreed anyway. How could he not?

"You really want me to go?"

"No! I want you here with me. We're a team, you and I. Life doesn't work for me unless we're together."

"Then…"

The lost look in her eyes took the breath out of his lungs—the belief from his heart. "Above all, Laura, I want you safe."

She dropped down to the stool on the kitchen island. "Safe?" He saw that she hadn't changed out of her work uniform yet. Because she'd just returned home? Or because she hadn't wanted to get undressed while she was at home alone?

Since the rape, she hadn't changed her clothes once without Harry in the house. He wasn't home until 6:30 on tae kwon do nights, and each time she'd been in her work clothes—which she used to get out of the second she got home.

"Until these guys are caught, you're a target—as long as you're with me."

He'd like to sit with her, take her hand. To reason together and figure out what to do. That was something else they'd lost these past weeks. The partnership that had always sustained them.

"So we're going to let them split us up? That's it? They win?"

"No!" At least he hoped not. But how did a man who loved a woman as much as he loved Laura let her live in danger because of him? The detectives were on to other cases now. The trail was cold. And he was afraid that the repeat cycle was upon them.

"Just until they're caught."

"They might never be."

He'd thought of that. All the time, lately.

"Then, until they commit another crime and we know it's not racially motivated."

"You want me to move in with my parents until we hear that some black-hooded guys break into another couple's home and *attack* them?"

It sounded ludicrous.

"I'm going to look for them myself, Laura," he said now, sinking onto the stool beside her. He stared at the tip of his shoe on the linoleum. Black on white. And then he glanced over at her. "I won't stop until I find them. You have my word on that."

"I don't want your word on that, Harry! I want you to stop! Now! All of this. I want you to let it go and to help me let it go. I want us to get on with our lives! Together!"

He had to wait for composure before he could speak. "Is that what we're doing, Laura? Getting on with our lives together?" His sight a little blurred by the tears he'd been unable to avoid, he tried to meet her gaze as the question slid softly out of him. "We sleep in the guest bedroom. You close the door when you shower. I can't even hold your hand...."

Regret gnawed at him when he saw the hurt—and then the confusion—in her eyes. "I just need time..." Her tone implored him.

"I know that, honey," he was quick to reassure her. "And I'll wait forever if that's what it takes. But I also have to know that what you went through...what I saw and heard and know you had to endure...because of me..."

Harry couldn't go on. Tears choked him and because he couldn't fall into the loving embrace of his wife's arms, he left the room.

She didn't need this. Didn't need his grief on top of her own.

She needed to move in with her parents until it was safe for her to come home.

* * *

A police car was cruising down the street when Laura got home Wednesday night.

She didn't want it there, marring the quiet landscaped neighborhood with reminders.

What if the men who attacked her saw it there? Thought it was her fault? What if it was pissing them off?

And what if, like Harry thinks, they're targeting you and plan to come back?

Laura pulled her Ford Ranger into the drive, pushing the button on her visor to open the garage door, going in, closing the door behind her. Slowly. Calmly.

She would not run. Would not cower.

The big metal door lowered, shutting out daylight, until the windowless room was in total darkness.

She grabbed for the door handle, missed and started to shake. Her wrists hurt. She could feel the ropes burning them.

And knew he was going to touch her. Hurt her.

With a cry, Laura grabbed for the handle again. She was in her truck. Safely in her garage.

But felt, again, her panties sliding down her legs, denim scraping her inner thighs, the roughness—

Her cell phone rang.

Frantically, Laura punched at the button that would turn on the little truck's interior light. She was fine. Had to breathe. Just breathe. Relax. She wasn't hurt. Everything was going to be okay.

The phone rang a second time. Someone reaching out to her.

She snapped on the light and flipped open her phone almost simultaneously.

"Hello?" The fear in her voice frightened her further.

"Mrs. Kendall?"

"Yes?" She should never have come home early. Especially not on tae kwon do night.

"This is Tiffany Simmons from Desert Fertility Center."

Laura blinked in the sudden glare of light, clasping the door handle, climbing out of the car, glancing behind her—and to both sides—before she pulled her purse out of the truck and shut the door.

Tiffany? Fertility center?

Oh. "Yes?" Her association with the center seemed like lifetimes ago.

"I'm sorry to have to tell you that the vials of specimen your husband left during your last visit six weeks ago have met with an unfortunate accident. A refrigeration device failed and the backup generator had been disconnected for service."

Specimen. Harry. Six weeks… Laura tried to keep up. Had a flash of memory of a woman, herself in some other time, walking down the steps outside the clinic, babbling about whether they'd have a boy or a girl.

Right now her system was so out of whack she wasn't even having periods.

"When your husband called to cancel the appointment a few weeks ago, he re-set it for the first of August. I just wanted to let you know that he'll either have to stop in before that so we can run tests on the fresh samples, or be prepared to participate, without pre-screening, on that date."

She had to get the door to the house unlocked before the woman rang off. Just in case. But the key slipped. Missed the hole. And again.

Willing her trembling fingers to still long enough for the key to hit its mark, Laura tried one more time.

"Thank you," she said. "I'll…tell him."

And she was in.

"Hi, Dr. Kendall. I didn't expect to see you sitting here."

"Denise, hi. Great comment in class today." Harry stood, facing his student across the small table in the crowded student cafeteria on U of A's campus. He'd been so busy watching, listening, he hadn't noticed Denise's approach.

"I've never seen you down here before."

He'd been a time or two. In the past week. "I had half an hour before going to the gym," he told her. "Thought I should get something to eat."

Drink, he amended silently, looking down at the lone bottle of raspberry freeze on the table. He was going to lift weights before his martial-arts class and hadn't wanted a full stomach.

She smiled, an expression on her face he'd never seen before. Not sexual, exactly, but certainly more personal.

And for the briefest of seconds, Harry was flattered. It'd been a tough few weeks, emotionally speaking.

"Well, I'd better be going," she said, backing slowly away, as though she'd stay if he just said the word.

He didn't.

He called Laura's cell instead, to reassure himself that she was packing to go to her parents' the way he'd suggested, although she hadn't actually agreed. After listening to several rings, he was switched to her voice mail.

Frowning, Harry hung up and tried again. Why wasn't Laura answering her phone?

Laura had been in the house for fifteen minutes and had paced the entire square footage twice, checking the alarm each time she passed to make sure the "home" light was on, before she got out her cell phone and called her mom.

"It's me," she said as soon as her mother picked up. Bob wouldn't be home tonight. Wednesdays were church nights for him. It was the night all the youth in the church gathered for their weekly activities. As a church leader, Bob Clark liked to put in appearances at all activities, particularly making himself accessible to the teenagers in his flock.

For a second, Laura wished she was one of them again, one of the sheltered young women who were so closely guarded. She'd left the church when she'd fallen in love with Harry. And hadn't once looked back. Until tonight.

"I've put fresh sheets on your bed and—"

"Mom, I'm not coming."

She'd made up her mind. No matter what any of them said.

"But I—"

"You all think you know what's right and best for

me," she interrupted, fueled by the thoughts she'd had all day—Harry's betrayal, siding with her parents against her. Pressuring her. As though *her* will, *her* choices, didn't count. As though she couldn't possibly take care of herself. "Yes, something bad happened. But I'm a grown woman. A wife. And I'll recover."

As if from afar, she saw herself hurrying around the house turning on lights in every room despite the bright Arizona sunshine streaming through the windows. If she waited, darkness would get in.

"Harry doesn't want you there."

Stopping with her hand on the bathroom light switch, Laura saw herself in the vanity mirror. That haunted face with the shadowed eyes wasn't her.

"Yes, he does," she said with effort. She refused to let them get to her. "He just doesn't want me hurt." She understood that. "But there are no guarantees in this life, Mom. I could be mugged at the garden tomorrow."

Not a good thought.

"Or killed in a car accident."

Oddly, that idea wasn't nearly as frightening as opening the closed door at the end of the hall. Harry had been in there—to get their clothes and toiletries. She hadn't. Not since that first day.

"Laura, until you know this wasn't a hate crime, just being with Harry puts you—"

"Some people hate Christians, too," she interrupted. "And Americans."

And she wasn't going to live her life in fear.

She wasn't. She reminded herself of that all day, every day.

It got her up in the mornings. Got her to work. And home. It was keeping her here.

"I won't be terrorized, Mom. I won't let them win."

The sigh on the other end made her heart heavy.

"I heard there was a problem at the fertility center."

Laura was only minimally surprised to learn her mother had heard about that. The center was managed by a woman from her parents' church, Grace Martin, which was why Laura had chosen it in the first place. She'd known Grace most of her life.

"There was a broken refrigeration unit," she said now, figuring her mother already knew the details, but playing along anyway. It was easier.

"What if it was more than that?" Sharon's voice sounded honestly frightened.

"Of course it wasn't, Mom," Laura quickly assured her. That hadn't even occurred to her.

"You don't know that, Laura. There are still a lot of people in the world who don't think black people and white people should marry."

People like Sharon and Leonard Clark. Her folks were polite to Harry, they were kind, but when they introduced him, it was always just *this is Harry.* Never "Laura's husband." Never "our son-in-law."

"Even if something had been tampered with, which I highly doubt, ours wasn't the only sperm there. Someone else could've been the target."

"I don't imagine there are too many white women with black husbands at the clinic trying to have babies."

"Mom, stop!" Laura's headache had moved to behind her eyes. "Just stop. I'm not coming home."

"At least promise me you'll think about it."

"No. I've made up my mind. I'm Harry's wife. I love him. This is where I belong."

She listened for her mother's acquiescence. Grudging though it would be.

"Laura? Have you ever stopped to think that maybe everything that's been happening lately is a sign? Including the fact that you and Harry can't conceive on your own? God and His angels can only take care of you if you let them."

Laura paused, taken aback by that remark. Her own spirituality was deep and true. It was also more compassionate, more tolerant, than her parents'. And she remembered how completely trapped and suffocated she'd felt living under their tutelage.

"God loves all His children, Mom,"

"Of course he does. But if you don't ask Him if—"

"I ask every single night. And every morning, too. I am meant to spend my life with Harry. My heart bears witness to me." She'd said it all before, countless times.

Ringing off before her mother could add any more pressure to shoulders that were unsteady at best, Laura noticed that she'd missed six calls from Harry.

He'd left one message.

He was on his way home.

11

At ten o'clock Wednesday night, Daniel Boyd was just drifting off to sleep when his cell phone rang.

"Boyd."

"I'm sorry to bother you, Detective…."

The second he heard Harry Kendall's voice, Daniel climbed out of bed, poured himself a stiff shot of whiskey to help him get to sleep when he'd once again shut his eyes—in about thirty seconds.

And promised himself he wouldn't shoot the guy. The man had called earlier to tell Daniel about their plans for Laura's move—to ask for extra patrols in Laura's parents' neighborhood instead of their own.

"Go to bed, Kendall." He grimaced as he gulped down the fiery liquid.

"Plans changed," Kendall said. "She's still here."

A string of curse words played themselves out quite satisfactorily in his brain. The pathetic bastard couldn't even manage something as simple as getting his wife out of his house.

"She's leaving tomorrow then?"

The younger man sighed. Not a common, everyday release of frustration—the kind Daniel exhaled a hundred times a day. No, this was the gut-deep sound of a man who was at the end of his rope. Boyd didn't want to hear it.

"Unfortunately not. She's staying."

"She's perfectly safe there, you know."

"Not if the attack was racial."

Daniel didn't have the brain cells to waste on another argument with the man.

"Relax, Kendall," he said, instead, impatience threading its way through his voice. "Miller's putting out feelers with every known hate group in the state of Arizona, and on the Internet. So far, he's turned up absolutely nothing."

"The rapists—they're at the university." Harry Kendall spoke as though the words were proven fact. "First my car, and then the voice."

Or maybe the husband who'd been made to watch his wife's double rape was being driven beyond his coping skills.

And there was nothing Daniel Boyd could do about that.

"I'll call right now and get the patrol back on your street," he said, figuring that was why Harry Kendall had called. He disconnected before Kendall could attempt to thank him.

Remembering the last time they'd gone to get milk, Laura stopped by the grocery store on her way home from work on Thursday. Considering Harry's state of mind where she was concerned, she felt it was safer that way.

For the rest of world, at least.

And for a few minutes, as she pushed her cart down aisles of food she didn't need, she actually relaxed. This was normal. This was everyday life.

There were fresh snow peas in the produce department. Harry loved fresh snow peas. Laura tossed some in the cart. And two cuts of beef tenderloin from the meat case. She bought baking potatoes, salad fixings. A bottle of wine.

She was going home to have dinner with the man she loved. What could be more normal than that?

The woman at the checkout called her honey. The bagger offered to help her out with her groceries. Aware of the line behind her, all people who'd need their groceries bagged, Laura shook her head. It was enough to know that the world was filled with good people. People who wanted to help. Not harm.

Somehow, over the past couple of weeks, she'd forgotten that.

Walking out to the sauna-like evening, keys in hand, Laura squinted against the bright sun, taking a second to notice the mountains in the distance against a background of perfect blue sky. No place on earth was more beautiful than Arizona in the evening.

She'd forgotten that, too. Forgotten to notice. Forgotten that her life was filled with things she loved.

Her Ranger was in the third spot of the center aisle, right where she'd left it half an hour before. The blue four-door sedan that had been parked next to it was gone, replaced by a much-older green two-door.

She pushed her cart up to the driver's door. She unlocked it, then turned back for the first bags of groceries—and saw that the left rear tire was completely flat, the silver rim lying against a puddle of rubber on the ground. There was no way she could drive on it. Not even the few blocks it would take her to get home.

She had a jack. She had a spare. She knew how to use both.

She could call Harry. And wait. Or she could attempt to get the full-size truck tire down from underneath the bed. She could—

"You need some help?"

Turning, the cart between her and the young man at the end of her truck, Laura hesitated, a smile and a *yes* hovering on her lips. Harry would kill her.

She couldn't talk to strangers.

Couldn't trust anyone.

"I can have this done for you in no time," the kid said. He looked about nineteen, with a bowl-on-the-head haircut, pants a little too short. Glasses.

Her rapists hadn't had glasses.

Had they?

"The jack's just behind your seat there," he said, not taking one step closer.

And Laura had a sudden vision of herself from his perspective. A woman standing there like a zombie, afraid to move, to recognize the helping hand of a stranger.

"Thank you," she said, embarrassed by the shakiness of her voice. "Let me move these things…."

He backed up, waiting while she pushed the cart out into the lot and around the Ranger.

"May I get the jack?" he asked, while she was on the other side of the truck.

He knew something. Had sensed her reticence. And was going out of his way to make her comfortable.

"Of course," she said, blinking back tears of sadness mixed with gratitude.

Regardless of what Harry needed her to believe, what her attackers had shown her, the world was not an ugly place.

Boyd wasn't answering the phone. Neither his cell, nor the extension on his desk. Hands shaking—with impatience and probably something more—Harry punched in Robert Miller's number as he drove to the Botanical Garden on Friday afternoon.

Slow down, man. Stay cool. The words repeated themselves in his mind again and again.

"Miller."

"Detective…" Harry introduced himself. "I just got a call from the fertility clinic where Laura and I have been patients for the past year."

"Desert Fertility Center." Miller named the place immediately. Either the detective just happened to have that page of their file open in front of him, or he was damned good. Figuring the chances of the former were slim, Harry relaxed a little.

"There's been some kind of accident." Harry gave the detective the details he'd only just found out— details his wife had known for two days. "Put that together with the bastard calling my dislocated shoulder by its medical term. I'll bet the guy works at the clinic, saw Laura and me come in together…."

"We've already checked them out," Miller's response

was prompt—and disappointing. "No one's aware of anyone having any racial biases, and every young male on the payroll had an alibi for the night of the rape."

"Maybe someone lied."

"Mr. Kendall, with all due respect, sir, you need to back off and let us do our jobs."

Maybe someone who worked at the clinic was also a student at U of A.

"What about the medical school on campus?"

"I looked into it myself, personally."

Miller claimed then that he had another call, and Harry had no choice but to hang up.

But he wasn't done with this. An accident, *right now,* at the medical facility where he and Laura were trying to make a baby. A rapist with medical knowledge. It was too much of a coincidence for Harry's peace of mind.

He was going to have to take this one on, too.

Turning into his wife's place of employment, Harry attempted to slow his mind as he slowed his Lexus.

One thing at a time.

He was there to make sure Laura's truck was safe. He'd been suspicious about yesterday's flat tire from the beginning. A new tire, completely flat. Not a slow leak. And a man miraculously there to help.

He'd received another call that day, too—from the garage where he'd taken Laura's tire.

There was nothing wrong with it. No obvious leak. No holes. The mechanic had concluded that the air valve had somehow leaked.

Harry knew differently. Someone had deliberately

let the air out of Laura's tire. And then been there to save the day.

And would that man, perhaps, have taken her if he'd had a chance?

He turned into the drive. He'd just check her truck. Make absolutely certain she'd be safe. Stop in and say hello. He'd wait until tonight to speak to her about the other phone call he'd received that day. The call from the fertility center.

He found her truck easily. She always parked in the same area. For the five years she'd been working here, she's always chosen one of the same three spots. He'd have to talk to her about that.

Predictability led to vulnerability.

The truck was fine. He examined it again just to be sure. Considered going home without seeing her. She'd no doubt accuse him of overreacting. Get annoyed. But Laura was sliding away from him and he had to stop that from happening.

It occurred to him that she'd been coming home from work when she'd gone to the grocery. It would've taken almost the entire time she was in the store to get all the air out of that tire. Which meant the perpetrator must've been there from the start.

And because Laura's visit to the grocery store was spur of the moment, the only way the guy could've known she was going to be there was if he'd followed her. From work.

Harry had already told Miller his theory. And been brushed off for his efforts.

Maybe he should take a quick look around. Find out if anyone had noticed anything....

He hurried up the walk toward Laura's garden. Until three weeks ago he would've been picturing his wife's welcoming smile.

Three weeks ago, she would've called him the second she heard that the vials at the center had been destroyed.

Slow. Calm. He reminded himself as he reached the experimental garden. She'd said she was spending the afternoon there. Running the first experiment on a new aloe species she and Kelly had bred.

Stomach churning in a way that had become far too familiar, Harry stepped inside the enclosure, seeking his wife.

"Do we have to do this here? Can't we talk at home?" Laura tried to keep her voice low as she faced her husband in the corner of the medicinal garden.

"Yes." Even his whisper was adamant. "Don't you see?" He stood so that she had to either look in his eyes or at his shoes. "They know about every facet of our lives. They know where we live. What clinic we use. Where I work. They have to know where you work, too. You're not safe here, Laura."

"Harry, you're being ridiculous." The expression on his face worried her. He was so sure. And so completely irrational.

"Am I?" Hands in the pockets of his slacks, tie loose at his neck, he took another step forward. "Why didn't you tell me about the vials?"

"I don't know." But she did.

"Don't do that, Laura, not to me."

Tears burned the backs of her eyes as she continued to hold his gaze, thinking about him. About them. Loving him so much.

And finding herself scared to death because it wasn't enough.

"I can hardly take care of myself right now." She voiced the thoughts she'd had three weeks before, just after the rape. The last thing she wanted to think about now was having a baby.

"But that doesn't mean we can't have everything prepared for when the time is right." He wasn't relenting at all. If anything, he seemed to be getting more agitated, rocking back and forth on his feet.

Laura had never seen him like this.

And wished to God she could figure out how to help him.

"It also doesn't explain," he said softly, but with growing intensity, "why you didn't tell me about it."

"I found out on Wednesday. If you remember, we were rather preoccupied by your insistence that I move home to my parents'."

A battle he'd lost.

"You didn't want me to know because you knew I'd draw the conclusion that the *accident* was connected to the rape."

Donna Jamison, one of her colleagues, passed by, waving. Starting to feel sick to her stomach, Laura waved back.

"Harry, please. Can we talk about this later?"

"No! Don't you see, Laura? After that thing with the tire last night…"

She frowned. "What?"

"That was no accident. I just heard from the garage. There was not even a pinprick in that tire. Someone let the air out."

His breathing wasn't calm. And suddenly, hers wasn't, either.

"They told you that?"

"No."

"What did they say?"

"The guy didn't understand it. Said it could've been an air-valve problem, but it didn't make sense to him. He doesn't know our circumstances, though, so he wouldn't consider the possibility that someone deliberately sabotaged that tire."

The area, with its misters, felt like a sauna.

"I think someone was waiting for you after work," Harry continued. "Maybe someone from here. I think they followed you to the grocery store."

Laura stared, searching the intense gaze in front of her for a hint of the man she knew.

"You've got to open your eyes, Laura. See what's happening. It's not safe here."

She *was* seeing. More than she wanted to. Harry was going off the deep end. And she didn't know how to help him.

He was in counseling already. It didn't seem to be making any difference.

"What do you want me to do?" she asked. "Quit my job?"

His hesitation surprised her, but not as much as it should have.

"No," he finally said. "I want us to do some investigating, try to find out if anyone here might know something. Maybe someone saw a stranger hanging around or—"

"Harry, we are not going to question my coworkers. The police have already done that."

"Laura, someone is out to get us. They know our movements. We have to find out who they are. We have to stop them."

She hated this. Hated the confusion. The helplessness. The growing paranoia—what else could she call it? She was sick. And tired. And had nowhere to run.

Her safest haven, Harry's arms, didn't feel safe anymore. Nothing did. She couldn't live like this.

Didn't Harry see that if they didn't stop thinking about the attack all the time, they were never going to get over it?

"Everything okay here?" It was Kelly, standing just behind Harry.

Laura's stomach settled a bit as she smiled at her friend. "Fine."

Harry turned, said hello.

"Hi, Harry. Good to see you."

"Tell me, Kelly, have you noticed anything out of the ordinary around here? Anyone lurking around? Asking questions? Anyone who's mad at Laura?"

Kelly glanced from one to the other.

"Nooo."

Laura sent Harry a pleading glance.

"You're positive?" he asked.

"Yeah. What's going on?"

"Nothing," Laura said quickly. "Harry was just leaving."

And then she did something she'd never done before. She escorted her husband to the exit. "Go home," she told him, praying that he would. "We'll talk there."

And sometime between now and then, she'd have to figure out what to say to him.

One thing was for sure. They couldn't go on like this.

Bobby had a job to do Friday evening. Or rather, one to oversee. An important job. A member of the Ivory Nation was about to earn his red shoelaces. Another loyal fighter for the cause, preserving God's world for His chosen people. He celebrated each one, showing proper gratitude to the source of all knowing for His assistance and guidance, for entrusting Bobby with this sacred task.

Grateful, too, that Tony would be home to look after Luke, Bobby put on tonight's uniform—threadbare jeans, boots and a T-shirt with the sleeves cut out so that his white-rules tattoo would be fully visible.

Not that anyone but his most trusted brothers would see him. Bobby was a businessman; he had an image to keep.

"I wish I could go," Tony said as he was getting ready to leave.

"I won't leave Luke with a sitter." Which was why he either worked from home or took Luke with him when Tony wasn't there.

"I know. I don't think you should. I'll stay and we'll

have fun, won't we, guy?" Tony grinned at the toddler on his hip.

Wide-eyed, Luke nodded back. "Tony, Tony, Tony," he chanted with the grin that broke Bobby's heart every time he saw it.

Bobby's smile was genuine, his love for his son and his new brother chaste and pure. He drove away as Johnny Rebel played on the stereo in his living room.

Harry was much calmer by the time Laura got home. He could breathe again. Think. And he knew he had to lighten up with Laura.

She'd come through hell. She was dealing with things he'd never understand. Alienating her was pointless—and it absolutely would not keep her safe.

He had dinner on the table. A glass of wine for her in his hand. And an apology on his lips.

Fear still crowded his heart, but he spent the evening watching television with his wife as though nothing had happened to change the shape of their lives.

At ten, the news came on. Sitting with Laura, their feet touching on the couch, Harry resented the time passing, knowing that within minutes she'd get up and go to the bed they shared, but in which they never touched at all.

Candidate George Moss was in the headlines again. "According to studies done by independent agencies, based on health records, traffic accidents and arrest reports, there are an estimated 55,000 illegal aliens in the United States," Moss was saying in answer to a question

Harry hadn't heard. "Costing the federal courts and prison system more than $1.6 billion in 2002 alone." The clip was from a luncheon with the governor earlier in the day.

"You know," Harry said, as much to keep Laura in the room with him as because there was something about the man that really bothered Harry. "In spite of that guy's expensive, perfectly pressed suits, he's the epitome of someone who stands for the idea that there isn't enough to go around."

"Illegal immigrant health care costs Arizona an average of $400 million a year," Moss's previously recorded image went on speaking.

"My folks know him," Laura said, gaze focused on the large screen. "They say he's great, but it seems to me that if you listened to him, you'd be afraid to walk down the street alone. It scares me to think of him actually getting elected—imposing his fear-mongering and prejudice on all of us."

Harry agreed, and yet the thought of Laura walking down the street alone scared him. "But what if he's right?" he asked, haunted by dangers that were becoming more and more apparent to him these days. Maybe Moss, repulsive though many of his ideas were, had understood all along that danger was all around them.

Border problems. Hate problems. Pornography. Social injustices and faltering families.

And crime statistics that were paralyzing.

How had he ever lived with peace in his heart?

It wasn't quite light, but it wasn't completely dark, either, when Laura opened her eyes on Saturday morning. Five o'clock. Harry had only come to bed an hour ago. She'd seen the clock on her nightstand then, too.

Turning over, she perused the sleeping features of the man she loved.

No matter what had happened, what continued to happen, the thread of feeling that bound her life to his hadn't weakened.

With that thought she drifted back to sleep.

Less than an hour later, his shudder wakened her. Worried her. As did the shadows under his eyes. He hadn't slept properly in weeks. Because of her. Because he needed so desperately to keep her safe.

As she lay there, still relaxed from sleep, images slipped through her mind. Of the sadness in his eyes as she shied away from his touch. The frantic worry when she refused to join his obsessive fight to do a job they weren't equipped to do. And of him sitting up night after night, unwilling to sleep until after the time the rapes had occurred. One thing became quite clear. She was hurting Harry by staying in that house.

She'd been adamant about staying because it had always been Harry and her against anyone who tried to split them up. It had become a way of life for her, choosing him over them. *Having* to choose. Her own parents had regularly put her in that position.

But this was different. Laura froze as she stared at him, seeing things differently now.

Harry wanted her gone so badly he'd appealed to *her parents* for help.

Not because he no longer loved her, or found her dirty or lacking or less, but because he loved her so much.

With tears in her eyes, Laura slid quietly out of bed.

By seven she had enough clothes packed to last the weekend. She could come back on Monday to get more. At seven-thirty she called her mother.

And by the time Harry woke at eight, there was little left to do but say goodbye.

Late Monday morning, Harry went to the Desert Fertility Center to fill a vial with sperm he never intended to use. Moss's predictions and even statistics he could ignore, but the man's warning of danger he couldn't get out of his head. Harry knew from his own reading that there were thousands of victims of hate crimes; Laura was only one. There was so much peril out there, peril for those who were blindly living as though the world was safe.

He couldn't bring a child into such a society. He wouldn't.

And still, there he was, thinking of his beautiful wife whom he could no longer touch, remembering the feel of her fingers on his chest, her lips on his. He reached for his penis, closing his eyes and telling himself over and over that the hand gripping him was Laura's. That she was there with him, loving him, needing their intimacy as badly as he did.

And when he was done, he zipped his fly and sealed the container, just as they'd shown him the last time he'd been through this. But rather than return to the nurse's desk as he had the day he'd visited the clinic with Laura, he opened the door a crack, waited until the hallway was clear, and slipped through the employee entrance to the back of the center.

"Oh, Kel, I'm such a mess…."

"No, honey, you aren't a mess at all." Kelly's soft voice, a balm to Laura's raw pain, drifted over her.

They were supposed to be having lunch at Kelly's apartment, which wasn't far from the Garden, so they could talk openly.

Instead, Laura had fallen apart before they could get the lettuce out of the refrigerator, and they were sitting together on the younger woman's sofa.

Laying her head back, trying to calm herself, Laura looked at the surroundings she'd loved since the first time she'd gone to Kelly's home. The sculpted metal group of colorfully painted women on the wall opposite her. The papier-mâché heart in maroons and golds and pale greens and purples.

And the angels. They were everywhere. In many mediums.

They didn't stop her tears.

"You're human, Laura," Kelly said, brushing back the hair from Laura's wet face. "You were violated in the worst possible way. Give yourself a chance."

"I love Harry," Laura said, looking her friend in the eye. "So much it hurts."

"I know."

"I'm *more* when I'm with him than I am by myself."

"He's a good man. And he loves you, too. He'll be there with you through this whole thing."

That was true but it brought as much pressure as comfort.

"I still get that excited feeling when he walks into a room, or when I see his number come up on my cell, you know?"

Kelly's long hair shadowed her face as she leaned forward, elbows on her knees, and glanced sideways at Laura.

"Not many people ever find what the two of you have," she said. "He gets a look in his eye when he sees you, like you're the most precious thing in the world."

"He doesn't look at me like that anymore." Laura's voice broke. "And the worst part is, I don't want him to." Hearing herself say the words aloud, feeling their truth, she just couldn't hold on anymore. Sobs wracked her body. Painful, gasping sobs that felt as if they'd never stop.

Kelly's arms came around her, pulling Laura against her, and it was as though a dam broke inside. She wasn't strong. Or capable. Or able to go on.

She was broken.

"I can't stand the thought of being around a man," Laura whispered half an hour later, her head resting lightly on Kelly's shoulder. "Sexually." She paused. "Not even Harry."

"Give it time."

Her counselor had said as much. There were rape survival groups she could join. But she wasn't ready to sit in a room with a brand on her forehead. Or to tell complete strangers what had happened to her. She didn't want to be one of them.

She didn't think she could bear to hear their stories. To know that other women had suffered as much as she had—some worse.

"What if it doesn't ever get better?" she asked now.

"It will."

Kelly took Laura's hand in hers and Laura held on to that lifeline. "I listen to my counselor talk," she said. "I hear what she says and logically, I understand. I know I can take control, that I'm stronger than I feel. I know I'm not to blame. That I'm not dirty or any of the other things they talk about." She was rambling, her voice little more than a whisper. "But knowing doesn't change how I *feel!*"

"Oh, sweetie. There hasn't been enough time yet. You're still in the first stages of recovery."

Maybe. Or she'd been permanently destroyed.

She was so filled with tension and defensiveness, with invisible walls hiding everything easy and hopeful and open inside her. The thought of a man—of *Harry*—coming near her, touching her, made her need to lash out, to hit and claw and fight and not stop.

The idea of ever again seeing the men who'd done this to her, meeting them face-to-face, left her immobile. Scared and quivering.

Tears dropped down her face. "I was a virgin when I married Harry." And now she'd been with two other men.

Kelly gave her a gentle squeeze, and Laura wanted to close her eyes and not move until unconsciousness took her and never brought her back.

She'd been away from Harry for two nights and

missed him so much she didn't feel whole. She was worried sick about him. Needed to know how he was. If he was eating.

She talked to him several times a day, and he said he was fine. She didn't believe him.

She needed to see his smile.

And, in spite of all that, she was ashamed to admit, even to herself, the relief she experienced every night when she went to bed alone. Free from the possibility of his touch.

For that, she did hate herself.

She wasn't the person she wanted to be anymore.

He might be a man who'd run out of luck, but Harry finally had something fall into place. Darting in and out of doorways, like some actor in a bedroom farce, he surveyed the private section of the fertility center. The rapist had said AC instead of shoulder. He had a medical background. And Harry and Laura had been due for artificial insemination the day after the attack.

Harry had come at lunchtime today, hoping most of the technicians would be out.

As far as he could tell, there were only a couple of people in the area. But he saw more cubicles than he'd expected.

Somehow, in that labyrinth of partitioned walls separating computer desks from lab counters and tables, he had to find payroll information. Or employee insurance paperwork. Or workers' compensation files. Something that would give him a list of the people who worked there.

A young Hispanic-looking woman with a mop was

cleaning a back corner of the room, directly down the aisle from Harry. She glanced up. He smiled. And she moved on.

So did he. From one cubicle to the next, one cubby to the next, opening drawers where he could, scanning desktops and in-boxes.

Someone had to be in charge of human resources. He'd gone through all the unlocked doors on either side of the office, and more than half the cubicles.

Hearing footsteps, Harry quickly slid behind a partition, flattening himself against the makeshift wall, eyeing what he could see of the corridor beyond. A man about his age walked by, dressed in a white lab coat, perusing some kind of flyer.

He was completely unaware of Harry. Sweating, Harry stepped back out and into the next space. He wasn't leaving until he found what he'd come for. He'd never get another chance like—

"Can I help you?" The woman was motherly in appearance, fiftyish, with a kind smile. She'd come up behind him, a large, lidded paper cup from a nearby fast-food establishment in her hand.

"I don't believe we've met," he said, as though he had every right to be wandering around the employee section of a medical facility. He failed to offer his hand for a shake due to the little cup he still held. "I'm Dr. Kendall and I'm looking for Dr. Barnes. Have you seen him this morning?"

Laura's fertility specialist had been planning a two-week sojourn in Europe and was scheduled to return after the fourth of July. Today was the second.

"I'm not sure," the friendly woman said with an accepting grin. "I'm just here from the temporary service, but I can get Dr. Samuels if you'd like to wait," she offered.

"That would be great."

Obviously the woman assumed, since he was back there, that he'd been granted admittance. The people in this place really needed to work on their security.

And he had, at his best guess, about sixty seconds to find what he needed and get the hell out. Something told him Dr. Samuels wouldn't be nearly so trusting.

Rushing from place to place, searching for anything that might give him a list of employee names, Harry heard the woman's voice again, talking to someone at the front of the room. They were coming in his direction.

Glancing around frantically, he saw the men's room just in time. He bolted himself in the fourth of five stalls across from a row of urinals, raising his feet with some inane thought that no one would notice the door was bolted shut, indicating that someone was inside.

He sat there, cramped up like some crazy lunatic, for a full fifteen minutes before he dared venture back to the door. He had a class to teach in less than an hour and a ten-minute drive ahead of him.

Maybe he didn't just look crazy. Maybe he *was* crazy. What the hell was he doing prowling around private property with the intent to steal confidential information?

Squaring his shoulders, Harry pulled open the heavy washroom door, relieved to see that the open areas of the workspace were either occupied by people too busy to notice him or were still empty. He'd make one confident swoop up the center aisle, heading straight for the door out to the public part of the clinic, drop off his sample and get back to his own life.

He took one step, and then turned. He'd heard a click.

A time clock.

Without taking a second to think, Harry grabbed all the time cards, shoved them down the front of his shirt and walked out.

He was at his car before he realized he'd failed to leave his little container behind.

12

"Hi, sweetheart, how are you?"

Holding the phone to her ear, Laura stared at the ceiling of the room she'd grown up in, remembering the days after she'd first met Harry in an undergrad English class ten years before. She'd lain in that very same bed, thinking about him.

"I'm fine," she told him now. Numb mostly. Had been since her breakdown with Kelly that afternoon. It was kind of nice. "How'd classes go today?"

He told her about a student who challenged him every step of the way, arguing about historical facts as though they could change them if they wanted to. You could argue accuracy, argue theory and interpretation, and Harry was open-minded and eager. Apparently this boy did none of that.

"I called Detective Boyd this morning," he added, just when Laura was starting to relax into the normalcy of the conversation. "I thought we should let him know you're staying over there."

Good idea. Call off the hounds.

She told him that preliminary tests were showing her new aloe hybrid to be four times faster at treating burns. Of course, she was talking about half a day of tests. And not on any living creatures.

Still, she was hopeful. And continued to stare at the ceiling.

"I miss you."

"I miss you, too, Harry. So much." But she didn't mention going home. He might be more rested now, having had two full nights' sleep, but nothing else had changed. Nor was there any change coming in the fore-seeable future.

Unless a miracle happened.

Which left her where? A grown woman living with her parents for the rest of her life?

Or a married woman living alone in an apartment? Safer because her black husband wasn't with her.

Divorced?

Harry's next words chilled her. "I'm making progress with my investigation, Laura." Laura pulled the covers up to her chin, holding them there with both hands.

"Please stop," she whispered. "Please, Harry."

"I'm going to find them, Laura. I got a list of the em-ployees at the fertility center today," he said, his voice picking up momentum, until he sounded more like a stranger than the man she'd devoted her life to. "I—"

"How'd you do that?" she interrupted, certain she didn't want to hear, yet knowing she had to.

"Doesn't matter how," he said. "What matters is that I compared it to a list of students at U of A. I started with the med school because that connection seemed the most obvious. And I was right."

"Right about what?"

"There's a guy, David Jefferson, who's a med student here who also works at the center."

The name was irrelevant. Not information she needed to process or remember. "You aren't doing anything illegal, are you?" Laura lowered her voice, in spite of the fact that her parents' bedroom was at the other end of the house.

"Do you understand what I'm saying, honey? I've made a valid connection. I'm calling Boyd first thing in the morning."

"Harry, don't! He's going to think you're crazy."

"He's going to see that I'm right about this being a hate crime."

"Because a med student works in a fertility clinic? That's like…like deciding someone's guilty of murder because he's a law student and works at the county attorney's office."

"Laura, I've looked up this David Jefferson. According to his time card, he was at the center the day the vials were destroyed. And it looks like he works every Monday and Wednesday morning, which means he would've been there for our last visit, as well. I know whoever did this is also on campus because I heard him outside my office."

"Maybe he was just there because of *you,* not because he was a student," Laura said dryly. Not because she believed a word of what either of them were saying…

"Laura—"

"Don't you see what's happening, Harry?" she asked

him, loving him so much and, at the same time, strangely afraid of him—of what he was doing, becoming. "You've let this eat at you until you've lost all perspective. Listen to yourself! You actually think some guy at the fertility clinic saw us together, decided to teach us a lesson and that, coincidentally, he also attends the university where you teach?"

"Those men were either someone who knows us or saw us together, and couldn't tolerate the idea of a white woman with a black man," he said stubbornly. "Their message was very clear."

That voice was back again, the one that had told her so succinctly that the gun he'd been loading would be in bed with them. Period. It was stern. Uncompromising. Everything Harry was not.

She might have cried if she'd had any tears left to shed.

"Call Detective Boyd if you must, Harry," she said now, closing her eyes. "But then, *please,* let him take it from here, okay? No more sleuthing. You're going to get hurt." Or get himself in trouble.

Neither of which she could tolerate.

"Please."

"I'll be careful."

"Harry."

"I want you home, Laura."

She didn't have anything to say to that.

On Tuesday, after an unsatisfying conversation with Daniel Boyd—who, Harry feared, was humoring him in his pledge to follow up on the David Jefferson lead—Harry once again sat in his office, planning his next move. Harry was convinced that someone in his life, or Laura's, was out to split them up. It might be Jefferson or some other person on the fringes of their lives, someone he had yet to ferret out. Maybe there were *two* people who didn't want him and Laura together. Two or even more...

"Hi, Dr. Kendall, may I come in?"

Turning, Harry saw his favorite grad student at the door, a shy, hesitant smile on her face. Such a contrast to the rest of his life.

"Denise, of course, come on in. What can I do for you today?"

"I just wanted to know if there's anything I can help you with. Papers to grade or anything. I'm Professor Anderson's T.A. this term, and I'm supposed to do at least ten hours a week, but he hasn't had anything for me recently and I don't feel right getting paid for doing nothing."

It was students like Denise Marshall who kept Harry from feeling jaded. Most of the kids he knew would take the money and run.

Frowning as he recognized the negative bent of his thoughts, he invited Denise in. And set her to work grading the papers he'd planned to spend a few hours on that night—and to resume the next day. The Fourth of July. His first holiday without Laura since they'd met.

"There's a special meeting at church tonight, honey," Sharon Clark said as Laura set the table Tuesday evening. Because she'd just declined an invitation to accompany her parents to a church member's home for a Fourth of July barbeque the following day, Laura listened, trying to find interest in the things her mother cared so much about.

"George Moss is coming to speak to us."

"The man scares me, Mom."

"Scares you? He's one of the good guys, honey. Your father knows a colleague of his brother and…"

Adding napkins to the knives and forks and spoons she'd already set out, Laura tried—and failed—to focus on her mother's voice, expostulating about the upcoming primary elections.

Still four months away.

Laura couldn't think four days away.

"You should come with us," Sharon said again.

"I'm tired."

"Your father thinks what George Moss has to say is important, Laura."

Her father, the respected securities attorney downtown who seemed to know everyone—and judged people as either *like them or not*. The "like thems" were accepted, included in their inner circle. The "or nots" weren't.

Harry had been an "or not." With the distinct understanding that even if he became "like them," he'd never be completely accepted as their daughter's husband.

They didn't want such a hard life for Laura. That was what they said, and Laura believed them.

What they'd never seen was that Harry made her life easier, happier, more peaceful than it had ever been living with them.

Sharon stepped in front of Laura, who carried a stack

of plates, and blocked her way. "I don't want to leave you here alone."

"And that's ridiculous," Laura said, moving around her mother to complete her task. "I'm not a child who needs coddling," she said, hating how weak her mother's love made her feel at that moment—yet welcoming her love, just the same. "I was raped, Mom. Past tense. I'm as safe now as any other woman, and you certainly don't have a problem with women being home alone—yourself included."

Sharon's silence, her stillness, was strange enough to bring Laura's gaze back to her. "What?"

Her father would be home soon. They had to get dinner on the table. And she wanted to call Harry. To make sure he ate.

And maybe ask if he'd come over. For a little while. She needed to see his smile…

"It's just…." Her mother hesitated, gaining Laura's full attention.

"Just?"

"What if Harry's right, Laura? What if it wasn't a random incident? What if someone really was sending you a warning?"

"Stop it," she said, more harshly than she'd ever spoken to her mother. "Just stop," she added in a softer voice. "Please."

"Honey, listen." Sharon grabbed Laura's hand, pulling until they were face-to-face. "I don't want to frighten you. Or make anything harder. But if you run from this, you might bring about the one thing you fear most."

"And what's that?" she asked, bracing herself instinctively.

"Getting hurt again."

"No, Mom, what I fear most is never getting my life back. I've already survived the hurt. I'm not running. I'm refusing to let fear control me."

"You're telling me you aren't scared?"

"Of course I'm scared," Laura said, blinking back the tears that always seemed to be pushing at the backs of her eyelids. "I'm scared that Harry and I will never recover from this. I'm scared of living in a world so out of control that we aren't even safe in our own beds. I'm scared that Harry's losing his grip on reality and is going to get himself in trouble, or worse. I'm afraid to close my eyes at night and to face myself in the mirror in the morning. I'm afraid of the future and scared to think of the past because I know where it leads. I'm afraid to go into my own bedroom at home. And I'm afraid I'll never get back in there again, that I'm going to be stuck here, waiting forever."

"Oh, sweetheart." She pulled Laura close.

And against her mother's shoulder, feeling the shudders going through her, Laura said, "But I can't let the fear win, Mom. You know? I'm not running away, I'm just refusing to give in. I have to keep pushing, keep moving so I at least have a chance."

With tears in her own eyes, Sharon nodded, gave Laura another silent hug, and went to pull her meat loaf out of the microwave.

"I can't, hon." Harry stared at the U of A map he'd been working on, sectioning off areas, dividing them among the days left in the week. If he spent four hours canvassing daily, he could cover most of the campus at least once each day. He was paying particular attention to the med school, but would include the remainder of the campus as well. He was looking for at least two men. And if he could get one, it would only be a matter of time until he got the other.

"Please, Harry? Mom and Dad are out and I miss you."

The note of pleading, of wanting, in her voice almost had him. Lines on the map in front of him blurred.

"I miss you, too."

"Then you'll come?"

He ran a hand over the top of his head, holding on to the back of his neck. "No."

"How about tomorrow? Mom and Dad are going to the Schusters for a barbeque. I'm not going."

"I…can't, honey."

"Harry, it's the Fourth of July! We haven't spent a single holiday apart since we met!"

"You think I don't know that?"

"We lived together for weeks after the attack, Harry. What's a few more hours?"

"I'm not willing to take the risk of finding out. They left a message on my car, let the air out of your tire, destroyed vials at the clinic—"

"You don't *know* that, Harry."

He did know. He just couldn't get anyone else to listen.

"Please, Harry, for me?" Her voice dropped, catching him in the groin, not in a sexual way, but deeper, at his core. A place only she could access.

"It *is* for you, Laura. It's all for you."

"You really aren't coming."

He'd hurt her. The one thing he'd promised himself he'd never do.

Biting back the string of curse words that ran through his mind, Harry tried to think, to weigh needs and priorities.

And saw again the vision of his wife, nightgown shoved up to her waist, legs spread wide. And heard the cry that had erupted from her when that bastard had shoved himself inside.

"We haven't found them yet."

"We might never find them." An unfamiliar note of hopelessness entered her tone.

And still, he couldn't give in. He had no choice. Someday she'd understand that. If they got to the other side of this nightmare and managed to reach that *someday*.

"They attacked you because you were planning to make a baby with me."

Her sigh was hard to take. "You don't know that," she said again.

He believed it, though. And he'd be letting her down in the worst way if he didn't follow through.

"Baby aside, Laura, this was a hate crime, enacted solely because you're a white woman married to a black man. White should stay with white, remember? I heard the words."

"But—"

"I *heard* them. And you heard something, too."

"I think I did, but…"

"Trust your instincts," Harry implored her. Boyd had moved on to other cases. He remained alert and watched incoming cases for similarities, but he'd done all he could based on the information he was prepared to accept as valid. "You know you heard something. What was it?"

Come on, sweetie. Come on. "…I'm not sure, Harry." His heart sank. "I might've imagined it, just like Detective Boyd said, and I don't want you running around playing cop because of something I'm not even sure I heard."

"You said you could hear that remark about white with white." Harry wouldn't back down. Nothing was more important than throwing these guys into prison and putting this behind them. Nothing was more important than having Laura back.

"Maybe, but…"

"Think about it, Laura," he continued now, jumping up from the couch to pace the living room. "Whoever did this knew us from somewhere. We'd just been to the center and made final arrangements to have the procedure. Then the day before our appointment, our house is broken into and the attackers not only say *white should stay with white,* they make some remark about a white baby. We both heard the one guy speak. He was articulate, and he said *injure* instead of *hurt.* He also said *AC* instead of *shoulder.* Medical terminology. Then I hear the bastard's voice outside my office at school. And it turns out there's a med student at the university who also works at the center."

"Med students extern at clinics all over the city, Harry. You can't go around bashing this kid's reputation just because he's a med student who happens to work at the center!"

"But Boyd can ask him where he was the night of the rape." And if he didn't, Harry would follow up on his alibi. Or find a way to do it himself.

"It wasn't a hate crime, Harry." Laura sounded tired—and like she thought he was crazy. The tension stretching Harry's nerves escalated. He was losing her.

God damn it, no! He *couldn't* lose her.

"The Power-Reassurance rapist picks his victim ahead of time, and breaks into her home at night," he said, knowing he had to convince her. One way or the other. "The Power-Assertive rapist finds his victims in bars, or other places, but he finds them—he doesn't attack randomly. We're dealing with both."

"And hate crimes are the product of rage, Harry." The evenness of her tone surprised him. "Neither of those men seemed at all angry. They didn't punish or degrade me beyond the obvious. They didn't blindfold me or beat me or do any of the other horrible things I've heard about in counseling over the past few weeks."

She *was* paying attention. Harry's spirits lifted. And then plummeted. She was drawing wrong, and potentially dangerous, conclusions.

"We're dealing with at least one educated man, here," he said, pacing again, collecting his thoughts so he could present them to her as succinctly, rationally and convincingly as possible. "These guys weren't stereotypical supremacist punks. They weren't out to punish you, but to save you. That's how they see it.

They were giving you a very clear warning. White women don't carry black men's babies."

"Their warning wasn't all *that* clear, Harry," Laura said immediately. "Because you're the only one getting it."

His chest tightened, locking the breath out of his lungs.

"Please just come over, Harry. Let's watch that Robin Williams movie, *RV.* My parents just bought the DVD and said it's hilarious."

"I…can't."

"Yes, you can. But you don't want to, do you?" Her tone changed. "You don't want to be around me."

If she'd started to cry, he would've felt better. The acceptance in Laura's voice scared him, as though she'd expected his reaction.

Frustration drove him to pace harder. Faster. "It's not like you to think—"

"It's okay, Harry, I understand. I really do. I'm a constant reminder of something you can't fix. I'm different now, I know that. Not the woman you fell in love with. I'm damaged, and neither of us knows if I'll ever get over it, but we're pretty much guaranteed that I'll never be exactly the same…."

13

"Stop!" Harry couldn't stand any more. "Now. Just stop," he repeated after Laura had fallen silent. "You're completely one-hundred percent wrong."

Not a good way to talk to her. He'd probably shut her down, which wasn't his intent at all.

"You have the right to your opinions," he said, in spite of an inner admonition to proceed gently. This was as gentle as he could be at the moment. "You're certainly going to draw your own conclusions and you can disagree with me about every aspect of this situation except—one. Only *I* can say what I'm thinking and feeling. Only I know that."

Her silence was hard.

"And on this matter, here is what I think. Your body was hurt, Laura. Your spirit was hurt. And in the end, I believe the suffering will make you stronger, not weaker. And even if that wasn't the case, I love you, Laura. I signed on for life, not just for who you were the moment I married you. I don't *want* you to be the same." She still said nothing, so he just kept talking.

Hoping she heard him. Needing the connection. "Look at how much we've both changed in the years since we got married. You're less afraid of conflict. You stand up to your parents when they disregard your beliefs. I'm a lot more compassionate and aware of others and their feelings. We've both gained five pounds."

He'd hoped for a chuckle. And didn't get one.

"Yes, seeing you hurt is painful, honey. Of course it is. Just as it'll be when I stand beside you someday to put your parents to their final rest…."

He knew the analogy was a bad choice before the words were even out of his mouth and continued quickly. "But while I can't change what happened, I *can* fix it. I can see that these scumbags are punished and I can prevent them from ever doing this again. I'll find them if I have to do it single-handedly. I promise you."

He wouldn't stop until he did. *Couldn't* stop.

And then, taking a deep breath, he tackled the issue they hadn't talked about. One that made him physically sick to his stomach every single time he thought about it.

"Seeing you suffer reminds me that I wasn't man enough to protect you in our own house—our own bed."

There. He'd put it right out there. The ragged blade that had been between them since the first rope went around Harry's wrist.

"Oh, Harry, no! You aren't to blame at all! And you're more of a man than either of those disgusting in-dividuals ever will be. There were two of them! They had the edge of surprise. And you were sound asleep."

Her love washed over him.

"But I'm fixing that, too, Laura," he told her, not really hearing her words because they'd been meant as a salve, not as conviction. "If I'd had the gun then, it would've made all the difference."

"Harry…"

"I've already scheduled my first testing in tae kwon do. I'll be a first-degree black belt in less than two years. And I'll be pressing twice my weight within months."

He'd made it back to the living room, was once again in front of the campus map.

"Workouts and guns don't make the man."

"No, but they give him the tools necessary to protect his family." He'd promised Laura and her parents that he'd love and protect her, and he hadn't been prepared. He'd pay for that lapse the rest of his life. But he would not pay for a second one.

"If you want to exercise, Harry, that's great. If it makes you feel good, then I'm all for it. But I need you to know that you don't have to prove anything. Not to me. You stood up to two men in the dark, lashing out at them in spite of bruises and a dislocated shoulder. You didn't cower or hide. That's all the man I need. Or want."

God, he loved her. More than life.

"Please come over, Harry."

Sinking back into the couch, Harry closed his eyes as it started all over again. This crazy roller-coaster ride through hell.

"I'm not risking your life any further," he told her, weary but determined. "If these jerks are watching us right now, I want them to see that we got their warning. That we're heeding it. I want them to believe we've split up. It's the only way I can be even half-sure that they'll leave you alone."

And that was killing him. He wielded the most power by doing nothing—except staying away from her.

"Until when, Harry?" Her voice had a new edge.

"Until we get them."

"And if we don't?"

"We will." *I* will, he amended. And he would. He had nothing left to lose.

"And you think that, assuming these two are caught and go to jail, we'll be out of danger? You think they're the only two white supremacists in the city?"

What he knew was that these two were after him and Laura. They were all that mattered.

"What about that?" Laura's voice jabbed at him. "How are you going to prevent some other small-minded prejudiced idiot from noticing us?"

He didn't reply. He *had* no reply.

"Don't you see?" she pleaded. "We can't let them do this to us. We can't let them rule us by fear. We belong together, you and I. We both know that, have since the day we met. And if other people have a problem with that—well, that's *their* problem. We won't let those problems separate us. Remember that? We promised."

He shook his head, picking up the pencil he'd been using to mark off campus buildings according to the mileage chart and his daily schedule. "I remember," he said, holding the phone with one hand while writing

with the other. "But those peole with the problem…
They've made it ours. I'm not coming near you until
these guys are caught."

He heard everything she *wasn't* saying and then the
click as she hung up the phone.

Harry sat up long into the night. He had a lot more
thinking to do.

And by morning he knew he had to take things one
at a time. First, he'd get the guys who'd hurt Laura. And
then he'd figure out how to tell his wife he loved her
too much to expose her to this kind of danger again.

Any way he looked at it, the outcome of the biggest
risk he'd ever taken in his life—marrying Laura—had
been determined.

He'd lost.

There were times Daniel Boyd came face-to-face
with his conscience. Not often. But it happened.

He didn't like it much. The experience *or* his conscience.

He'd worked with many a cop over the years whose
conscience was pretty undemanding, easy to get along
with. Malleable. Not Daniel's. No, his internal compan-
ion was a pain in the ass. A strict taskmaster. He tended
to stick to a pretty straight and narrow path—consist-
ing almost entirely of work—so he could avoid the
damn thing.

Harry Kendall, the black professor who—even if he
didn't know it—was as much a victim as his wife, was
bringing out the worst in Daniel.

His heart bled.

His brain had long since grown impatient and still he couldn't walk away.

And Harry's worst sin of all—he'd roused Daniel's conscience.

He'd promised to look up David Jefferson. He'd done so.

He'd assured the overzealous, amateur detective and distraught husband that he'd call.

Picking up the phone, working on the Fourth of July because work was what he did—*all* he did—Daniel cursed aloud and dialed.

"David Jefferson is a model citizen as far as I can tell," Boyd said without preamble when Kendall answered. Feet propped on his desk, he stared at the scuffs on the toes of his black shoes. He'd been there since six. Miller was home with his kids. Officially they had two days off. "He's never even had a speeding ticket."

"That's it?" Harry Kendall's voice was getting sharper with every conversation they had.

"I talked to him myself. He has an alibi for the night of the break-in."

"What alibi?"

"He was at the medical building studying all night. His friends can vouch for him."

"They were there at three in the morning?"

"One of them was. And another at four." What was it about college kids that made them most productive when the world was asleep?

But then, maybe they had something there. He'd sure get more work done during the daylight hours if he didn't have people like Harry Kendall slowing him down.

"College kids have been known to lie for each other," Kendall said now, exhausting Daniel. "There was that case just last year, at the campus in Colorado. Those two students raped a mentally disabled girl behind the library and then took her, nude, outside town and left her there. The poor kid was so confused by the time she was discovered, wandering around that she couldn't give any reliable testimony. And when she finally did see one of the guys again and claimed he'd been one of her rapists, his fraternity brothers came forward with a solid alibi."

In the end, the cops had charged seventeen men with obstruction of justice. The perp had been sentenced to ten years.

For demoralizing, dehumanizing, a helpless young girl.

"That case was exceptional," Daniel said. "Listen, I talked to several students, a couple of doctors and the office manager at the clinic. They all give David glowing reviews. The two guys you were talking about were flunking out of school and had several priors for drug charges."

"What about the suction cups? Or the leather gloves? Did you check to see if he's purchased either?"

"Yes. Miller ran a check for his name on the relevant store records. There was no match." Rubbing his eyes, Daniel thought about the vending machine around the corner.

And a chocolate bar. Enough of them might kill him—eventually.

Put him out of his misery.

"Before you ask," he heard himself continue. "No one's seen him in a black leather jacket or gloves. He wears a size twelve shoe. If I had anything to go on, a prior, a shoe size that matched, even an unpaid parking ticket, maybe I could look more closely, but I don't."

"So what if I find him, hear him talk, identify his voice? That would be enough to get those subpoenas, wouldn't it?"

Who was Kendall fooling? He'd recognize that voice if he'd never heard it before in his life. Daniel couldn't set him loose on an innocent med student. Kendall had lost all perspective.

"It's time to stop, Mr. Kendall," he said, no longer trying to humor the man. Kendall was going to get himself into serious trouble and there'd be nothing Daniel could to do to help him out.

"I can't."

"Yes, you can. And what's more, I'm telling you to. You've already been arrested once, and you're skating perilously close to doing things you won't be able to take back. You and Mrs. Kendall have been through a tough time. Deal with that. Continue to get counseling. Move on. Don't let it ruin your life."

"You ever been married, Boyd?"

Kendall's question surprised him. Tilting back in his seat, he dug deep and found a little more grace to offer. If only the younger man would let go of his insane obsessions.

"Yes."

"You still married?"

"No." And then, without understanding why, he

added, "I'm divorced. Didn't take Jess long to figure out she didn't want to be married to a cop. We lasted six months. Twenty years ago."

"Got any sisters?" Kendall's next question was quiet.

Daniel Boyd's chair came down with a crash.

"Her name was Sheila, wasn't it?"

If his hand wasn't frozen to his ear, he'd have hung up. Kendall was trespassing on territory that was not open. To anyone. Period.

The unusual holiday quiet of the precinct crept over him, trapping him by memories he refused to acknowledge.

"I found a newspaper article on the Internet," Kendall continued, his voice softer now, filled with an understanding—a compassion—Daniel didn't want. Or need.

"She was older than you by five years, wasn't she? You were the younger brother mentioned in the article. You're *that* Daniel Boyd."

He felt a tic at the corner of his mouth. Daniel rubbed at it with his thumb. Thought about Jess. A couple of stiff whiskeys. Getting lost in the arms of someone who understood him.

"The article said you were only thirteen."

Fuck the article.

"I...the thought of—I'm thirty-one years old and I can't handle the things I saw happen to Laura. I can't begin to fathom how you must've felt, how horrendous that must have been, standing there while your sister was raped in broad daylight in your own living room." By a black man.

How had he felt? You don't feel. Tapping the desk with one hand, Daniel stared at the archway leading to the hall. He wasn't in the mood for chocolate. Maybe some vanilla cream cookies. Dipped in milk. He hadn't had those in thirty years.

You don't ever feel again.

"I just wanted you to know," Kendall was saying, "how very thankful I am that you're there, doing what you do. If anyone can find the guys that hurt Laura, you can. And if they hadn't already found the man who hurt your sister, I'd go looking for him myself."

Daniel had underestimated Harry Kendall.

She was overreacting. Laura knew that. She'd missed her period because of the stress. That was a given. It had happened before. Many times. Starting when she was a teenager. Anytime there was conflict of any kind, her monthly cycle was disrupted.

The doctor had said her emotion-based irregularity could've had something to do with her inability to get pregnant. She'd wanted it so badly, stressed so much over their desire to have a baby that she'd probably been her own worst enemy, making conception impossible, especially with Harry's low sperm count.

That was how powerful stress could be.

She'd taken the morning-after pill following the attack. It had a 75 to 89 percent success rate. It was that 11 to 25 percent she had to annihilate.

It was noon on Thursday, and she was in the guest bathroom at Kelly's apartment. She pulled from her work satchel the box she'd stashed after her stop at the drugstore that morning. She couldn't do this at work. Couldn't do it at her parents' house.

She didn't have to do it all, except to calm her nerves. Kelly needed five minutes to put the salad together.

Laura needed two to three.

She'd refrained from drinking for the last two hours in an effort to prevent dilution. She was three or four weeks past ovulation.

Undoing her shorts, she eyed the sealed package in her hand. And the toilet. Considered dropping the package in the trash.

She sat instead. Opened the package. Followed the instructions. And, her heart pumping so furiously she could hardly breathe, she waited.

"Hi, Dr. Kendall."

"Denise!" The girl's innocent smile was like an infusion of air in a life that was suffocating him. "How're you doing today?"

"Good. Just wondered if you have anything for me."

"Professor Anderson still doesn't?"

Denise shrugged. "Some papers to grade, but I finished them." She held his gaze. And then she didn't.

Harry wanted to invite her in. To sit and chat about the Civil War. Martin Luther King. Vikings. Hell, he'd delve into a rousing discussion of cavemen if it would take his mind off the challenges he faced.

"Not today," he said, instead, eyes narrowed as he stared at her bent head.

His refusal was rewarded with another quick smile as the pretty young woman said she'd check back later, leaving Harry to wonder if he really was losing his mind.

For a second there, he'd thought Denise Marshall was coming on to him.

Laura released her hair from its ponytail and refastened it. She smoothed her shorts, pulled down the edge of her Botanical Garden shirt. Fixed her socks. Checked the laces on her shoes. Shoved the trash, stick back in its ripped packaging, into the deepest recesses of her satchel.

She opened the bathroom door.

Stepped out. Noticed the colorful metal girls dancing across Kelly's living room wall. Avoided the angels.

Kelly, rounding the corner from the kitchen, salad bowl in one hand, two plates in the other, looked at Laura and froze.

"What?"

Laura stepped forward, grabbed the bowl, set it on the table in the windowed dining alcove. Pulled out a seat. Sat. Put her napkin in her lap.

All with her satchel still on her shoulder.

"You're white as a sheet," Kelly said. "And you were in there kind of long. Are you sure you're okay? You're not getting sick?"

"I'm not sick at all." Laura could help herself to salad. Pour dressing from a bottle in front of her. She could pick up her fork. Mix in the dressing. She couldn't meet Kelly's gaze.

And she couldn't get the fork past her lips.

Kelly's hand on hers was Laura's first indication

that her own hand was shaking badly. The salad in her lap was the second.

"Come here," Kelly said, dragging her from the table to the couch. She sat, pulling Laura down beside her.

Perched on the very edge of the seat, Laura examined the swirled patterns of brown in Kelly's beige carpet.

"Tell me what's wrong."

Wrong. Yes, that was it. *Wrong.*

"I'm pregnant."

During the summer months, when the university had a much lower enrollment, Harry took a shift one afternoon a week at the guidance office. Academic counseling. The job, which used to be a labor of love, had become a tool in his investigation.

Because he could access student records. And when Boyd came up with yet another dead end, leaving Harry in the cold, he'd done what any man would to protect his wife.

He deliberately broke the university's code of ethics and looked up David Jefferson's class schedule.

And on Thursday afternoon, twenty minutes after he'd finished his lecture on the effects of bureaucracy on American wars, he was at the other end of the campus, standing outside a medical microbiology lecture, waiting for David Jefferson to leave class.

He'd been unable to find a picture of the pervert. There'd been nothing in the campus-news archives, and he hadn't been in the undergraduate nor the graduate yearbooks.

The bastard kept a low profile. And Harry knew why.

* * *

"My God, Kel, what am I going to do?"

Sitting in the front seat of her Ranger after work, Laura stared at her friend.

"We're going to talk about this, that's what." Kelly grabbed Laura's hand, held it on the seat between them. "The first thing you need to know is that you aren't alone."

Laura concentrated on Kelly's touch, the warmth and softness of her friend's hand pulling her back from the dark abyss into which her mind had been slowly sinking.

Kelly had wanted her to call a doctor at lunchtime. To take the rest of the afternoon off. But Laura had needed to work. To have *something* in her life that was normal. From five at night until nine in the morning, she floundered between despair and a desperate attempt to hold on. From nine to five, she was a botanist, tending to plants that provided life-sustaining oxygen.

Plants might appear fragile. Yet they were the source of life.

"Honey?"

Blinking, Laura became aware of Kelly's concerned gaze. And could no longer fight off the frightening thoughts that had been stabbing at her consciousness all afternoon.

She was in her five-to-nine time now. The numbness was wearing off. She'd avoided looking at her stomach all afternoon. She hadn't been able to touch it—or even let it brush up against anything.

"They raped me. Forced their bodies on me. *Inside*

me." She heard the words come out of her mouth but didn't recognize her own voice.

She could hardly form coherent thoughts.

"And now this?" she muttered.

Kelly looked at her with compassion. Laura closed her eyes.

"I now have a life growing in me that comes from one of *them?*"

She couldn't take in the horror of it. "Do you have any idea what this is going to do to Harry? He's already on the verge of fanatical…."

Dear God. Harry. This would kill him. She was afraid of what he might do, whatever action the news would prompt.

She'd had sex with him the night after the rape. Dare she try to convince him the baby could be his?

Laura's head fell back against the seat, her mind foggy. She felt like throwing up.

Harry would never believe the baby was his. They'd been trying for years to conceive. His sperm count was too low for unassisted conception.

She didn't believe it was his, either.

"You don't have to have this baby, honey." Kelly's whisper barely reached her.

Kill her baby? After she'd spent the past five years praying she'd *have* a baby?

Laura's thoughts were suddenly paralyzed. She could feel herself shaking, couldn't get warm.

"Hey." Kelly scooted closer on the bench seat, putting an arm around Laura's shoulders. "Come on. Talk to me. I'm right here."

Elation seemed bizarre at the moment. But…she was finally pregnant after all the dashed hopes.

And the child she carried was conceived of the devil.

She was trapped. And there was no way out.

"Laura…" Kelly's voice slid over her. Through her. "Talk, honey. Don't hold it in. Don't put yourself through this torture."

Laura stared at her friend.

"What are you thinking?"

Watching Kelly's lips as her friend spoke, Laura said the first thing that came to her mind.

"I'd like to put my head on your shoulder and sleep forever."

14

Harry tried to go home Thursday evening. He packed up his briefcase. Turned off his computer and the lights in his office and walked out, just as he'd done every other evening for the past five years. He greeted his peers, nodded at students, stopped to answer a question about a final exam that was coming up in a matter of weeks.

The faculty parking lot wasn't far from his office. There weren't many students to observe walking between the two, but he looked anyway. Every male he saw was the rapist. And yet not one fit the description—minimal though it was.

He threw his briefcase in the car and meant to get in. He couldn't—couldn't go home to that empty house.

The microbiology class might have been a bust. As had the behavioral science class before that. They were the only two classes the man was taking during the summer session. At neither had he seen anyone who'd sparked even a glimmer of recognition.

Needless to say, David Jefferson wasn't going to be walking around campus wearing a name tag.

And while a couple of the students he'd asked knew who Jefferson was, college students, especially graduate students in med school, were pretty single-minded. No one knew for sure if David had been in class that week. Or they weren't saying.

He stopped short of grilling the instructor.

He did learn one piece of information, though.

David Jefferson had blond hair. Just like Laura.

Picturing his wife's hair in the rapist's fist, Harry slammed the car door. A walk around campus might calm him down. Give him something else to think about.

Or an idea he hadn't come up with yet.

One thing was certain; he had nothing better to do.

"I have to go home." Laura gave Kelly a weak smile as her friend sat quietly beside her in the passenger seat. "My folks'll be worried about me."

"Call them," Kelly said. "Tell them we're having dinner."

At the moment, nothing sounded better to Laura— except maybe one of those sleeping pills the hospital had given her the night of the rape.

Sleeping pills she didn't dare take considering her present condition.

Oh. God. Heavenly Father. You are the giver of life. But all life? This life?

Laura listened, but got no response. Not even a twinge of feeling. No guidance or comfort.

God's child the offspring of a rapist? Didn't seem feasible.

She needed to get home. To the safety of the room she'd grown up in. The familiarity of sameness. She needed to go to bed and let this day end.

But when she thought of facing her parents, Laura looked at Kelly and nodded.

Harry walked for an hour. And then another. Sweating, he went from one end of campus to the other—finding much of it deserted this late on a summer night. During the school year, those same fields and sidewalks would be bustling with sound and movement. With laughter. A game of football or Frisbee.

Tonight, if there was anything going on, it was happening indoors. The 110 temperature didn't invite outdoor activity.

Dusk was falling and Harry checked his watch—almost 7:30. Hours to go before he could expect to sleep.

Turning the corner onto the broken sidewalk of the Tucson street bordering the campus, Harry considered going back to his office.

Or hitting a bar. There had to be a place med students hung out. There had to be a drink that could offer him at least a moment of solace.

Frat houses lined the street beside him, lights blazing in some, not in others. Probably deserted for the summer, Harry thought. On a hunch—or because he was irrational, just like Laura said—he headed down an old residential street, quiet and dark. Many of the homes belonged to fraternities and sororities. All were campus housing. Maybe one was filled with med students?

Harry crossed the street. And moved on to another. He was getting lightheaded from the heat, a lack of water, the need for food. The idea of a drink, sitting in a bar among other human beings, was looking more and more appealing. Running through a mental list, he tried to figure out which bar was closest—and least likely to be blaring with loud music on a Thursday night.

Maybe he should wait till he got home, then go to Grady's. It was only half a mile from the house. Probably better to drive first, drink later.

Harry stopped abruptly. Listening. He'd just heard the voice. Hadn't he? Had that sound been in his head? Or was it real?

God knew, he couldn't seem to escape the images and sounds from the night of the rape.

Glancing at the two-story house on his right, the front window a few feet away from him, Harry stood there, holding his breath. Would he hear it again?

He couldn't see any lights. Or cars in the driveway. There was no sign of life at all in the house.

But he couldn't just leave. What if they were in there? What if they'd seen him out here, a sitting duck on the sidewalk? What if they were laughing, punching each other on the arm as they watched him? Drinking a toast to themselves at Laura's expense?

Maybe the bastard had spoken on purpose. Just to provoke Harry, make him crazy. Haters grew bolder as their hate progressed. According to all the reading he'd done, escalation was mandatory to keeping the hate alive. Maybe they were taunting him—because they planned to get Laura again.

Harry couldn't let that happen.

Continuing down the street, he waited until he was out of view, slipped between two homes, hopped the wall into a backyard and then hopped another wall to the backyard next door. Taking his time, having to criss-cross to avoid a dog, he made his way to the frat house he'd been standing in front of. Lights were on in the back rooms of some of the houses. Music blared from one. Careful to stay in the shadows, Harry hoisted himself up on yet another wall, lost his balance and came down hard. The skin from his elbow to his right wrist burned.

He'd snagged his slacks. Scuffed his shoes. And now scraped his forearm. None of it mattered.

He was in the backyard, only yards from the house. There were two rear windows. One was dark. The other wasn't.

And, oddly enough, considering the Tucson temperature, the window was open.

They went back to Kelly's apartment. It was comfortable. Beautiful. Safe.

Once Laura had called her parents and Kelly confirmed that she was all right to drive, she'd left her to climb into her Jeep. Laura had followed her into a drive-through to pick up chicken, then helped set the table.

They talked about work while they ate. Discussed a meeting they were going to have with a federal-grant board the next week to present their experimental data to date. Kelly was as excited as Laura about the preliminary aloe and prickly pear results.

That half hour allowed Laura to escape again—if only for long enough to get some food inside her. Regardless of what happened, what she decided, she had to eat.

And then the respite was over. One look from Kelly and it all came back.

"Stay here tonight." Kelly's suggestion was unexpected. And completely welcome.

"I don't have clothes. For tonight. Or tomorrow. Or a toothbrush or—"

"I have pajamas you can borrow and we'll throw your clothes in the wash, it's not like anyone's going to know if what you have on is yesterday's uniform or one you wore last week."

Laura smiled. A real smile.

"I have a couple of those free toothbrushes from the dentist. And a drawer full of sample makeup from bonus days."

Could anything really be that simple? Her parents would object. That was a given. They'd tell her Harry wanted her with them—even though most days what Harry wanted didn't carry much weight with them.

"Listen, hon," Kelly said, leaning forward to hold her gaze. "You're human, okay? You've been through hell and back this past month. Give yourself a break. You don't have to make any decisions tonight. It's not like you can even get a doctor's appointment at this hour. You don't have to tell anyone yet. Take some time to rest. To ponder. Wake up tomorrow and see how you feel…"

Her words felt good to Laura. Right. If she was

hiding, so be it. Running, fine. For this one night, she wanted to leave Laura Kendall and her pain behind. To rest her head in a safe place, close her eyes and not find demons waiting there.

"You have sheets on the bed in the spare room?"

"Hold it a minute."

Harry stopped breathing. He didn't move. All senses tuned, he stared at the open window, flabbergasted.

He'd know that voice anywhere. Anytime. Every cell and sinew in his body recognized it. The articulation. The commanding tone. The tenor.

When the ensuing silence went on for too long, when he started to fear that if he waited any more the voice might disappear, Harry slid forward along the side wall toward the open window. He could make out a couch, set in the middle of the room, perpendicular to the window. A light flickered, as if from a television set.

That voice hadn't been on TV, had it? No way. He'd recognized it. He was sure of that.

With everything inside him, he was sure.

A couple of steps closer and he could make out a body sitting on the couch. A relatively small person. No more than five two or three, Harry figured. And along the back wall was an expensive-looking computer station with more technological gadgets than Harry would know what to do with.

He recognized the emblem of a popular gaming system.

When he'd gone to college, he'd been grateful for his

refurbished laptop that had weighed at least ten pounds and hadn't had enough memory to do more than write term papers.

Another step. And another. He could see the person more clearly now. A woman. With curly hair falling around her shoulders. She changed her position on the couch, resting her back against the arm, her head still facing the television.

The top half of her was completely nude.

Kelly had a glass of wine. They threw in a load of laundry and then, with Laura settled in front of an old Doris Day movie she'd never seen, Kelly did some paperwork. Took a shower. And had another glass of wine.

"I envy you, you know," she said, joining Laura on the couch as the movie ended.

"Envy me?" Laura couldn't imagine that. Not for a second.

"Yep." With a lopsided smile, Kelly took another sip of wine. "What you and Harry have… I've wanted that my whole life."

Had. What they had. Nothing was ever going to be the same again. That much was undeniable.

What they'd end up with remained to be seen. For better or worse.

The events of the past month had changed them both.

"When I first started college, I dated this guy…." Kelly never talked about her past. Or much about her present, either, aside from school and work. "I really loved him," she said. "He was kind and warm, and had the greatest smile."

"So what happened?"

"We couldn't keep our hands off each other."

Shocking herself, Laura had a glimpse of another time, feeling for a brief second the desire Kelly was describing. Only instead of her friend and a nameless boyfriend, it was her and Harry. "And this was a problem?"

"I wanted to wait until I was married to have sex. I'd grown up in a religious household, with a strong sense of morality, of right and wrong. And we were freshmen in college. Far too young to be thinking about lifelong commitments. Yet every time we were together, we got closer and closer until one night…"

Laura knew what she was going to hear. She and Harry had slipped up, too, despite everything she'd been taught. And afterward, when Laura hadn't been consumed with guilt as she'd expected to be—when, instead, she'd felt beautiful and peaceful and happier than she'd ever thought possible—she'd known that the things her parents had taught her, the things they believed, weren't true for her.

Harry was.

Kelly sipped. "…we ended up in his bed at the dorm, completely undressed, and I got scared. I didn't understand the power of what we were feeling and I was afraid I was going to ruin my whole life. I was afraid I was letting myself down."

The thought had never entered Laura's head that night with Harry. Very few thoughts had. She'd been too busy feeling…

"I got dressed and left as quickly as I could and the next time I saw him, I broke up with him."

"Why?"

Kelly sighed. "I was so afraid I was going to lose control and make a mistake I'd regret forever."

"Did you ever see him again?"

Kelly shook her head. "Not for a long time. I missed him, though, so much. I missed talking to him. Being with him. I missed having someone in my life who believed in me as much as I believed in him. He really liked me, you know? He listened when I talked and cared about what I had to say, even when he didn't agree with me."

Laura did know. Kelly could've been describing her and Harry. Until a month ago.

"But I still thought I'd done the right thing," Kelly continued. "I had pretty strong ideals...."

Laura considered what might have happened if she hadn't slept with Harry. If, instead of allowing the love between them to flourish, she'd run away. And knew, even as sat there pregnant with a rapist's baby, that she wouldn't change her original decision.

"Did you ever regret the choice?" she asked.

Kelly's chin puckered, as though she might start to cry. Turning her head, she faced the darkened window. And then she spoke.

"I regret that choice just about every day." Kelly's intensity reached through the numbness surrounding Laura.

"Because you never found that kind of love again?"

"Because what I'd saved myself for turned out to be an experience in the front seat of a car."

Frowning, Laura watched the unusual bitterness flash across her friend's expression. She'd never seen that side of Kelly before. For a second there, it felt as if she didn't know her at all.

"And if you weren't going to wait for marriage, you would have preferred the first guy?"

Kelly lost her apparent battle with composure. The eyes that met Laura's were filled with tears, and before Kelly could say a word, Laura's own throat constricted, her heart breaking wide open as she somehow recognized, on an emotional if not a conscious level, what was to come.

"We were making out. I…liked him. A lot. Things got a little out of hand and he had my pants down…"

Laura didn't need to hear any more. Didn't want to.

"I stopped him," Kelly said. "Told him no. But he wouldn't listen…"

"He raped you." The words were torn out of her.

"Eventually, yes."

As she sat there on her friend's couch, not a victim but suddenly an understanding caregiver, Laura's entire world shifted again.

Harry noticed the breasts. They were large. Firm. Creamy white. With nipples puckered as though from cold. Or stimulation.

As far as he could see, the woman was experiencing neither. It couldn't be cool with the window open to 110 degree heat. And there didn't appear to be anyone else in the room.

Where was Jefferson? Or whoever owned that voice?

With her gaze still turned toward the television set—

Harry couldn't tell what was on—she leaned forward, picked up a sandwich, and took a bite.

What the hell was going on?

For another fifteen minutes Harry stared at those breasts. That woman. For another fifteen minutes she sat there and watched television. Alone.

So maybe she was an exhibitionist. Except that she was presumably alone, unaware that anyone was observing her.

She was probably just hot as hell, without air-conditioning on this blistering hot summer night—as evidenced by the open window. And the fan he could see, blowing with minimal effect.

Neither assumption explained the voice.

Harry had heard it.

He knew he had.

Unless Laura and Boyd and everyone else was right and he'd gone completely over the edge.

15

"Did you press charges?" Laura asked her friend, still sitting on the couch with her later that night. They'd talked for hours, and for the first time since her attack, Laura was beginning to feel stronger.

She wasn't so odd, so marked, so alone, after all.

Kelly sipped from her fourth glass of wine. "No."

"Why?" Laura asked, while silently admitting she probably wouldn't have either. But she'd like to know that the guy had paid dearly for what he'd done to her friend. Even now, after eight years, Kelly bore the scars.

"It would've been my word against his," Kelly said. She looked directly at Laura. "I would've been put on the stand in court, his attorney would have pointed out that I was in his car with my pants down, no doubt claiming I'd agreed to the sex but that we'd had a fight later and I was trying to get back at him." Kelly's voice was low, resigned, and it didn't sound anything like the upbeat, confident woman Laura knew. "The truth of the matter is, we did have a fight afterward. I wanted to claw his eyes out. He took me back to campus and as I was getting out of the car one of his friends heard him say that he never wanted to see me again."

"But surely a good attorney could have explained that…" Laura didn't finish what she'd started to say. Explained what? That a woman wouldn't claim rape if there hadn't been one? Not always true. Or that any woman who'd been raped had every right to see the perpetrator punished?

"They would've dragged my reputation through the mud, and it would've been a fifty-fifty chance at best that the jury would convict him."

Her own case was different. Yet Kelly's words chilled her to the bone. Wasn't being raped enough? Could she really, at some point, be expected to sit in court and have her reputation put on trial, her every action laid out for strangers to scrutinize? Did physical rape lead to rape of another kind?

Yet what was the alternative? To allow men like Kelly's date, or her own two attackers, to move about freely, preying on innocent women and ruining lives?

"You never said anything about this…afterward… when I told you…"

"The last thing you needed to hear right then was about some other bastard wreaking havoc."

Maybe. "But you had to be reliving it…"

"It was a long time ago, Laura. Mostly I've come to terms with it. I just…sometimes I wish…I don't know. I hate that I didn't ever have it good before I had it bad."

Like Laura had. Suddenly she began to understand. And to see that, in spite of everything, she *was* lucky.

"You don't enjoy it," Laura guessed, with sudden

understanding. Was this why Kelly, at twenty-eight, was still alone?

"I don't dislike it."

"But you haven't…"

"I'm an onlooker," Kelly said matter-of-factly. "I hover somewhere above my body and perform. You know, he's doing this, I should do that. Or…maybe he'd like it if I did this. Other than those first few times of almost doing it—with a guy I loved—I've never just *lived* the experience, letting it take control."

"Have you been to counseling?"

Kelly shrugged. "On and off. But what happened to me was nothing like what you went through. I knew the guy. I let him touch me."

"But that doesn't give him the right to take more than you offered!"

"Of course not."

Shaking, Laura said, "It wasn't your fault."

"That's an easy one for the head to grasp, but a lot harder for the heart, huh?"

Her eyes moist, Laura held Kelly's gaze and nodded. In that moment they were sisters, sharing a common bond of pain and understanding that no one who hadn't endured what they had could ever fully grasp. To know that something wasn't your fault was one thing; to feel blameless was another. And feelings always seemed to take precedence.

Harry called Laura's cell phone from his car. It was only a little after ten. She'd still be up.

He got her voice mail. She had her phone off.

Leave it. She just went to bed early. Needed some un-interrupted sleep. Bobbing his foot as he waited for a light, he told himself the same thing over and over.

Until something else occurred to him. She'd gone to bed without attempting to tell him good-night.

That had never happened before, not since the night they'd first kissed.

Something was wrong.

Horns honked behind him as Harry quickly called Laura's parents. And cars were left in the dust when he heard that she wasn't there.

That she was spending the night with a friend.

Like a young girl who had her own life and was living it.

She hadn't even called to let him know where she'd be sleeping.

It was with a heavy heart and confused thoughts that he walked into the bar not far from his house.

His house. Not his and Laura's.

First thing Friday morning, Harry left a message on Boyd's voice mail, identifying the voice at the frat house as the one he'd heard the night of Laura's rape.

Denise was with him, making copies of some transparencies he needed for his lecture on Monday, when Boyd called back mid-afternoon. A medical student named David Jefferson was at the station. Boyd needed Harry to come in for witness identification. Laura would be there within the hour.

Leaving a bewildered Denise behind, Harry flew out the door.

* * *

Boyd met him at the door of the station again, just as he had the last time, giving Harry the drill for the upcoming proceedings.

"I hope you're right about this one," the detective said, frowning as he led Harry back. "Folks aren't real happy with me for dragging this guy in here on your say-so alone."

Tight-lipped, Harry nodded. *Please, God, let this time be different.* His nerves on edge, he glanced around the precinct. "Is my wife here yet?"

"Not yet," Boyd said.

And only then, when he felt the disappointment, did Harry realize how much he was looking forward to seeing Laura. It had been six days.

It seemed like six years.

He needed her.

Leading Harry straight into the room, Daniel Boyd closed the curtain on the one-way mirror.

"We're going straight for voice recognition this time," the detective said. "Five guys'll be lined up on the other side of this curtain. They'll each be asked to step forward and speak. You'll have as much time as you need with each one, and you'll be able to request any of the possible suspects to repeat themselves. Any questions?"

Harry shook his head. Then he asked, "If we don't get him by his voice, will we do the pictures again?"

"*We* aren't going to do anything, Mr. Kendall. Just make absolutely sure you know what you're talking about if you nail this guy."

Harry met the detective's guarded eyes. "You think it might be him, too, don't you?"

Not saying a word, Boyd stared at Harry. And then turned away. But not before Harry had seen a reluctant softening in the other man's expression.

"I think it's possible," Boyd admitted, opening the door, giving Harry a brief glimpse of Detective Miller a few yards down the hall, facing them, before leaving Harry alone in the sterile, cinder-block room with its cold tile floor and two rows of chairs in front of the black curtain.

Bobby Donahue paced. He swore. Taking aim, he shot a bird out of the sky. He had tears in his eyes as it fell to the ground. A symbol.

He had to take down one of his own. One of his brothers had acted under his own cognizance. He'd jeopardized the cause and had to die.

With another shot he took a branch off a tree several yards away. And another went straight through the middle of a leaf without removing it from its branch.

It was all in how he aimed.

Each shot had been carefully executed. With perfect results.

In the private compound a few miles from Flagstaff that served as his storehouse, retreat and secret hideaway, Bobby shot a bullet straight into the ground.

How long would it be for victory to be won? Would it happen in his lifetime? In Luke's?

He feared for his boy, growing up with all the evil

forces in the world. He was just going to have to work harder. Be smarter. Make more money. Push. Take more risks.

And make darn sure that the rest of his brothers got the message loud and clear.

Salvation depended on their obedience. On acting as one.

Individual choice spelled disaster for all.

God was counting on them.

The door opened. Turning expectantly from the corner of the room where he'd been standing, Harry felt disappointed to see that it was Miller, not Laura.

"Oh, I didn't realize anyone was in here," the detective said, quickly leading a handcuffed man to the door on the opposite wall.

The door into the lineup area.

The blond man stared straight ahead, with the exception of one quick, knowing look at Harry. Shaking with rage, Harry watched him.

Heard every step of the man's red-laced black boots.

David Jefferson.

That bastard had raped Harry's wife.

He was going to kill him.

"Sorry." Miller was back. "I thought Boyd was holding you up front until we were ready."

Harry had assumed Robert Miller had seen him when Boyd left the room. "No problem," Harry muttered, only half aware of what he was saying. On the other side of that window was the son of a bitch who'd ruined his life.

The door opened and closed again and Boyd was there.

Harry wanted to tell him Jefferson was the one. But he knew he had to do this right, had to let this play out according to the rules.

"Is Mrs. Kendall here yet?" Miller asked. Tension tightened Harry's shoulders when the other man shook his head.

"Okay, let's get going here," Boyd said, speaking into a microphone mounted on a table in front of the first row of chairs.

"Suspect number one, could you please step forward and read the line you've been given."

They heard the faintest sound of shuffling feet and then, loud and clear in the small room, a voice said, "Unless you want more than a dislocated AC, you'll remain still."

Harry, standing with his back straight, facing the curtain, didn't move a muscle. It wasn't him.

He could feel Boyd watching him, could see the detective's deceptively casual stance out of the corner of his eye. "Suspect number two, could you please step forward and read the line you've been given."

One by one the men were called forth.

Harry listened to each of them. And felt nothing.

"Suspect number four, could you please step forward and read the line you've been given."

Miller scooted lower in his chair to Henry's right, leaning on one elbow as he waited.

"Unless you want more than a dislocated AC, you'll remain still."

That was it. With control he could hardly believe

he had, Harry nodded, one short, succinct movement of his head.

He'd just found the man who'd brutalized his wife.

Boyd began to call number five.

"That was him," Harry said, his voice curt.

"I need you to listen to all five suspects, Mr. Kendall, and then tell me what you think."

Protocol. Harry had been told the first time around that they had to act very carefully during every step of the investigative process to protect the integrity of the case. They weren't giving these bastards any shot at getting evidence thrown out of court.

He listened attentively to number five. Or at least stood still. Waited for the proper steps to be concluded. He declined the opportunity to hear them all again.

"It's number four," he said, raising his voice, wanting any recording device in the room to pick him up clearly.

With a nod at Miller, Boyd was gone, presumably to give directions in the lineup room.

Harry was led out the other door.

He smelled Laura's sweet lilac scent, but he didn't so much as look in the direction from which it came. She'd be sealed in another room—until they moved him out of there, anyway. There'd be no opportunity for anyone to say he'd given his wife even a hint.

The order of the suspects would change anyway.

No one had told him he'd properly identified David Jefferson. He didn't need them to. He was that certain.

He prayed Laura would recognize the voice, too, and tell them with the same confidence.

Left in the reception area, Harry sat down to wait.

* * *

Feeling the weight of the world on her shoulders, and that of an unknown and frightening life inside her, Laura looked straight ahead as she walked down the hallway at the Tucson police station. Once again she had to face the past she'd tried so frenziedly to forget.

After yesterday, there'd be no forgetting. This was her life. She was going to have to stand up on her own.

Laura refused the chair Detective Boyd offered her as she entered the small room where they'd told her Harry had already been.

"It'll just be a minute," the detective said. Laura nodded.

She couldn't smell her husband's aftershave. And as much as she hoped he'd waited for her because she so desperately needed to see him, she also hoped he'd left—was on his way back to school, or home or out to eat. Because seeing him would be too hard, knowing she had a baby growing inside her.

She wished she could pretend it was his but dismissed the idea. She wasn't going to hide, play games with herself or Harry, or go into this blind. She and Harry had been trying for more than five years to have a baby.

And after one night of sex with someone other than Harry she was pregnant.

That could only mean Harry's low sperm count had definitely been the problem.

"Ready?" Boyd interrupted her thoughts, and Laura met his gaze long enough to nod. She stared at the black curtain. Miller stood on the other side.

"Suspect number one, could you please step forward and read the line you've been given?"

"Unless you want more than a dislocated AC, you'll remain still."

The second Laura heard the words, her heart froze. Just like that all movement in her body stopped cold.

It was him.

Oh, my God.

It was him.

She teetered, felt herself floating.

And never even knew that it was Miller' arms that came around her and prevented her from hitting the floor.

16

What was taking so long? Harry paced. Had Laura not been unable to identify the suspect? Would they hold him on Harry's word alone?

Had Boyd released David Jefferson? In that case, were they giving the man time to get away before they told Harry?

Where was Laura? Had she left by a back door, too?

Which wasn't necessarily bad if they'd escorted her out to keep her safe.

People came. People went. A very drunk and foul-smelling man was hauled past him. Down on his luck. Poor fool.

A father escorted out a long-haired, punk-looking teenager with a sarcastic glint in his eye and tattoos covering both arms.

And then, suddenly, she was there.

"Laura?" Harry got to his feet, but wasn't sure if he reached for her, or if she threw herself into his embrace. He just knew that as he stood in that police precinct, oblivious to all the people coming and going, nothing had ever felt better than Laura's arms around him, her body against his.

This was home.

Laura didn't register a lot of what was going on in the small room Detective Boyd ushered her and Harry into half an hour after they'd finished their identifications. Miller was handling the suspect. The orange juice the detective gave her was cold. Harry's hand, holding hers from his seat beside her, was warm. Vital.

She'd only fainted for a few seconds; she'd been able to complete the identification process. But she didn't feel like herself.

"We've got enough to book him, but I have to tell you voice IDs are the hardest. They don't always stick in court. Having them from both of you helps tremendously."

"It was David Jefferson, wasn't it?"

Laura saw Boyd's head lower once, slowly. Giving Harry the affirmation he'd needed.

And scaring Laura to death.

Harry had found this man. Harry with all his irrational theories.

"Did he have red laces in his boots?" Harry's next question confused her. And it wasn't just the words. It was the way he'd said them—with such foreboding.

Daniel Boyd tightened his lips. Nodded.

"Members of the Ivory Nation wear those boots. The red laces signal a brother who's shed blood for the cause." Harry's fingers were still warm and strong in hers, but he was pinning Detective Boyd with a hardened stare that she didn't recognize at all.

What was he talking about? Red laces? Boots? How did he know what they meant? And what was the Ivory Nation?

Her gaze flew to the detective, looking for any sign at all that Harry had completely lost his mind.

"I'm assuming Jefferson didn't give up the other man."

Frowning, the detective hesitated before answering. "He claims he doesn't have any idea what I'm talking about. He's never heard of either of you and wasn't anywhere near your neighborhood."

"He's lying." The conviction in Laura's voice surprised her. But only because she didn't usually speak so strongly, not because she had any doubt whatsoever about that man, who was being held in some other part of the building.

"All I can tell you is what he says. I offered to help him if he helped me, but he wasn't having any of it."

"He's covering for both of them," Harry said. "He has to or he's as good as dead."

Growing impatient, uneasy, Laura turned from one to the other. "Why?"

"Those laces are like a banner, advertising him as a member of the Ivory Nation." Harry looked straight at her, speaking as authoritatively as though delivering a lecture. "It's one of Arizona's largest white supremacist organizations, suspected in more than a hundred first-class felonies, including rape, murder, drug-running and burglary, but so far no one's been able to bring them down."

The detective nodded. "Your husband's done a lot of

research, Mrs. Kendall—Laura," Daniel Boyd said. The glance he and Harry exchanged puzzled her. Obviously the two had gotten to know each other better during her absence. "If Jefferson turns on one of his own," Boyd continued, "the rest of his pack would silence him immediately. He knows that. That's how they work. They hang together or die. It's what makes them so hard to break."

Laura started to feel sick. Something terrible was going on. She was the only one in the room who didn't know about it. And what she'd just learned was horrifying beyond words.

This afternoon's identification, the man they'd brought in—did this confirm what Harry had been saying all along? That her attack hadn't been random, but aimed directly at her and Harry, because people hated that they were together? She was being punished for her choice to marry a black man?

If so, the baby she was carrying was the direct result of a hatred so vile she couldn't even imagine it.

"We got a warrant to search Jefferson's apartment and car," Detective Boyd was saying.

"And the frat house," Harry added.

"No." The detective's face was drawn tight. "He doesn't live there. Nor does anyone place him there. The judge denied that warrant."

"But the voice…"

The detective sat forward, his hands in front of him, glancing up at Harry across the table in the small interrogation room.

"I have to be straight with you, Mr. Kendall. The fact

that you found this man was a fluke—and a lesson to me not to get too sure of myself. But I didn't bring Jefferson here because I found him at the frat house. I brought him in to get you off his back. Pure and simple."

"You arrested a man to protect him?"

"I didn't arrest him. I convinced him it was in his best interests to submit to a lineup. And I did it to protect *you*. I knew you weren't going to rest until you had that chance."

Listening to the detective, hearing the mixture of exasperation and compassion in his voice, Laura said, "You thought Harry was wrong."

"Not after I picked the man up and saw the laces in his boots."

"So why did Jefferson come?" Laura asked, not wanting to know anything about her attacker, but needing to understand.

Boyd shrugged. "I can only speculate, but my guess is that he was playing his best chance. If he refused, I'd have reason to suspect him. If he didn't and you guys missed the call, he'd be free to go with the assurance that we'd leave him alone. I'm guessing he didn't think you guys heard enough of him to worry about."

"And now that we've been proven correct, the judge still won't let you look in the frat house? We have another man to find and I'm betting he's there."

The detective shook his head. "Jefferson claims he's never been to that frat house in his life. I showed his picture around there this morning, and no one recognized him. There's no link between him and the fraternity, as far the rosters show, so no reason to invade their privacy."

"I heard him there." Harry's words were no less strong for their low tone.

"Your word about hearing a voice from a house where you saw only a woman alone, is not convincing. And certainly not enough justification for a judge to issue a search warrant." He raised his eyebrows. "And let's not forget that, by your own admission, you were trespassing."

Harry ignored that. "So we need more evidence."

"No!" Detective Boyd's voice was angrier than Laura had ever heard it. "No, Mr. Kendall," he said more calmly. "What we need is for you to go home, be a teacher and a husband. Take up a sport. Continue with counseling. And let us do our jobs."

Harry didn't move. "There's another man out there, Detective."

"I need your word, Mr. Kendall."

Harry stood, saying nothing.

Boyd stood, too. "If you go near that house again, you're going to be arrested for trespassing."

Laura's heart clamored in terror for her husband when Harry met the man's gaze head-on, not backing down at all. If what the two of them had just said was true, if some white supremacist organization was really behind all of this, then Harry was in even more danger than she'd feared.

* * *

"Dear God, I am sick and sorry. Please forgive my ignorance."

Bobby stood at the desk in his home office; Luke was playing on a blanket spread out on the floor.

"Forgive my ignorance, Father," he repeated, watching his son.

Luke glanced up. Gave him a wet grin. The boy was teething.

"I should not have trusted, Father. Forgive me," he said, more softly, as he came around the desk, leaned down to the toddler, looking the boy straight in the eye.

Luke was learning many things. How to put shapes in openings. To hold the big crayons with his right hand as he colored. To play with cars and trucks and trains and guns. And to be humble in the face of his creator.

With a quick kiss on the boy's head, Bobby stood, checked his watch and made a call on the cell phone that was practically attached to his hip.

Tony answered on the first ring. *Thank you, God.*

"You on your way?"

"Yeah." The young man sounded harried.

And he was late. Bobby stood, stared out the window, teeth clenched. He didn't need another challenge that day.

"What's wrong?"

"Nothing's wrong," Tony said quickly. Hearing the Johnny Rebel music in the background, a CD Bobby had given him for his birthday, one Tony always listened to on the drive from Tucson to Flagstaff, Bobby relaxed slightly. "I was just," Tony began. "Just…you know…"

Not today he didn't. "What?"

"Beth wanted to…you know…"

Ahh. With a grin, Bobby understood. And opened his heart to his little brother again, allowing Tony's love to fill him. He'd almost let the unfaithful actions of one man corrupt his soul.

He'd been double-crossed. But the situation was under control.

Some people were just bad. Evil. Even some white men who claimed to share their quest. But he couldn't let one man lead an army astray.

He was going to have to rid the brothers of a lost soul. Something he hated to do, but accepted as necessary. Look how close he'd come to letting the actions of one man make him doubt his beloved Tony. If this got out, others would react the same way—begin doubting where there was no cause to doubt.

Tony. He'd turned his most precious compatriot over to the tutelage of a traitor—to a man who'd acted on his own, putting the entire organization in jeopardy. David Jefferson would die for his disobedience.

Bobby felt no compunction at ridding the world of this particular evil, but he'd have to tread carefully. Choose his man with precision and care, and get it done at the first opportunity. Word couldn't leak out. Not now.

Not with the senatorial primary just months away.

Laura said she had to speak with him. Fortifying himself against more warnings of danger, or pleas to give up, Harry followed her to Kelly's apartment. Laura's friend was out for the evening, and it was a place where the two of them could have some privacy and yet be relatively safe.

Unless someone was following them from the police station, which Harry doubted. Jefferson was in jail. And his accomplice, even someone as bold and confident as white supremacists were known to be, wouldn't likely be hanging around the police station right now.

It looked like he was actually going to have a few minutes alone with his wife.

Maybe Kelly would have a bottle of wine and a snack they could buy from her. It was no secret that Kelly liked her wine.

Maybe he and Laura could just sit and talk about life, their jobs, something other than rape and violence and fear.

Maybe she'd let him hold her again like she had in the police station. Even for a minute…

Kelly had wine. Laura didn't want any. She didn't want to sit on the couch, either. So Harry sat with her at the table, trying not to panic.

Was she going to warn him to back off? Or tell him she wanted to come home? *Please, God, let it be that.* She couldn't come back yet—especially now that they were getting so close. But he wouldn't mind hearing that she still wanted to.

Feeling a trickle of sweat start at the base of his neck, the swarming in his stomach, Harry casually laid a hand on the table and waited.

"I…Harry I…" At the look she gave him, he broke out in a full-blown sweat. It seeped from every pore. Chilling his skin.

Was she trying to ask him for a divorce?

He'd known it was inevitable.

Not yet! His mind screamed the words. He wasn't ready. Wasn't strong enough. He had to get the other bastard first.

Then he could afford to fall apart.

"What?" he asked when what he wanted to do was beg her not to say the words.

The memory of holding her in his arms, against his body, a few hours earlier that day haunted him. Was that the last time?

And then he saw the tears in her eyes and knew he had to make it easy on her.

This was Laura. He'd die for her.

"Honey, it's okay," he said, leaning forward so he could look her in the eye. "When I told you I loved you for better or worse, I meant it. When I told you I'd love you forever, I meant it. And when I told you I'd support you through all your choices and decisions, I didn't just mean when they coincided with mine. I meant all the time. Whatever you need, just tell me. I'll do everything in my power to see that you get it."

Instead of calming her, his words had the opposite effect. Laura burst into tears.

"Oh, Harry…" She hiccuped. Twice. "You can't…" She shook her head, took a deep breath.

It was painful to watch the effort it took her to compose herself. Compelled by a need to act, and feeling helpless at the knowledge that he couldn't, he sat. And waited.

"You can't fix everything," she finally said, wiping tears from her face.

"I know that."

"You can't fix this."

He stiffened from the inside out. Determined to listen calmly—to take it like a man.

"I...Harry..."

She was so beautiful. So perfect.

"Oh God, Harry. I'm pregnant."

He sat. Waited. Until the frightened look in her eyes got through the confusion in his brain where her words hadn't.

He replayed them.

And turned stone cold.

"You're...pregnant," he said when he had the ability to produce a coherent sentence.

She nodded, her breath catching. "I...I don't know, Harry. I don't understand why this is happening to me. I feel trapped. I hate myself. And I'm so scared."

He wanted to hold her. To tell her everything was going to be okay. He wanted to kill the bastard sitting in his cell in the county jail a few miles away.

He wanted to kill every single bastard who'd ever thought he could stick his dick someplace it wasn't welcome.

Sitting there, Harry caught on fire, burning up, searing himself with a pain so intense he didn't think he could bear it.

"Don't be afraid, love." The words weren't his; they just came out of his mouth. "It'll be okay. I'm right here with you. You're not alone. You're never alone."

What was he saying? And why?

They *weren't* going to get through this. Not together. She wasn't safe with him.

And she was pregnant.

With another man's baby.

17

How many twists of a knife could a man's heart take? How much rage could he choke back?

How much love did he have to feel before he could be numb to this kind of pain?

"Who else knows?" They were the first rational words that came to his head. He felt odd asking that question; it showed him how separated he'd become from his wife that this would even occur to him.

"Just Kelly. I did the home pregnancy test here. On my lunch hour. Yesterday."

Which explained why she hadn't gone home the night before. Harry had no idea why that should matter at a time like this, but he felt better knowing. Thank God Kelly had been there for her.

Harry held her hand in his on the table. "We don't have to have it."

She didn't recoil. Didn't seem to notice that he'd said *we,* not *you.* Didn't pull her hand away.

"I think I do." Her face contorted, she held his gaze with moist eyes. "But if it's okay with you, I really need to wait until I talk to Dr. Barnes before I make any decisions. There're so many questions, genetics, laws, rights...."

Her voice trailed off, leaving him overwhelmed at the implications.

"Have you called him?" he finally asked.

She nodded. "I was on the line with him when Detective Boyd called. He said he'll squeeze me—us—in at ten tomorrow."

Saturday morning. The fertility specialist had been good to them, and Harry was confident the man would take care of Laura now.

He'd been counting on Dr. Barnes to see Laura through the pregnancy they'd hoped would result from the insemination procedure they'd been scheduled to undergo.

And here they were. No procedure. But Laura was pregnant.

Just what they'd been hoping for for years. She had a baby in that flat stomach across from him.

He knew it. But he couldn't believe it.

"Barnes is a straight shooter," he said, feeling disoriented. "He'll steer us right."

"This baby is mine, Harry, when it should be ours."

Lips tight, he refused to cry. "What's yours *is* mine." And then, as a defensive mechanism, a way to bear the anguish washing over him, Harry forced himself to think rationally, logically. Or at least attempt to.

And something occurred to him.

"We should be able to get DNA from the baby to convict the father."

The proof they needed.

In a form he'd never once considered. And had he been given the choice of a conviction at such a cost, Harry would rather have the bastard go free.

She was nodding, her gaze growing vacant. She looked far too young to be dealing with such tragic events. Completely overcome. Lost.

Whatever happened, now or in the future, Laura came first.

"Honey, whatever you need to do, we'll do," he said, finding strength in giving. "I'm here. If you need to talk, we'll talk. If you aren't sure what to do, we'll look for an answer together. The main thing is that you understand you aren't alone in this. From beginning to end, I'm with you."

He couldn't think beyond the words—couldn't consider what that promise might eventually entail.

The tears that had been filling Laura's eyes fell, trailing slowly, unevenly, down her cheeks.

What could he say that would help?

"Only Kelly knows you're pregnant. If you decide to stop being pregnant, no one will know other than her and she'd take the information to her grave. It'd just be between us and the doctor."

He couldn't change the facts, but if he could ease the pressure…

"Did you tell anyone about the vials being destroyed?" he asked, fairly certain that she hadn't.

Still looking dazed—worn-out—she shook her head.

"Then if you decide to keep the baby, no one would have to know it isn't mine."

Except that her rapists had been white. And Harry wasn't.

"My mother would. She knows about the accident at the clinic."

Chills spread through him. "You said you didn't tell anyone."

"Mom heard from Grace Martin."

He'd forgotten the center's manager went to her mother's church.

And his in-laws had made no pretense about their reservations regarding Laura's choice to have a baby with Harry. That baby would be a "half and half," as they'd crudely put it. A child with two cultures, who'd never fit completely into either, who'd never know the security of true acceptance.

Feeling completely cold, Harry had another horrifying thought. How far would his in-laws go to prevent the inevitable?

And what the hell was he doing even having that thought?

Harry glanced at his wife, almost to reassure himself that she hadn't known what he was thinking.

She couldn't possibly know.

It was crazy.

"I'm sorry." The way her voice rose, as though in a plea, ripped a new hole in his heart.

"Laura." He leaned forward, held her hand to his chest. "Don't you ever, ever think you've done anything wrong here. You loved me. That's it. The sum total of your crimes. Even if everything in life goes downhill from here, I will still die a happy man, knowing I had that."

She smiled, her eyes moist again. Then, very slowly, she leaned toward him, until her lips were touching his.

And Harry forgot everything but how much he loved her.

Harry was being wonderful. Watching the rearview mirror as he followed her to her parents' place, Laura couldn't help falling in love with him—the man she'd married—all over again.

It wasn't altogether a sweet feeling. With a love that immense, came responsibility. And pain.

How could Harry look at her, knowing she was finally pregnant, and not with his child? How could he stand that heartbreak?

How could she?

Somehow, doing no more than living their lives, she and Harry had been presented with a challenge that was unlike anything they'd ever faced.

And the worst wasn't necessarily behind them.

If supremacists were after them, they'd only begun. Because if they'd really intended to leave her pregnant with a white baby, they wouldn't be content to let Harry raise the child.

And from the little she'd learned about hate organizations, taking one member down didn't stop them or destroy their cause.

But before she could worry about that, she had to get through the next few hours. Once again, she battered down her heart for a storm it might not survive.

Her folks were waiting for them in the front room,

their expressions serious. Her phone call of half an hour before had warned them that she and Harry had some disturbing news.

She started by telling them that one of her attackers was in jail. At which they both visibly relaxed. She followed that news with the man's suspected white supremacist ties and watched them exchange worried, knowing glances.

And then look at Harry.

"It's clear to both of us," her father began, "that the only way for our daughter to be protected from further harm, the only way for her to have any kind of normal life, will be for the two of you to divorce. This isn't going to end here. Not if a group like the Ivory Nation has taken notice. I have a lawyer friend to whom I've already spoken and we can have this done as quickly and painlessly as possible. I'm prepared to cover all of the expenses and—"

Even Laura, who'd been dealing with her father all her life, was shocked.

"No!" she interrupted, her voice uncharacteristically sharp.

"Laura, listen to your father—" Sharon's eyes were marked with concern as she gave her husband a nervous glance.

"I said *no,*" Laura interrupted again. "I am not divorcing Harry. And certainly not on your say-so. My marriage isn't up for discussion by you or anyone else, and I resent the fact that you'd even go so far as to see a lawyer on my behalf."

Laura had no idea where the words were coming

from. Or how. For a woman who'd spent her life avoiding conflict, she was doing a pretty good job of bringing it on herself.

Maybe she was finally fighting back, regardless of the outcome.

Or maybe Harry meant that much to her.

"Laura…" Harry's voice was soft, but held warning.

"No," she said a third time, with a quick glance in his direction. "I'm sorry." The words were directed at her parents. "I mean you no disrespect and I love both of you very much. But I need you to understand me on this. I love Harry. I won't divorce him. If the Ivory Nation, or whatever they're called, is really behind this and one of their own is in jail, they're going to be very careful about coming anywhere near us again. They'll know they're being watched."

"Laura…"

"Besides," she added when everyone sat there looking at her as if she didn't have a clue, "they've already made their statement with us. What more could they have to gain?"

"Splitting the two of you up," Len said. "You have to realize they might not stop until that's done."

He was scaring her. Saying things she couldn't think about right now. Afraid to look at Harry, to see his affirmation of her father's words, she raised a hand.

"Wait." The word was half statement, half question. "Please. We've got something else to talk about. Something of more immediate importance," she said, apprehensive as she faced the possibility that her news was only going to further her parents' cause.

"I'm pregnant."

Telling her parents was almost easy, much easier than telling Harry had been. Watching the horror, the anguish, cross their faces was not.

For once in her life, they were at a complete loss. Neither spoke at first. They sat there, silent, without answers.

The acid in Harry's stomach had burned its way through to his heart as he sat quietly in the upscale living room of his in-laws' home and heard them talk to Laura about divorcing him, as if he wasn't even there.

They meant well. He understood that. They adored Laura and wanted what was best for her—something he shared with him. And the one thing that had kept him quiet.

Because they were right.

And now, they were devastated, as well. Something else he shared with them.

"My gosh, no." Sharon Clark's cry, when it fell into the silence, was weak, her eyes bleak with an agony Harry could relate to. "You said—but—"

She turned to her husband, as though he could somehow explain what was going on, make it palatable.

Len's lips were thin. Tight. A pulse beat at the side of his jaw.

"—but the vials were destroyed!" Sharon blurted.

She was having a hard time facing what she already knew. And he wondered if his in-laws would find it more acceptable to have their daughter pregnant by a white rapist than by the black man who was her husband.

He hated himself for the thought.

Still, Sharon had known about the vials. Before Harry had, apparently. Maybe even before Laura had. She obviously had an inside line.

Could it be that she had more than that? That she'd somehow been instrumental in the accident at the clinic? Or that Len had?

"You're right about the vials," he said now with as much calm as he could muster, taking Laura's cold hand in his. "We never went back for the insemination."

"Then that means…" Sharon's voice faded. He could feel her and Len staring at him. And met their gaze with difficulty.

"It means that the precautions taken at the hospital after the rape were not effective."

"Or," Laura said, looking at each of them in turn, "by some incredible miracle, Harry and I managed to make a baby on our own."

"After all the years of trying?"

Watching his mother-in-law, Harry tried not to see signs that she was equally horrified by that unlikely possibility.

"There's certainly a chance," Laura added, but without much conviction. Harry wished *he* could believe her.

An hour after Harry left, promising to be there in the morning to take her to see Dr. Barnes, Laura crawled into bed.

The same twin bed she'd slept in all those years. It was hot. She was cold, dressed in sweat shorts and a tank top, the covers pulled up to her chin. It wasn't late. She wasn't even lying down. She just needed the day to end.

"Can we talk for a bit?" Sharon stood in the doorway.

Laura had shut the door. She searched for the "no" that had rescued her from her father's divorce pressures and couldn't find it. Against her will, she nodded instead.

Still wearing the navy, short-sleeved dress she'd worn to a church retreat earlier that evening, Sharon came in and sat, the bed dipping beneath her weight. Like she'd done countless times before, she took one of Laura's hands in both of hers, signifying to Laura that the conversation they were about to have was serious.

Laura had always wondered about that hand-holding thing. Half the time, she'd loved the comfort. The other half, she'd felt manipulated. What did it signify? The depth of the bond between them? Or the power a mother has over her child?

She'd made it pretty clear she couldn't handle any more serious conversation that day.

"I know what you said earlier, sweetie, about not wanting to divorce your husband. And I respect that. I really do. But I've lived a lot longer than you have." Sharon leaned closer, giving Laura a sad, understanding smile. The kind that told her she wasn't going to like—at all—what her mother was about to say.

But she'd already guessed that much.

"I love you, Laura, and I want what's best for you. That's all I've ever wanted."

"I know that," she said, honestly, when Sharon paused.

Her mother nodded, the lines around her eyes more pronounced than they'd been even weeks before. Or maybe Laura was just more aware of the sadder things in life.

Loss. Aging. A society where you weren't free to live by the dictates of your heart.

"I'm begging you, Laura, *please* listen to your father on this divorce issue. I'm not asking you not to love Harry or even see him on occasion, as long as you're discreet—not that I'd ever want your father to know—but please, please end this marriage."

More frightened than she could ever let on, Laura considered her mother's request. Not because of her and Harry, but because of the baby she carried. The rapist's baby. The racist's. It could be either of them.

If they'd killed her, it might have been kinder.

Instead, they'd left her with this baby.

Would they be coming back for it?

Seeing the lines of concern on her mother's face, the love and pain reflected there, she said, "I'm tired, Mom. Can we talk about this tomorrow?"

It was a conciliatory gesture—holding out that hope, as though they'd really talk this through another day—but it was all Laura could manage. It was how she'd always coped.

Sharon nodded, running her palm along Laura's cheek. "Of course, honey, I'm sorry. I should've been more sensitive. I'm just so scared and…"

"Me, too," Laura said. "Me, too."

Standing, Sharon paused.

"I know you and Harry said you weren't going to discuss anything about the baby until after your appointment tomorrow…."

After she and Harry had reached that agreement at Kelly's, they'd held her parents to it. Not that anyone had really been prepared to discuss anything. Or even consider the questions that were waiting for answers. They were all still in shock.

But, for the first time that day, Laura had a feeling she could give her mother what she needed to hear.

"I'm not planning to abort the baby," she said.

She wasn't planning much of anything. Hadn't made a single decision, and wouldn't. Not until she had the facts. And talked them over with her husband. But there were some things that just seemed obvious.

"If anything, I think I'd give it up for adoption," she said, tears springing to her eyes again as she watched them form in her mother's.

Maybe, sometime during the course of the past twenty-four hours, she'd made one decision.

The life growing inside her was real.

And she was going to do what she could to see that it had a chance.

Sharon nodded and knelt down to kiss Laura's forehead. "I love you, baby."

"I know, Mom. I love you, too."

_18_

At nine o'clock Friday evening, Daniel Boyd stepped up to Jess Robbins's front door, bottle of scotch and steaks in hand.

"Sorry I'm late," he said by way of greeting when she answered his knock.

"I'm just glad you're here."

Straight from the mouth of a woman who loved you, Boyd thought, knowing he shouldn't be there—Jess deserved so much better—but knowing, too, that he wasn't strong enough to walk away.

"These are ready to go," he said, holding up the bag of meat. "I'll light the grill."

"It's already done." She took the steaks. And the bottle.

Watching her ass in the tight denim, Daniel followed her out to the kitchen. And downed in one gulp the first drink she poured for him.

Another three or four and maybe, just maybe, he'd be able to get it up for her.

Or not.

Sex had never been easy for him.

But Jess made it safe to try. Jess—the woman who'd been his wife so briefly such a long time ago, the woman who'd insisted on having her own life, apart from him. Jess, who was more often in a serious relationship than not, but who still saw him every time he called, and who called him when he didn't.

"I take it, since you're here, that you got the guys in the Kendall case?"

Because it seemed that the only time he could get a hard-on was after he'd put another sex-crime offender behind bars—after he'd saved another female from atrocious violation. And Jess was the only human being on earth, besides himself, who knew that.

She removed the white paper securing the steaks.

Daniel reached for a plate to carry them to the gas grill on the patio outside her sliding glass door.

"We got one of 'em."

"He's not talking?"

Pausing for a sip, Daniel watched her season the meat. "Oh, he's talking," he told her eventually. "He lawyered up. And repeatedly attests to his innocence. In spite of the fact that we turned up a pair of suction cups in the trunk of his car. And I found a sales record at a local leather store with his name on it. The suction cups are for changing out car glass, he says, a job his buddy does on weekends and for which he borrows his car. And since when is purchasing a black leather jacket a crime? According to his lawyer, he's innocent."

With one lifted brow, Jess glanced at him. "And you're sure he's not?"

Daniel finished the second drink. *Slow down, buddy. You won't even make it through dinner at this rate. Jess doesn't deserve that.*

"If you'd seen Laura Kendall, the second she heard that voice…"

"Okay, so he did it. You've got him. And little does he know, you're a master at getting someone to give you what you want."

There was no double entendre in the words—although Jess had every right to imply one. Instead, her tone—and the look she sent him—was completely serious. And she was right. Most of the time.

"He's a red-shoelace-wearing member of the Ivory Nation."

Jess dropped the saltshaker.

And Daniel decided to skip the steaks and get right down to finding the forgetfulness only Jess's arms could bring him.

The dark-haired twenty-six-year-old woman moved slowly around the side of David Jefferson's apartment building with packs weighing down her shoulders. She watched for any sign of surveillance, anyone who might see her as she approached the outside staircase leading up to David's third-story unit. She'd purposely waited until the moon had crossed to the other side of the sky, leaving the partially enclosed flight of steps in dark shadow.

Exhausted and sweaty from more than twelve hours spent on the streets of Tucson, blending in with the homeless, she was eager to get behind a locked door once again. To shower. And sleep.

Up one flight of steps and then another, stepping softly, she worried about David—not because she wanted him home, but because without him, she had no home. He was her keeper, her warden and jailor, but he was also her protector.

Up the last flight, and she slid her key in the lock, turning quickly, quietly, glancing over her shoulder. Everything was still—immobilized by the ungodly heat and dryness. Like the breath stuck in her throat.

Inside, she didn't turn on any lights—and didn't plan to. Not until he was home again. She'd hidden in the closet when they'd come for him that morning. But he'd said they were coming back with a search warrant. He'd asked her to shove his black leather jacket and hood in the packs she'd been living out of in the year since her disappearance. Backpacks that were always kept ready, just in case. And he'd asked her to leave….

There was no sign, at least in the darkness, of anyone having been there. If they'd searched, they'd done so neatly.

Did that mean they hadn't come yet?

That they'd be back in the morning?

Would David want her to spend the night on the streets, too?

He'd said they wouldn't be able to keep him long, but he wasn't here.

Too tired to go back out, more scared of the streets than the police, she dropped her packs, stripped off her clothes and slid under the sheets without so much as washing her face.

* * *

"You're right at four weeks," Dr. Thomas Barnes said, glancing between Laura and Harry as they sat across from him in his office on Saturday morning.

Gritting his teeth against the anger building inside him, Harry forced himself not to move as he held his wife's hand and listened.

"I'm putting down March tenth as an estimated due date."

Reading glasses perched on his nose, the doctor wrote on the file in front of him.

Harry and Laura remained silent. Dr. Barnes set down his pen, crossing his hands on top of the file.

"Okay, let's get down to what we're really looking at here."

Laura's hand was slippery with sweat, or maybe it was his. Regardless, Harry held on.

"First, physically, there's no reason to expect anything other than a perfectly normal pregnancy. It's too early to tell much, but I've been seeing Laura for, what, a year now? She should have no problems should you choose to carry the baby to term."

Harry, trying to keep an open mind, to let Laura drive the situation, latched on to the last thing the doctor had said.

"You think we shouldn't?" he asked, aware of how desperately he needed this part to be over.

Those bastards had already infiltrated their lives enough. Surely Laura couldn't be expected to give birth to their offspring, too.

And surely he couldn't be expected to watch, a small, shameful voice said.

Barnes perused them for a moment, then tossed down his glasses, leaning back in his chair.

"That's never an easy decision." When he finally spoke his voice was grave. "But in a situation such as this one, it's certainly easier to understand if you wish to terminate. I could put you in touch with someone who performs extenuating-circumstance terminations," he continued. Harry was hanging on his every word. "It would be done in a hospital setting, with anesthesia if you'd like.

"Living with a rapist's child will always, to some degree, remind you of the violent attack you two suffered. And naturally, you might find it difficult to fully love the child…."

Right. He was so right. They had to abort.

And they'd do a DNA test on the fetus and either get the bastard in jail to hand over his accomplice in exchange for a lighter sentence, or have the evidence necessary to get the other one.

Only then could they begin to put all of this behind them.

"However…" Barnes started to speak again. "Considering Laura, her heart and emotions, her upbringing and beliefs…"

Harry's stomach dropped.

"I'm not sure abortion would be the best thing for her. Would it?" The doctor's kind gaze settled on Laura.

Returning his look, Laura shook her head. "I don't find it morally wrong—for other women," she said slowly. "I just don't think *I* could do it. Not if the baby's healthy. It's nine months of my life weighed against a lifetime."

Barnes didn't react. Didn't appear to have any judgment at all, one way or the other. But Harry's heart lurched at her words. The decision had already been made.

Barnes had Laura pegged exactly.

"Could you put me in touch with a good adoption agency?"

Her next question obliterated any doubt, and Harry settled in for another long haul.

This time, instead of watching as his wife was forced to submit to the brutal violation of other men, he was going to watch her body grow large with a stranger's child.

With Harry's support, Laura made it through the appointment at the doctor's office. He was a rock, sitting there beside her, holding her hand, when she knew this had to be breaking his heart into painful shards.

Which was why, when he started asking questions, as though he was taking control of whatever aspects of the situation he could, she wanted to jump up and celebrate. Everything from her diet and rest to future physical activity was discussed, with her opinions sought every step of the way.

This was her Harry. The man who always came back, ready to face head-on whatever challenges were before him.

With logic and calm.

"There's a suspect in custody," Harry said to the doctor when Laura thought they were through. "If all goes well, he should be going to trial within the next three months. Is there a way to get DNA from the baby in time to use it as evidence that this man raped my wife?"

No. Laura held her breath. They'd identified the man. She'd have to testify during the trial. Surely they weren't going to put the baby inside her on the stand, as well.

"The test can be performed using amniotic fluid," the doctor said, and seeing the sudden gleam in Harry's eye, Laura pulled her hand out of his. "However, it will only rule someone out if his DNA is not present, or include him if it is. At that stage, it cannot tell us conclusively who the father is. Only who definitely isn't the father—or who *might* be."

Thank God. Too tired to be ashamed of the relief she felt, Laura wanted to go now.

"That would help our case, though," Harry said.

Dr. Barnes nodded. "If it doesn't rule out the suspect."

"How dangerous is the test?"

"It carries a fairly high risk of infection, but nothing we probably can't deal with."

Great. Potential problems. Court evidence. She was struggling to put one foot in front of the other already, and they were talking about adding even more to her load.

"It always comes with a fairly significant risk of miscarriage," Dr. Barnes was saying.

"If I'm at risk, anyway, you mean?" she asked.

"No. The procedure itself can cause fetal distress or hemorrhaging, and can result in miscarriage."

"If that happened, maybe it was meant to be anyway," Harry's words shocked Laura. "Maybe it would be for the best." They were talking about a *life* here. And other than her emotional and physical discomfort over the next eight months, there was no reason she couldn't do this. She was healthy. She had insurance and a good job.

"Dr. Barnes." Laura sat forward, compelled to bring up something she'd decided not to let herself think about. But if there was even a chance...

"The night after the rape, I..." She stopped, felt herself getting hot. She might have come out of her shell a lot in the past years—and weeks—but there were still so many parts of Laura that were most comfortable left inside.

"There's no chance, Laura," Harry said, his voice firm. Dead. As though, like her, he couldn't even allow himself the hint of a possibility.

"What happened the night after the rape?" the doctor asked.

"I...we...made love," Laura said. And before the doctor could think Harry was some kind of beast, she added, "I begged him to."

"I understand." Dr. Barnes was all business, with a measure of kindness thrown in. "So what you want to know is whether there's any possibility this baby could be Harry's."

"In your opinion," Laura qualified. "Considering everything you know about our situation."

The doctor scrutinized them. Laura slid her hand

beneath Harry's on his thigh. The strength with which she held on reached clear inside her, and only at that moment, did she realize, admit to herself, how much she'd been hoping.

"I have to be honest with you," he finally said, and a wave of nausea swept through her. "While there's always that possibility, with Harry's low sperm count, the chances aren't good."

She'd known. Which was why she'd promised herself not to ask.

Dr. Barnes listed all the months and years they'd been trying to have a baby, the various steps they'd taken, which included just about every available aid on the market, drugs, temperature regulation, everything. All to no avail.

"However," the doctor said, frowning, "I can't completely dismiss that possibility…"

Her heart started to pound as she waited for him to continue.

"Although Harry's sperm count is low, there's still a chance that your infertility was also, at least in part, emotionally based. As we discussed before, you wanted a baby so badly you were blocking it from happening. Your stress, every time you tried, interfered with the hormones that were trying to do their job."

"Wouldn't that be even more reason for her not to have conceived that last time with me?" Harry's voice was hoarse.

"Not necessarily."

The doctor's words shocked her. Laura was cold and hot at once. Sweaty and chilled. She clutched Harry's hand until she could feel her fingernails digging into his palm. And still she couldn't let go.

"That night, probably for the first time, the last thing on your mind was conceiving a baby," the doctor said. "I'd guess that if you'd been asked, you would've said you didn't want it at all."

She nodded. Remembering when the clinic had called about the vials.

"I've seen more than one case where that's all it took."

"So what are you saying?" Harry asked, clearly tense now. "That there's as much chance the baby's mine as that it's one of the rapists'?"

"No." And just like that, all the good feeling that had been rising in Laura vanished. "I wouldn't go that far."

Harry nodded, his jaw taut. "How far would you go?"

"On a scale of one to ten?"

"Yes."

"I'd give you a one."

"Ten-percent chance." Harry said what she was thinking.

"About that."

"It's not enough," her husband said. "I think we should do the DNA testing."

And that was where they differed. And where she wasn't going to budge.

"If there's any chance at all that I am finally pregnant with my husband's baby, I will do nothing—nothing—that will put this baby at risk." Her strength was back.

"Wait a minute." Dr. Barnes sat forward. "I don't want to mislead you here," he said, "or have you going through the next eight months hoping, only to be disappointed."

Bitterly crushed would be more like it.

But Laura was resolute. "It's too late, Doctor," she said. "A one percent chance was all I needed. You multiplied that by ten."

"If we did the test, it would show us *now* whether or not there's a chance the baby's mine," Harry said.

"And there's a chance we'll find out it is—and then lose the baby because of the test," Laura responded before the doctor could.

So much for consulting her husband. She'd made up her mind.

Arizona Daily Sun
Flagstaff and Northern Arizona's Source for News
Saturday, July 7, 2007

Tucson police have arrested a man suspected of raping a Tucson woman while her husband was forced to watch. David Jefferson, 26, is a medical student at the University of Arizona, and a card-carrying member of the Ivory Nation, one of Arizona's largest self-proclaimed white supremacist organizations. The victim, whose name has not been disclosed, is a thirty-year-old Caucasian. Her husband is black.

Flagstaff former prosecutor Janet McNeil Green, whose brother was a member of the Ivory

Nation and who spent five years bringing supremacist activities to light, was unavailable for comment.

"Detective Boyd?"

"Yes."

"This is Bobby Donahue."

"Yes."

"I'm calling on behalf of an organization with
which I'm involved and which, for too long has suffered under false accusations and long-standing
rumors that the organization no longer wishes to
tolerate." Donahue's speech was oddly formal, it
sounded rehearsed.

Daniel responded in kind.

"We're speaking of the Ivory Nation, Mr. Donahue?"

"Yes."

"And what is the purpose of this call?"

"I want to help you."

"Then you don't mind if I record our conversation?"
Donahue had probably been counting on that request.

"Not at all. I read in the paper this morning that you
have a man in custody who has been incorrectly identified as a member of our organization."

"Yes."

"He is not a member of the Ivory Nation. I have been
asked to inform you that we are willing to cooperate
fully in the prosecution of this man. We wish not only
to clear our organization's name of any suspicion
relating to this heinous crime, but to prove, once and

for all, that we are good men doing God's work, not the evil cult members we're often accused of being."

"Who asked you to make this call?"

"Our membership is greatly disturbed by the continued negative and completely erroneous press we receive. As a result we voted, unanimously, to put our efforts and resources into correcting these negative assumptions. Starting right here with rumor control."

"Are you the leader of the Ivory Nation, Mr. Donahue?"

"God is our only leader."

"But you are in a position to know about the organization's dealings and to discuss them?"

"Yes."

"So what can you tell me about David Jefferson?"

"He attempted to align himself with the Ivory Nation, to the extent that he received an invitation to attend our Sunday-evening worship services during July of last year." Translated, that meant Bobby had recruited him. And he'd bet July was when Jefferson had earned his laces, not when he'd first attended.

"Did he become a member of the Ivory Nation?"

"No. He did not. We found him to be filled with hate, mean-spirited and prone to violence. He tried to convince some of our younger members that only with force would we be able to sustain God's work on this earth. We asked him to leave." Daniel detected no discernible truth in those statements.

"And did he?"

"Eventually." More like Bobby had a hit out on the guy, he thought cynically.

"Peacefully?"

"Yes. He came back twice. He was particularly intent on getting his way. But each time, after multiple requests to leave our premises, he did so."

"Do you know anything about Jefferson's possession of a set of suction cups used to lift heavy pieces of glass?"

"I didn't know he owned any, but he told me once that they're readily available and described how they're used. This was while we were installing a piece of stained-glass art in the alcove beside the front door of an antique shop."

Convenient.

"Mr. Donahue, have you or any members of the Ivory Nation, to your knowledge, ever worn black hoods during any part of your work or worship?"

"Never. We are a peace-loving group who seek only to restore God's earth to the glorious state He envisioned during the days of creation."

"What can you tell me about the red shoelaces Jefferson was wearing when he was arrested?"

"Nothing. David Jefferson's attire has nothing to do with me or the Ivory Nation."

Bullshit.

"But members of your organization wear red laces as a symbol of full brotherhood, do they not?"

"We wear them to church—as a symbol of Christ's blood that was shed for us. Just as other religious groups drink grape juice or wine to commemorate His sacrifice."

"Out of curiosity, Mr. Donahue, how does a member of the Ivory Nation earn those laces?"

"Just by loving God, Detective. Just by loving God."

_19_

At his desk on Saturday afternoon, Daniel was going
through every tiny piece of information he and Miller
had collected during the Kendall investigation, looking
for the one small discrepancy that he'd missed, the
one little clue that would lead him to Jefferson's
partner. Daniel had just hung up the phone from a conversation with the infamous leader of Arizona's largest
and most powerful white supremacist organization
when his cell rang.

As usual, he thought about ignoring it. Almost
did—a challenge Jess had issued twenty years before,
when his job had come ahead of her every single
time there'd been a choice to make. But then flipped
open the phone. Seeing who it was, he didn't answer
right away.

Jess was right. He had to learn when to quit. He'd
arrested a rapist the day before and still hadn't been able
to perform with Jess last night. Instead, she'd held him
while he slept.

And had kissed him goodbye with an understanding smile and tears in her eyes after she'd made him breakfast that morning.

On the fourth ring, he pressed the send key. "Boyd."

"Detective…"

"Mr. Kendall. What's wrong?" The younger man's tone of voice had the hair on the back of Daniel's neck standing up.

"Laura's pregnant."

Shit. Goddamn it to hell. Fucking sons of bitches. Daniel's blood raced through his veins, inciting an anger he could barely contain.

He was going to kill the bastards. In cold blood. With his own hands.

He'd cut off their cocks, cram them down their throats and suffocate them.

"When they find out, they'll be back for her." Kendall's words were more statement than question.

"*If* they find out."

"They're going to find out, Detective." Harry had never sounded so exhausted.

Or hopeless.

Daniel's mind sped up. Looking for a way to defuse the situation—to save Harry Kendall's ass.

"They know who she is," Kendall continued. "And they're watching her. It's their M.O."

God, he wanted to deny that.

"They'll leave her alone," he said instead.

"And what about after she has the baby?"

"We'd better hope to God it's black." The detective didn't give that response. The man did.

* * *

With a last tug on the double knot, Bobby Donahue finished tying the red laces on his boots and straightened. Tony stood in the doorway.

Bobby's eyes narrowed. "I didn't hear you come home."

Tony stared at Bobby's boots. "Luke's still asleep?"

It was after four on Saturday, and the child was always up by three. "I didn't manage to put him down until almost two." He could hardly speak, could hardly breathe. He'd personally chosen Tony's mentor in Tucson. The betrayal—if there'd been a betrayal here—was his fault.

And then he looked up. Tony's gaze was direct, his eyes filled with tears. "I saw the paper," he said. "I know you didn't tell Jefferson to rape that woman. You wouldn't. He acted without authority, didn't he? Betrayed you. And I had no idea…"

Bobby said nothing. Tony rambled on.

"I should've known," he was saying. "Should've seen the signs. But I was too distracted by Beth—just like you warned. I let you down, let the brothers down. I'm ready to take my punishment. Whatever it needs to be. I'm so sick about this Bobby, so sick. And so sorry…"

Tears streamed down Tony's face and Bobby knew they were going to be all right. Tony would be punished; his sense of guilt would be far more painful than the lashes against his thighs. But they would be okay. He wasn't a traitor.

Thank God.

* * *

The first day of the second summer-session classes barely hit Harry's radar. He reviewed rosters, delivered syllabi and lectures, answered questions and filled out the necessary paperwork on automatic pilot, going through the motions with most of his mental faculties absent.

For the past forty-eight hours, his life had consisted of work-related obligations and hanging out around the frat house where he'd heard David Jefferson's voice. Sometimes he was in a car across the street, or down the road. Occasionally in the backyard. He'd fallen asleep there, propped up against the wall behind a desert willow bush, the night before.

His cell phone was always at the ready, and anytime anyone came or went, he snapped a picture. Most of them were of young, good-looking women. All white.

He showered at home. He'd been to bed once since dropping Laura off at her mother's house on Saturday after the doctor's appointment. He'd eaten a time or two.

But no matter where he was or what he was doing, the visions tormented him. His wife on the bed, writhing in agony. The half-naked young woman sitting aimlessly on the couch eating a sandwich. The sight of those red shoelaces in David Jefferson's boots. Like a slide show with no end, they continued to parade inside his head.

Harry picked up another roster from the pile on his desk and dropped it immediately, shoving his finger in his mouth. Tasting blood.

He pulled it out and studied the quarter inch slit spurting blood on the pad of his right index finger. Too wide for a paper cut. Not deep enough for stitches.

What the hell?

Lifting the roster more carefully, Harry stared.

Underneath it, shoved between the papers on his desk was a broken piece of glass. With a soaped inscription.

Stay away or die.

Jefferson's accomplice was at the university, too.

Monday afternoon, ten minutes after his final class, Harry was in a rental car, just in case they were watching for his Lexus. He'd parked across the street and down a block from the frat house, more certain than ever that it had some connection with Laura's rape.

Boyd could sit at the station, analyzing glass and soap, interrogating David Jefferson, putting together theories and warning Harry to cease and desist.

Harry was convinced the frat house was going to lead them to Laura's second rapist.

Based on the topless young woman he'd seen the week before and the number of women who'd been coming and going—usually alone—on this deserted street, Harry was sure something sexually deviant was going on. But what?

Had the two rapists—Jefferson and the other man—been holding the topless woman hostage? And what about the others?

Was Laura's second attacker there, in the house, going on without him?

A slender blond woman, mid-twenties, came out of the house, looked both ways, crossed the street and started toward him.

She moved slowly, her body alluring even in old shorts and flip-flops.

Had they seen him? Had she been sent to approach him? Could he talk her onto his side without their being any the wiser?

Would she shoot him point-blank and leave him to die in a pool of his own blood?

Maybe, if he could convince her to get in the car, make it look like he was abducting her so they wouldn't hold her accountable, he could explain why she should help him. He could offer to help her.

No matter what she was involved in, he was sure Boyd would help her cut a deal if she turned state's evidence.

Once she heard about Laura, the baby, surely she'd see that these guys were evil and had to be stopped....

As she drew closer, he stared, frowning. Her makeup was impeccable, her eyes thickly outlined, her lips deep red and glossy. And her nails were painted to match, both fingers and toes. Kind of a contrast to the old shorts and tank top and flip-flops. He knew it meant something.

She was almost upon him. Harry tensed, one hand on his door handle, the other on the ignition, waiting to see what she did before he made his move.

What she did was walk right by without even glancing at him. If she knew there was a black man sitting in a midsize nondescript car on the street, she sure didn't seem to care.

If she knew Harry Kendall was watching her, she pretended not to.

He kept her in sight in his rearview mirror, debating. Should he wait until she turned the corner and go after her? Try to get her to talk to him? Over the past two days, he'd followed several of the other women. He'd seen a couple of them go into an office building on High Street—so maybe they knew each other from work? Several had disappeared around the corner before he could get to them. One had been speeding away in a car by the time he'd managed to climb over a neighbor's wall and follow her. Another, he'd seen in a coffee shop, kissing a young man who'd apparently been waiting for her. A young man he'd never seen before and hadn't seen since.

So maybe he'd better continue to watch the house for...*what?*

Some guy to come out with a sign that said he wore a size-eleven shoe? Or march around in his black hood and gloves with part of the thumb bitten out?

He didn't know. He just knew that the answer to finding Laura's second rapist was in that house.

And he wasn't giving up until he found him. He was going to sit right there, renting different cars every day for the rest of the summer—or the year—if that was what it took and—

His cell phone rang. Fumbling with the holder at his belt, he grabbed the phone and flipped it open before it could peal a second time. Maybe it was Laura. Maybe she'd decided to consider the amnio DNA test, after all.

It wasn't Laura.

Boyd wanted to meet him at the station.

Eyes narrowing as a nerdy-looking young man walked toward the frat house but cut through a side yard a couple of buildings away, Harry snapped a picture and took the now-familiar route to the station.

"Laura? Can I talk to you for a second?" Kelly caught up to Laura in the parking lot on Monday afternoon as Laura was leaving.

"Sure," she said, warming as her friend drew closer. If there was a bright spot in anything that had happened during the past month, her new closeness with Kelly was it.

"You're leaving early," Kelly said, frowning as she studied Laura's face. "You aren't sick, are you?"

"No." Laura told her about the counseling session for unwanted pregnancies she'd agreed to attend.

"Thank God at least one of the guys who did this to you is off the streets," Kelly said, hugging herself in spite of the hundred-and-ten-degree heat. "Anyway, I won't keep you, but I just…I…"

"What?" Kelly seemed upset. "What can I do for you?" Laura asked.

Shaking her head, Kelly rocked from one foot to the other and then abruptly stopped. "Nothing. I've just been debating all day whether or not I should tell you this."

Placing her purse and keys on the seat of her Ranger, Laura turned back. "Tell me, Kel. I can't stand any more secrets."

"But I might be causing trouble where there isn't any."

So there was someone at work involved in all this. Just like Harry thought. He'd been right about Jefferson, though they hadn't proven yet that the man had anything to do with the destroyed vials. And they might never be able to do so.

"If you think something's wrong or you saw something—"

"Okay," Kelly looked her straight in the eye. "I'm just going to tell you, and then we'll figure it out together."

"Good." She wasn't alone. She never felt alone when she was with Kelly. "What's up?"

"I was on campus this past weekend, buying books for my second-session class that starts tonight…"

She'd forgotten that Kelly was going to the second session. She'd skipped the first.

"Yeah?" she prompted, sensing that she wasn't going to like what she heard.

And that this had nothing to do with anyone at the gardens.

"I was at the bookstore nearby so I walked over to take a look at that frat house you told me about. I had no idea which house it was, but you'd mentioned the street and…"

Laura was sweating again. And chilled, too. It was never going to end. Everything always came to the rape.

"What did you see?" she asked. She wasn't going to be able to escape. To move on. Especially now that she was carrying this baby…

"Not what—who." Kelly paused. "Harry."

"Detective Boyd told him to stay away from there."

"That's what you said, which is why I'm telling you. I'm really worried about you guys. You've got to talk to Harry."

"What was he doing?"

"I saw him get out of a car and follow a couple of girls down the street and around the corner."

He was going to get himself arrested. Or worse.

He was going to antagonize these people until they came after them again.

On her way to the counseling session, Laura had only one thought on her mind. She'd threaten to move back home if that was what it took. Somehow she had to get Harry to stop.

"The photo lineup was inconclusive." Sitting across from Daniel Boyd in a coffee shop a block from the station, Harry heard the news over a cup of cappuccino.

"What does that mean?" he asked, bitterness spreading through him.

"Miller had pictures taken of several angles, blew them up five-hundred percent. There was no sign of scabbing or scarring on Jefferson's penis."

"So he healed."

"Yep."

Frowning, Harry eyed the older man. "You agree with me."

"I was with your wife when she heard Jefferson's voice," Boyd said, his gaze direct. Weary, but direct.

"There's no doubt in my mind that he was one of the two men in your bedroom on June seventh."

And for the first time since that horrible night, Harry took a breath that wasn't completely filled with the pain of betrayal and the tension of defensiveness.

"So how important was that identification?" he asked now, wondering how far out on a limb Daniel Boyd was willing to go.

The detective shrugged. "I won't lie to you," he said, loosening his tie. "The voice recognition is strong, probably strong enough to get us to trial, but after that it's anyone's guess. With only one solid piece of evidence…"

"You think the jerk might walk?"

"What I think is that we don't have much time to find his partner and get one of them to squeal on the other." Boyd's voice was unrelenting, the look in his eyes hard as flint.

"We?" Harry didn't miss a beat.

"I didn't give twenty years to this job without learning a lesson or two," Boyd said. "The most difficult one being that arresting these guys doesn't always mean the innocents are safe. A conviction has to go along with the arrest to do that."

Boyd took a sip of coffee. He grimaced as though he didn't much like the stuff. Harry pictured the man more at home with a bottle of beer in his hand.

He wouldn't mind one himself right now.

"The second thing I've learned is that sometimes you have to cross a line or two to ensure that conviction."

"Okay."

"My hands are tied in ways that yours aren't."

Harry nodded, unable to glance away from the weathered face across from him.

"I figure you're on to something with the frat house," Boyd was saying. "And I suspect you pose no threat to these guys. You're their victim. They're toying with you. I'm sure you're aware of the similarities between white supremacists and the rapist profiles. Ultimately it's about power, control, a desire to dominate. You hanging around just feeds their sick sense of power."

Harry had figured that out a while ago.

"Which makes you the perfect person to use as a cover."

Sitting up straighter, Harry took another deep breath.

"If this is going to work, it'll have to be between me and you," Boyd cautioned. "I don't even want Laura to know."

"You, me and Miller," Harry clarified, heart pounding with something besides dread and fear.

Boyd shook his head. "He's a good cop," the detective said, his voice level, "but he plays by the rules. Takes off when his shift is over. He's the perfect husband and father. Votes conservative." Boyd met Harry's eyes. "What does that tell you?"

"He wouldn't agree to this."

"Right."

Harry thought over everything Boyd had said—and the dealings he'd had with the detective over the past weeks, understanding one thing. Daniel Boyd was spending his entire life making up for the hideous crime he'd witnessed as a thirteen-year-old boy. As though it had been his fault. He spent his entire life

saving other women as an attempt to atone for the
sister he couldn't save.

"Say something," Boyd demanded.

Harry didn't even hesitate. "I'm in."

Laura called Harry late that afternoon. The counseling session already forgotten five minutes after she'd left
the room, she was dead set on getting through to her
husband.

"I'm coming home," she insisted the second he
answered.

"No, Laura."

"Harry…"

"If there's anything you need I'll bring it to you."

"I need *you.*"

"I know, babe, but it's not safe, especially not now.
With Jefferson in jail, his partner's going to be getting
nervous. Besides, there's more bad news."

Her heart sank. "What?"

"The photo ID was a bust."

Laura listened as Harry gave her the details, and
wondered why Boyd hadn't called her, as well.

"We've got the voice recognition, and of the two,"
she said, "that one's stronger. Miller and Boyd are still
gathering evidence…"

"We have a size eleven print and a man who wears
a size-twelve shoe." Harry's voice was brusque. "A
black leather jacket that's like a million others in this
city and no sign of the glove I marked."

"We knew we wouldn't have that until we found the

other guy—the smaller one. It was his glove you bit and he was obviously the size eleven."

"We've got suction cups that apparently have an alibi, a defendant who has people willing to lie about Jefferson's whereabouts the night of the attack and—"

"And we've got two positive IDs on his voice," she reminded him softly, trying to take back control of the conversation. To persuade him to let this go before she lost him. To jail. Or worse.

"You've got to do the amnio DNA, Laura." Harry's next words sent her spinning again. "We both know it's him and he's going to get away."

The fear in her heart made her shudder. "No, he isn't."

"Let them do the test, okay, Laura? Please?"

"Harry, I'm not going to risk the life of a child over something that won't be conclusive anyway. That evidence wouldn't be any stronger than the suction cups and the leather jacket. Even an amateur defense attorney could convince a jury that there's room for doubt if all the prosecution has is inconclusive evidence." The calmness of her voice was the result of habit, not anything she was or wasn't feeling.

"But the more evidence there is, the stronger the case will be."

As she drove, she glanced around the quiet Tucson street where she'd grown up, noticing how tall the saguaro had grown, then slowed before she reached her parents' home. "I'm worried about you."

"Me?" His voice rose an octave in tone, but was still quiet. "Why?"

"Kelly told me she saw you at the frat house."

"You had Kelly checking up on me?"

"Of course not! She was at that store around the corner buying books and walked down the street because I'd told her about the house."

She paused and when he said nothing, continued. "She said you followed a couple of girls."

"I'm telling you, Laura, there's something going on in that house. These girls come and go, usually alone but not always. As far as I can tell, they don't stay long. Maybe they're dealing drugs."

She hadn't thought of that. But it made sense. It also had nothing to do with them.

"They've got Jefferson, Harry. Detective Boyd really thinks that as soon as the bastard sees he's going to get a conviction, he'll be ready to take a plea in exchange for information."

"That just means he'll get out of jail earlier, Laura. We don't want that."

"We also don't want *you* in jail. I'm going to have a baby, Harry," she said, ashamed of herself for playing that card, but desperate enough to do it. "Maybe yours…" She waited to let that sink in. "I need you here with me," she said when she got no reaction.

"Not if we don't get these guys, you don't," he said. "Because they're going to hit us again. And from what I've read about these people, they don't merely repeat themselves. Every act escalates in violence compared to the previous one."

She couldn't listen to this. Couldn't live her life in

this kind of fear. Fear for Harry's immediate safety was another matter.

"Harry, please, stay away from that house."

"There's something going on there."

"I agree, it sounds like there is. But it's got nothing to do with us."

"I'm pretty sure it does, Laura. There's a connection…"

"Let it go!" She tried one more time. "Please, just do it for me?"

"I am doing it for you. That's the whole point," he came back, and Laura knew she'd lost. Harry had his own demons to fight. She just prayed that they wouldn't destroy him in the process.

Very late Tuesday night, sitting in another anonymous rental car, on the opposite side of the street and closer to the frat house than he'd ever been before, Harry slid down in the driver's seat, leaning his head back against the leather upholstery. Boyd had him continuing his stakeouts, as amateurishly as before, since he didn't want to alert anyone to his involvement. He wanted anyone who might be watching Harry to think he was an aggrieved husband bent on avenging his wife's attack. The only difference was that now Harry wore a wire. And had a direct line to Daniel Boyd twenty-four hours a day.

He didn't dare sleep much, but dozed on and off during the early hours of the morning. There was little or no traffic in and out of the house after midnight.

Kind of strange for a party place.

Boyd had run all the pictures Harry had taken on his cell phone. Other than a couple of girls implicated in a minor drug bust a few years before, nothing had turned up. None of the young people were on file anywhere.

Eyes closed, Harry thought of Laura, her voice on the phone that evening. She'd laughed at some stupid quip he'd made—

The blast came so suddenly, Harry had no time to move. Or press the button that would connect him to Daniel Boyd. Heart pounding, he lay in the darkness, unmoving, a black man dressed in black, lying against a black leather seat, trying to figure out what was going on. Something had whizzed by his ear.

There was a hole in the windshield.

A puncture that he recognized. One most people saw only in the movies. Smooth and small, leaving the glass intact, a bullet had just flown through his car— missing him by inches.

She'd been there alone for four days—without turning on any lights or the television. Hadn't heard a word from Jefferson, which, she assumed, meant he was still in jail.

That surprised her. It usually didn't take that long.

The first days alone had been good. The best two days since she'd been abducted the year before. She'd read, finishing one of Jefferson's psychology textbooks. And made herself an omelet every day.

She'd worn shorts and a T-shirt to bed at night and slept uninterrupted from early evening until daybreak.

But now she was out of eggs. And cheese.

Someone had been outside the door that morning.

If Jefferson was still in jail, then he'd been abandoned by the Ivory Nation. He was as good as dead.

Unless he *was* dead.

Arms wrapped around her naked body as she stood in the shower, she thought about running. No one was actively searching for her. She could get away, flee to another town, another state.

But that would mean leaving her baby with the devil.

She couldn't do it.

Huddled in a corner, she started to pray that David Jefferson would come home.

"The bullet's a .22 caliber. Fired from a shotgun, but you knew that."

Jess sent a weary glance in Daniel's direction as she faced him across a table in her lab just before dawn on Wednesday.

He nodded, sorry for waking her up and dragging her down here in the middle of the night. But he'd put an innocent man's life in danger when he'd involved Harry Kendall.

"What else can you tell me?"

"You mean have I seen anything else like it recently?"

He looked her straight in the eye, knowing full well that he was putting her job on the line again with this unreported investigation. "Have you?"

Her gaze fell. "No."

"If he'd been sitting up, he'd be dead."

"Sounds like he'd better be careful." Dressed in a lab

coat and a pair of tight jeans, Jess busied herself sanitizing an already clean table.

"He's refusing to back off. Getting shot didn't deter him at all."

She raised her eyes then, cutting Daniel to the quick. "Sounds like someone else I know."

She was right. He didn't know when to quit. And not just with work. They'd been divorced for twenty years and he still couldn't stay away.

And she couldn't tell him no.

"Thanks," he said, then turned and left her in the secured police lab all alone.

Kelly missed work on Wednesday. Calling to see how her friend was feeling, Laura wandered back to the garden, not looking forward to the long day ahead. She needed people around her. Someone to talk to. She needed her husband. Plants weren't enough anymore.

On Thursday of that week, Harry stopped by the university food court after class for a burrito before heading out toward the frat house and Carlisle Street. Today he was going in the back way, watching the area between the houses. Twice since Monday, that same nerdy-looking young man had cut between those houses. Boyd wanted to know why. So did Harry.

"Dr. Kendall, hi."

Half the chicken burrito consumed, Harry nodded as Denise stopped beside his table. He'd seen her coming.

"Hi. Haven't seen you around this week," he muttered.

"I've got an archeology class and it's gone until at least four every day."

"Archeological Clarification of Palestinian History?" he wondered, knowing how time-intensive the upper-level class was during the brief summer session.

"Yeah."

She stood there, backpack hanging off her shoulder, hands on the back of the chair. Her low-cut jeans and tank top made it hard for Harry to avoid seeing the exposed skin of her stomach from his seated position.

He made a point of looking away.

"Um…do you mind if I sit down for a second?" she asked.

He did. But wasn't free to tell her why. Reaching over, he pulled out the chair.

"I…have something I want to ask you." Her words came quickly.

Harry bit into his burrito. Chewed. Waited.

"I…it's just…something's going on, isn't it? Something bad."

He took another bite. Chewed for a long time. Swallowed. "What makes you think that?"

Not a great answer. It was the best he had at the moment. He'd spent the last three nights on stakeouts. Dozing in a car that was more often hot than cool, as he didn't want to leave it running for long in case it drew attention.

Once again he'd seen women come and go. And determined that three or four young men were living in the house—based on the laundry and food they carted in and out.

"You haven't been yourself." At Harry's raised brow, she looked down. "I'm sorry, I shouldn't have said that. Like I know you or anything. But…you seem tense and…tired, I guess. And you're not positive like you usually are, you know?"

He did know. But he couldn't say so. Not to a grad student at the university where he taught.

"And then…" Denise looked him in the eye again. "Last Friday, you got that call, and the expression on your face, like you won the lottery or something, and the way you ran out without really saying goodbye or locking your door or anything, well…I don't know…"

She seemed genuinely concerned. Upset. As though he mattered to her more than a teacher should.

A complication he absolutely did not need.

20

Harry meant to tell Denise that she was imagining things. To give her some vague explanation for the previous Friday's hasty departure. But faced with the very real and sincere emotion glistening in her eyes, he said, "Five weeks ago tonight my wife was raped."

"Oh, my God. I'm so sorry…."

Denise looked as awkward as he felt. He should've held his tongue.

"Is she…okay?"

He nodded. Met her gaze. "No," he heard himself say, regretting the indiscretion, and at the same time, finding some kind of peace in saying it. This was exactly what they'd prescribed in counseling; speaking out instead of continuing to bear the silent, unwarranted shame. "She's hurt and afraid and her refusal to accept what's really going on here could put her in more danger."

"What do mean? What's going on?" Denise picked up on Harry's lapse before he realized he'd made it. He was even more tired than he'd supposed.

Because he trusted her, because he'd spent hours talking with her about the social and political history of minorities, because she was as black as he was, Harry told her what they now knew for certain. "The attack was racially motivated."

Denise's features were grim. She'd met Laura. Leaning forward, lowering her voice. "White supremacists?"

"Yes."

"Do you know what group?"

"Yes."

"Wow." With a dazed shake of the head, she dropped her pack to the floor. "Wow."

Boyd had told him to go with his gut—acknowledging that while Harry's instincts had certainly been off the mark a time or two, they'd also led them straight to Laura's attacker.

Harry wanted Denise's perspective. The young woman was not only intelligent and educated, she'd been aware of hate groups ever since her half brother back in Alabama had been beaten up by one.

"So what are you doing about it?" The question was filled with a conviction that he would—that he must—do something.

"I sent Laura to live with her parents." He glanced at the woman who was only a few years younger than he was. And made up his mind to trust her.

"There were two of them," he began, and related everything to her, minus his private conversations with Laura—and anything about the baby. The results of that night had nothing to do with finding these sons of bitches.

"So you think the whole fraternity is white suprema-cist?"

"I'm not sure. The idea has crossed my mind."

"They could be running drugs. It's one of the most common ways underground organizations make money for guns and propaganda."

"But that doesn't explain the women."

"It could be like you said. Maybe these guys watch out for interracial relationships on campus and then lure the girls there."

Uncomfortable, remembering the sound of that bullet cracking through his windshield—and Daniel Boyd's assumption that it hadn't been just a random drive-by—Harry looked around. The room was mostly deserted. "But to what end?" he asked. "That's where I'm getting stumped. Are they trying to lure them away from other relationships? Like some kind of quest? Have sex with them as a means of power, manipulation, control? Do they promise to love them, too?"

The idea was too ludicrous.

"Maybe they impregnate them."

Harry had thought about that, too, though for obvious reasons had chosen not to disclose that particular theory.

"This Jefferson guy worked at the fertility clinic. That's how you found him, right? When you got the time cards?"

"Right."

"So the baby connection makes sense. He knew you two were planning to have a biracial child."

Yes, and that was what bothered him. Maybe it was

like Denise said. Maybe these bastards were a group of young men—a species of vigilante—who were out to save the white girls on campus. And the attack on Laura had been a side venture—because one of the supremacists happened to work in a fertility clinic and saw Laura there with Harry.

"We need to see if any of these women are pregnant," Denise said excitedly.

"We?" He'd wanted her perspective. Nothing more.

"It's too much, Dr. Kendall," Denise said. "With all due respect, you can't do this alone."

He wasn't alone. But he couldn't tell her that. Couldn't tell anyone that.

"I'm *not* bringing you into this."

"That's where you're wrong—and too late. You already have. And at this point, knowing what I do, I can't just walk away. This is exactly the kind of thing we've spent the past five years talking about—the ways certain social groups try to control others…"

Harry listened, trying not to be drawn in by her intensity.

"I think I should get to know one or two of the women."

Denise's last statement caught Harry's attention. "Get to know them how?"

"Show me your pictures. Maybe I'll recognize someone. But if not, we watch the house. As a student, I can follow one or two of them a lot more easily than you could. Even, say, into a ladies' room. I strike up some kind of conversation, you know, like, you wouldn't happen to have change for a tampon, would you?"

Mind racing, Harry sat quietly, letting her talk. He'd have to get Boyd's okay, but Denise might have a good idea here—she had an in neither he nor the detective had.

And they were running out of time.

"What then?"

"Then I come up with a way to keep her talking until we discover something we have in common and I'm in."

"Doing this, you're going to find out what those women are doing in the frat house?"

"It's worth a shot. It probably wouldn't take me long to learn if she's pregnant. Maybe that office building you've seen a couple of them go into is a doctor's office. We could check all the suites in the building. See if a there's a doctor. Don't you think my plan could work?"

Harry almost nodded. And then didn't. "I think you're a black woman walking right into a white supremacist trap and there's no way I'm going to be part of that." Boyd wouldn't allow it, either.

"Then I'm going alone."

She stood up. Grabbed her pack.

"Wait!" Harry couldn't let her go. If anything happened to her…

She turned and said over her shoulder, "This is me you're talking to, Dr. Kendall. I haven't spent the past five years of my life studying the history of disenfranchised people so I can go sit in a classroom someplace and spout off theories. I didn't see my little brother's face all swollen and hear him crying and afraid to go to school, just so I could ignore what's going on around me. I'm going to make a difference."

He couldn't have her out there running into God knew what, all alone.

"You don't know which frat house I'm talking about."

"But I know you're going there again. So, how I figure it, one way or the other you're going to show me."

Harry stood, too, trash in one hand, briefcase in the other. He didn't have a lot of time. She obviously wasn't going to wait.

And he *couldn't* wait. He had business to attend to. Every moment that slipped by took Laura further away from him.

"I have an appointment," he said. "But if you'll give me until this evening to get back with you, I promise to seriously consider your offer."

"Okay." Her voice lifted, as though what he'd asked was only reasonable.

He studied her for another minute before—against his better judgment—he took out his cell phone, pulled up the pictures stored on the internal memory card and showed them to her.

She didn't recognize a single person.

Nope, that would've been too easy.

"Write down your number and I'll call you tonight," he told her.

She scribbled it on a clean napkin.

As soon as Harry got settled on Carlisle Street, he was calling Boyd's private line. Although the detective was angry with him for not keeping his mouth shut, he agreed they'd have to use Denise's help. But she wasn't to know about him. She'd be working on her own, as Harry was—without official police protection.

Another life in danger.

Things had gotten far too messy.

Bobby could hardly contain his impatience as he waited for Luke to fall asleep Saturday night. He'd been praying all day and, just before dinner, had received confirmation from God that the action he'd been pondering was correct. And now that he knew, he couldn't put it off. Time was critical. Tomorrow would be their church meeting and then Tony would be driving back to Tucson.

He smiled as his younger "brother" leaned down to give Luke a soft kiss on the temple as the two of them finally laid the boy down. And stood back to let Tony raise the bar on the crib.

The boy was ready for a regular bed. Bobby hated to lose this last part of his babyhood. Raising Luke was going to be glorious, he knew that, his best work. But he still hated to say goodbye to the innocence of babyhood.

The love ahead would be tougher, filled with discipline and hard lessons, not children's games and cuddling.

As Tony joined him in the hallway just outside the baby's room, Bobby tapped his arm gently.

"Let's go in here," he said, pointing to the master bedroom.

Tony followed him, taking a seat on the sofa beneath a bay window that overlooked the back half of the wooded lot. Carefully placed security lights illuminated the uncurtained view.

Sitting on the edge of the adjoining chair, Bobby rested his forearms on his knees and took a deep breath.

"How's Beth?"

Tony's grin was answer enough. "Great," he said. "She's everything I've ever wanted. Beautiful, smart, funny, and she's got this gentle way about her, you know?"

Bobby nodded. Amanda had been that way. At first.

Later, after the baby, she'd changed some, become fierce, but only to protect her baby. Like any mama bear with a cub.

"Yeah," Tony said. "She makes these little sounds when she makes love." Tony's face glowed. "And she's not real wild. She just lies there and…waits for me."

In spite of his commitment to celibacy, Bobby felt his dick harden against the zipper of his shorts. A testimony to Amanda.

"I'm telling you, Bobby, sometimes it's hard not to think about making love to her again, but I'm doing like you said, controlling my mind, putting my thoughts on the bigger picture."

Bobby sat back. Smiled. "Tell me about that."

And for the next half hour, as he listened to Tony talk about his work in Tucson, his political science classes, his ideas and the strides he was making, Bobby knew again that he'd made the best choice.

"I have a question to ask you," he said when Tony finally fell silent. "And I want you to take a few minutes before you answer. Understand?"

"Of course." The boy didn't hesitate, didn't bother to hide his eagerness, either, and Bobby's heart exploded with a fresh burst of love for his brother.

"Are you ready for red shoelaces?"

Tony earned Bobby's highest regard as he sat there, unmoving, pondering the question. The young man showed neither excitement nor alarm. He respected the seriousness of the moment. The question. The vow that would be required—all of which they'd talked about many times over the past year.

Tony stared straight at him for a full ten minutes, his focus unwavering. And when he looked away, Bobby knew he'd come to a decision.

It was the one he'd needed to hear.

On Sunday night, when she'd tried repeatedly to reach Harry for their nightly call and couldn't, Laura grabbed the newspaper and went to her room. She changed into an old pair of shorts and a T-shirt and dropped down to the bed, making it look as though she was in for the night. Her parents were out but wouldn't be late. Ten or so.

And as soon as they got home and said good-night, she was going to slip out, even if she had to climb through the window like she'd done as a college freshman and wanted to see Harry. She was going to find her husband.

She didn't know the exact house he had under surveillance, but she knew the street. She wasn't going to sit by idly while Harry got himself arrested. Or worse.

He was intent on infiltrating evil territory. And while

Laura had never paid much attention to stories about the Ku Klux Klan, mostly because she believed they were of historical interest, not anything that existed in today's more enlightened society, she'd read enough true crime books to know that bodies could simply disappear.

A local department store was having a twelve-hour weekend sale, she saw in the paper. Baby clothes were illustrated in the ad. She turned the page.

The whole state had heard about one of those bizarre cases last year—the one in which a woman, mother of a two-year-old boy, had disappeared in Flagstaff and her body had never been found. Her car, as Laura remembered it, had been in some kind of accident and abandoned.

Shortly after that, some guy in a Phoenix jail, who claimed to be a white supremacist, had hanged himself in his jail cell with white-power graffiti all over his walls.

The manufacturer of the makeup Laura used was having bonus days next week. If she purchased at least seventeen dollars worth of merchandise, she'd get a bag of free samples. A twenty-dollar value.

She had a shelf full of those samples in her bathroom closet at home. Along with most of her home remedies. She missed them.

Tomorrow would make it two weeks that she'd been here.

It was time to move on. Either home or someplace else. One thing was for sure; she couldn't stay under her parents' roof much longer. She loved them, but their conservative beliefs were confining. Not only that, because of their sincere love for her, those attitudes and expectations began to subtly manipulate her until she lost sight of what was her and what was them. They made decisions based on the fear of negative consequences.

Laura wanted to quietly reach for the stars.

As she turned pages to get to the real estate ads, a picture caught her eye. A quarter-page head shot of the man her parents had been talking about at dinner.

George Moss. According to Len and Sharon Clark, and their friends and fellow church-members, the world would change for the better if this man was elected. And if his opponent won the senatorial race, they were all in danger of destruction—from inside America—and out.

Laura read about a speech the man had made that day. And when she was done, she wadded up the paper and shoved it in the trash. She wasn't going to buy into the scarcity mentality. This was a land of wealth and bounty—there should be enough for everybody. Yes, there was bad in today's society, but there was also great good. She had to believe that.

She wasn't going to live her life ruled by fear.

She just wasn't.

She moved resolutely to the computer in her parents' family room, determined to educate herself so she could speak out against everyone who was trying to make her afraid. Afraid to walk alone in the world, afraid to live by her heart. That group included her parents and—for different reasons—her husband.

If she listened to them, if she bought into a set of beliefs like the one George Moss espoused, she'd divorce Harry. And spend the rest of her life only half-living.

It didn't take her long to find more information than she wanted on white supremacists. Or to find out that the problem was much more extensive than she'd imagined.

And as she read, tension filled her limbs and chills slid down her spine.

It was all about secrets.

The groups claimed their cause was gleaned from Christian teachings. And somewhere, somehow, things got twisted. Christian beliefs, like *love your neighbor,* became love the neighbor you think God meant you to have. Not the one you did have.

But, judging by several sites on the Internet, the new recruits didn't understand how Christianity had been distorted—perverted—by these groups. They were largely male, young, idealistic loners looking for a cause in which to invest their passion, for something to believe in, a place to belong. And in a process of slow indoctrination, they were being drawn into a belief system that was beginning to spread through American society.

Laura started to shake. She closed the Internet site. Checked all the doors. Grabbed the throw at the end of her bed.

And sat down in front of the computer again.

She wasn't going to look anymore. Or, rather, she'd just look at the search engine. She'd found a site that made the problem seem huge, that was all. If she went back, she'd see there wasn't much else.

Except there was.

She came across a Web site that played the most vile songs she'd ever heard. Someone called Johnny Rebel, whose songs ranged from "Fuck You, Osama Bin Laden" to horrible, vile things about African Americans. Things she couldn't even bear to read in a song title.

Johnny Rebel had a lot of fans. They praised his music on a message board.

Laura clicked. Clicked again. And discovered probably the most frightening document of all. It was written by a respected law-enforcement organization, and cited facts that were so frightening, she began to wonder how she and Harry had managed to live peacefully together for the more than ten years they'd known each other.

White supremacy was escalating. Changing. Leaving behind some of the gang-war tactics. Cleaning itself up. Growing money. Infiltrating white-collar walks of life.

And the secrets continued.

Because even when a white supremacist is brought to trial, his crime will usually be exposed, but his white supremacist ties will not. Any defense attorney worth his salt will move to have any white supremacist allegation or alliance suppressed. And any judge upholding the law would have to grant that motion on the basis of prejudicial evidence.

Laura shut down the computer, took her blanket to the couch and curled up in a corner, waiting for her parents to come home.

She'd always felt safe when her dad was around.

* * *

On Monday, Harry stopped at the campus bistro for a late lunch, on his way to a coffee bar where he was meeting Denise. That morning, she'd been having coffee with one of the women she'd met, someone named Chelsea.

Anxious to hear what she'd learned, feeling as if they were finally making progress, he almost missed the young man in line over at the university food court.

The nerdy kid from the frat house. Harry hadn't seen him all weekend, and now, suddenly, there he was. Forgetting the sandwich he'd ordered and paid for, Harry walked away, positioning himself behind a pillar where he wouldn't be seen but could see.

The kid was with a conservative-looking middle-aged man in a shirt and tie—attire that stood out on the Arizona college campus in the midst of a summer heat wave. Harry couldn't hear what they were talking about, but the older man seemed inordinately interested in what the young man had to say.

Trying to get closer, to find out what they had in common, or even who they were, Harry managed to keep them in sight as they ordered and then were served their food—in take-out bags.

They were leaving.

And he couldn't let them get away. A college-age kid whom he'd frequently seen on Carlisle Street, and an older guy who looked like a respectable businessman. What was their connection?

The relationship?

Was the man the kid's father?

That would explain it. And make Harry out for the fool he'd been more than once during the past weeks.

Maybe he *was* a fool. But he had to follow his instincts, and they were telling him to follow these two men.

With a quick call to Denise, putting off their meeting for a couple of hours, Harry walked into the hot afternoon sun.

21

Laura left work early on Monday. She hadn't been feeling well all day—the result of a bad night's rest, she was sure—and before Harry had a chance to leave class and do whatever he was doing these days, she wanted to talk to him.

He called her every morning. And every night. But he was telling her nothing.

And that wasn't good enough.

A vision of herself the previous night, sitting in the corner shaking when her parents walked in the door, renewed her resolve.

Her folks had been great. Loving her. Comforting her. And proposing solutions that she'd been ready, in her weakened state, to agree to.

Which was why she had to get out of there.

Because living like a scared rabbit was a waste of the spirit God had given her. A waste of her life.

If Harry wouldn't let her move back home, she was going to get her own place. This week. She'd rent something fully furnished and pay cash.

Out of habit, she checked the tires on her truck as she approached. And, as she did every day, breathed a little sigh of relief when she saw they were fine. So much for Harry's theory that someone had tampered with the tire to make her vulnerable.

She would get through this.

But the thought of what lay ahead still made her queasy.

Keys in hand, Laura pushed the button to unlock the door. Heard it click. And with her hand on the alarm button, she climbed inside the sweltering cab, then locked the door. It wasn't as if her coworkers would hear the alarm from out here, but a guest on the other side of the parking lot might. And if someone attacked her, the blaring sound might scare them off.

She was in.

She threw her bag on the seat beside her, hand with the keys halfway to the ignition before she stopped. Turned. Looked at the seat. Her bag was where she'd just thrown it.

But had she seen something else on the seat? Was it there, under her bag?

Laura's truck was pristine. Everyone teased her about how clean she kept it. And she could swear she'd just seen something white on the black cloth seat.

She stared at her bag, afraid to touch it. Which was ridiculous. Just as cowering on the couch had been. They were all getting to her, dammit, and she couldn't let them.

White supremacists. Harry. Her parents. George Moss and his paranoia, his scarcity mentality. His illegal alien statistics and broken family theories.

Still, she couldn't tear her gaze from the purse. And couldn't touch it. There was something underneath. She was sure of it.

"It's just a receipt." She spoke to the sweltering interior. Had to turn the truck on and get the air started before she died of heatstroke. She didn't move.

"It fell out of a bag...."

But then why didn't you see it this morning? You would've noticed.

Would I? I'm a mess. I could miss anything at this point. I can't trust myself.

The thoughts passed through her mind, almost in slow motion as she sat there, helpless.

She couldn't trust herself.

That was what they'd robbed her of. Trust in herself, her own judgment and perceptions. And until that moment, she hadn't even known what she'd lost.

Laura reached for the damn bag. If she found anything, there'd also be a perfectly logical reason for it. She was not going to run scared.

A piece of white paper, ordinary typing paper, lay folded neatly in the middle of the seat. Exactly in the middle. Not as if it had fallen out of anything.

As if someone had placed it there.

She was being ridiculous.

And to prove it to herself, Laura picked up the sheet. Her hands were trembling so hard she had a hard time unfolding it at first. Fumbled. Dropped it on top of the bag on her lap and snatched it up again.

The edge of the paper slid along her finger, stinging her as it fell open.

DO NOT ABORT.

That was it. In capital letters that had been meticulously cut from magazines and glued on the sheet.

"No!" Laura screamed, throwing the paper as far away from her as she could. She screamed again. They'd been inside her locked truck. *How* had they gotten into her truck?

"No! Leave me alone! Whoever you are, leave me *alone!*" She was crying. Sweating.

Blood from her finger dripped onto her dirty white shirt.

Denise wasn't anywhere to be found. Harry waited for her at the coffee shop half an hour past their designated meeting time. He asked from table to table, and at the service counter, but no one had seen her.

It wasn't like her to miss an appointment. Not once in five years. She'd never even been late to class.

Something was wrong. He knew it. Something was horribly wrong.

He rushed out of the restaurant, cursing himself for the false lead that had made him reschedule with Denise, for the instincts that had told him to follow the nerdy college kid and the businessman. They'd led him to the man's BMW in the parking lot, where they'd shaken hands in a father-son way, and the man had driven off. The kid had disappeared into a dormitory that was accessible only to occupants.

He ran to the corner, looked down the street. There was no sign of a beautiful young black woman. Same thing at the other end of the block. Forgetting his car, he hurried down to Carlisle. The road was deserted, except for the cars that were always parked in front of the same houses every single day. The street was quiet. Not even a leaf stirred.

So where was she?

Inside the house?

Had she gone against her word? And his orders?

He checked the earpiece to the two-way radio Boyd had provided for Harry to use with Denise, making sure it was on, then checked the instrument fastened to his hip. Both were in perfect working order.

Panting as he came to a stop, Harry tried to figure out what to do next. He didn't know who to contact, knew none of Denise's family or friends. Other than a permanent home in Alabama that she hadn't visited since Christmas, he had no idea where she lived.

If anything had happened to her...

Calling Boyd, Harry headed back to his office, with the slim hope that Denise had left word for him there.

Maybe she'd stayed late at her archeology tutorial, which was where she'd said she was going when he'd called to move their meeting time. She'd lost track of time.

Maybe she'd just plain decided to be done with all his craziness. He hoped to God that was the case. Denise was sweet and idealistic and far too young to be involved in the mess that had become Harry's life.

Rape and devil's babies, hatred and insanity.

And fear. Always. Everywhere. Inside. Outside. On everyone's faces. In George Moss's speeches. In the hearts of men. And women.

Boyd was on another call—another crime scene. He told Harry to stay close to campus and let him know if he heard anything. He'd get away as soon as possible and see what he could find out. From the morgue. Hospitals. Housing records.

Harry's office door, which he'd left locked, was open a crack. Slowing, he glanced around, smiling at the young woman passing in the hall, nodding to the adjunct teacher in the office next door. Everything seemed to be in slow motion. He was always conscious that there might be a second shot. One that would hit its mark.

Pushing open the door with one finger, he studied the room—and gasped the second he spotted Denise half-lying, her head back, in the chair by his desk.

"Hi." She spoke as if this was any ordinary greeting, any ordinary day. "Sorry I missed the meeting. I tried to beep you but I forgot to charge the radio."

Rushing to her side, Harry took in the swollen skin beneath her left eye and quickly scanned the rest of her body for injury. Scraped skin on her knee, and knuckles. A black smudge on her yellow tank top.

His face grim, he stared at her. "What happened?"

"I crashed."

"Your car?"

She shook her head, then, laughed, wincing as she did. "My bike. I was so hell-bent on playing sleuth, looking over my shoulder, I didn't notice the car that pulled in front of me. I ran right into it. Stupid, huh?"

Kneeling, Harry took a closer look at her injuries. They didn't seem too bad. All superficial.

"How fast were you going?" He took a first aid kit out of the bottom drawer of his file cabinet, removed an antibiotic cloth and knelt down again.

"Not very, thank God."

Denise grimaced when he touched her eye, but then sat there docile as he cleaned the wound and tended to her fingers and knees.

"I feel like such an idiot."

"Well, don't." The whole situation felt…off. "Tell me again what happened."

"I'm not really sure. I didn't get anything out of Chelsea this morning, except an invitation to apply for a job. Guess she works at some temporary agency on High Street. I knew you were hoping for more, and when I finished my tutorial, I still had some time, so I decided to bike through the neighborhood, see if I recognized anyone. I thought I heard something behind me, glanced back for a second and the next thing I know I'm lying on my stomach on the curb."

He put a Band-Aid on her knee. The scrapes on her knuckles were barely noticeable now that they were cleaned up.

"And you're sure you didn't see the car before?"

"No, but then I was pretty focused on the houses, looking for people in or around them."

"But you'd have noticed a car if it drove past you."

"You'd think, but I didn't. Anyway, I was a little dazed at first and was afraid I might need to lie down so I didn't want to wait at the coffee shop and I didn't have your cell number so I just came here. I still had the key I got from Nadine the day you left in such a rush."

He'd told the division secretary Denise was approved for admittance to his office the year before, when she'd done T.A. work for him.

"What'd the car look like?"

She frowned up at him. "Dark. A sedan, I think. It all happened so fast and—"

"You didn't see it afterward?"

"Uh uh." Denise sat up, her forehead still creased. "Kinda strange, huh? I mean, I wasn't really hurt or anything, but they didn't know that."

A hit-and-run. On Carlisle Street. Another warning. He wondered what Daniel Boyd would have to say about that.

"You're done," he told her. The words were emphatic.

Standing up, Denise met him nose to nose. "No, I'm not. It was an accident, Dr. Kendall. My own stupid fault. And I'm fine."

She was. But she might not have been. Might not be next time. His own life was worth the risks he was taking. Hers was not.

"I will not have another woman hurt at my expense."

The tips of her shoes were almost touching his. "I'm doing this at my own expense, thank you." Harry wasn't used to such boldness in a woman. Wasn't sure he liked it. And wasn't sure he didn't.

He stood there, staring her down. He couldn't just let her go. She'd do exactly what she'd done this morning and work on her own.

He couldn't keep her there, either. The warm, almost needy look in her eyes told him something had changed. He couldn't say when. Maybe in the past five minutes. Maybe the other day when she'd approached him and he'd broken his hard-and-fast rule to not mix his personal life with his students.

Maybe over weeks and months and years of knowing her.

How had he let it happen?

He was going to take a step back. Think. Figure out a way to get her to back off—a threat if he had to resort to that. He'd fight his own battle.

His foot received the command. It didn't respond. And as Denise's head came forward, his face didn't respond, either. The touch of her lips was a shock. And yet…somehow expected.

Without thought he returned the kiss. An instinctive reaction from a man pushed beyond endurance.

He opened his mouth to Denise's tongue for another reason. Her moist warmth, the closeness and intimacy, felt so damned good. Not because it was *her,* but because his life was balancing on a precipice and this moment was real. Alive.

"Wait." He gasped, jerked back, breathing heavily. "I'm sorry." He stepped away. And at her stricken look he added, "I shouldn't have done that. I'm sorry. It won't happen again." *It can't.*

She seemed confused when he took the blame for something they both knew she'd initiated. And then sent him a smile of relief. "It's okay, Dr. Kendall. You aren't yourself right now. You couldn't possibly be. Just forget it."

And so would she.

They exchanged the silent promise. Harry moved behind his desk.

He didn't look up until she was at the door, when his gaze finally met hers.

"Thank you."

Her smile was slow in coming but genuine. "You're welcome."

She left Harry standing with the late-afternoon sun coming through his office window. He picked up his phone and called Daniel Boyd.

Laura had no idea how she made it to the police station. One minute she was shaking in her car, trying to get out of the parking lot, and the next she was parked in front of the precinct she hadn't known was there until five weeks ago. She stepped outside the truck, checking her doors for damage. She saw nothing.

She should call Harry. And she would. But not until she'd been to see Detective Boyd. She needed calm, levelheaded action right now. Not more fear.

And she was scared to death of what this new development would do to Harry. What it would cause *him* to do.

Still shaking, the back of her shirt soaked with sweat, she pushed tendrils of hair back into her ponytail and walked inside the air-conditioned building.

Detective Miller was there within thirty seconds of being called. Boyd was out, apparently on another case.

"What's up?" The detective asked, his voice friendly. Concerned.

"*This* was left in my car." She handed him the note.

His face unsmiling, he studied the sheet. And then, long moments later, he asked, "Anyone else seen it?"

"No one."

"You called your husband?"

"No." Laura wrapped her arms around her. It was freezing in there. "Not yet."

Holding the page down and to his side, the detective drew Laura into an alcove, lowering his voice.

"I'm not going to tell you what to do, Mrs. Kendall, but until I get a chance to follow up on this—which I'll do immediately—I'm going to suggest we keep this between us for now."

The man was professionally trained to keep her safe. She waited to see what else he had to say.

"In my opinion, your husband's on the brink of explosion. This is the closest we've come to solid evidence, and we can't have him interfering." He gestured with the folded paper. "This could send him over the edge. Detective Boyd and I are doing everything we can to watch his back, but we can only do so much. We aren't being paid to protect people from themselves."

She nodded.

"This letter must've come from the second rapist."

But she didn't see how he could've known she was pregnant. The people she'd told could be counted on one hand. Unless the second rapist came from the fertility center, too.

"We'll get on this," Miller said. "In the meantime, I want to arrange for a police escort to follow you home."

Laura nodded again, listening.

"If you were pregnant, this would be a high-level threat, intended to instill even greater fear," he continued. "But he took a huge chance in his choice of scare tactics because it only works if you're pregnant. He's gambling that you are. And considering the situation, his odds aren't good. It's the type of gamble only a kid who's still young enough to be overconfident would make."

. She'd been raped by a kid? It sure hadn't felt like…

"I am pregnant."

The detective stopped mid-breath. "What did you say?"

"I *am* pregnant." It was like she was talking about someone else.

"Why weren't we told about this?" He sounded as though he had some personal stake in knowing. And Laura relaxed just a little. The man's obvious caring made her feel safe.

"I just found out recently and it doesn't have anything to do with the investigation."

"Apparently it does," he said, eyes narrowed. "Who else knows?"

"Harry. My parents. My closest friend and my doctor."

"That's it?"

She nodded.

"How do you know one of them hasn't told someone else?"

"I don't, of course, but my doctor can't, and the others wouldn't. They're more concerned about me than I am." Of course, another employee at the fertility clinic— maybe the second rapist?—could have confiscated her records. If Dr. Barnes had reported them in the first place.

Did she dare hope this latest scare could actually turn out to be the clue they needed? That this could all be over soon?

"You said the note was in your truck. Was it locked?"

Laura's nod was definite, her fear returning full-force.

"Was the door jimmied?"

She shook her head. "Not as far as I can tell."

"Do you have keyless entry?"

All she could manage was a second shake of her head.

"So whoever did this had a key."

"I guess." She'd hoped there was some other way—some criminal tool—that could have allowed entry without marking up her truck.

The detective closed his eyes and when he opened them, they were wary. And revealed an unmistakable compassion. "What I'm about to say isn't easy, but I need you to listen, and at least consider the possibility," he said and Laura knew what was coming.

"It's possible that this note isn't from the rapist at all."

Laura waited for the rest of it.

"By all accounts, you have three people in your life who want you to believe you're in danger so you'll agree to stay away from Harry. Am I correct?"

She tired to swallow but her throat was too dry. Laura nodded instead.

"Any of them have access to your truck?"

One did.

Detective Miller's next question was spoken very slowly, as though he understood that each word would be painful for her to hear. "Is there any conceivable way you could see Harry doing this? Trying to scare you?"

A month ago she would've said *no*. Absolutely not.

Today, Laura just didn't know.

"So, let's keep quiet about this. Don't say anything to Harry and let's see if he tips his hand. If he did this, he's bound to be suspicious, angry even, if we don't tell him."

Laura hated herself when she nodded one more time and headed with him toward the door.

"In the meanwhile, I'll run this through forensics and see what we get."

As Laura turned to go, the detective's cell phone rang. She left.

"Detective Boyd."

Daniel didn't believe in fate. But the moment he recognized Harry Kendall's voice on his cell phone, he felt the need to put his back to the corner. Look over his shoulder. And in front of him.

An instinctive reaction due to too many years spent dealing with the ugliest parts of life and not enough moments enjoying the good.

"Yes, Mr. Kendall," he said, seeing his partner using the computer at his desk as he returned to the office.

"Denise was hit by a car on Carlisle this morning."

Frowning, Daniel turned away from the crowded room. "Where is she?"

"At home," Harry said. "At least I hope that's where she went. She wasn't badly hurt—a few bruises and some swelling."

Daniel saw Sheila, dead on the floor, a pool of her own blood spreading out around her hips.

"We have to pull her off this," he insisted.

"She'll just go out on her own."

"What's with you two?" Daniel said, not bothering to hide the irritation in his voice.

"You know the answer to that as well as I do, Detective," Harry Kendall said. "You get kicked around enough, you have to fight back or die."

Swearing under his breath, Daniel promised to put an extra patrol on Denise Marshall and wondered what lie he was going to tell to make that happen.

If either of these amateur detectives got hurt, his life was over.

Reminding Harry to be careful, Daniel rang off.

When was this going to end?

But even when it did—if it did—there'd be another victim, another crime, another heartless bastard.

22

Harry hadn't seen his wife for a week and two days. And the past couple of nights, when he'd talked to her, she'd been different. More remote.

He was losing her.

Maybe he was losing everything.

Coming from his first class, wondering how he was going to stay awake for the second, he pictured himself years from now, walking on the very same campus, teaching the very same classes and then heading home to an empty house.

He was going the distance. He'd find the second rapist. Sit through the trials, testify, tell the humiliating, vile story as many times as necessary, in order to see those two bastards sent to prison.

And then he was going to divorce his wife.

In spite of his pleas, which had become demands, Denise had refused to back down on her quest to help Harry uncover the mystery behind his wife's attack. Daniel had found two doctor's offices in the building those girls had entered. One a gynecologist. Tomorrow morning, since she didn't have a class, Denise was planning to make an appointment there. She was also going to phone her new friend Chelsea to take her up on the offer of a job with her temp agency. Just in case.

Turning the corner to go up the walk toward his next lecture hall, Harry almost missed the man he'd seen in the café the other day with the nerdy kid from the frat house. Alone this time.

Dressed as before, in a white shirt and tie, his black leather shoes shined to perfection, he was once again heading toward the parking lot, where he'd said good-bye to the young man.

So who was he? A father who visited campus every second day? Maybe father and son met for lunch regularly. There was nothing wrong with that.

But it was a little odd.

Of course, the kid was kind of odd. A loner with a short, little-boy haircut slinking between frat houses.

Harry took the first step into the building. He turned and saw the man's straight back as he strode purposefully away.

As though he was going somewhere important.

Suddenly, without warning, Harry had to know where that was. Had to know the man's business and what he was about. Rational thought didn't enter his head as he whirled around and sprinted across the campus, bumping into a couple of students on the way. He ignored the dirty looks, the startled glances.

His car was in the front row of the faculty lot. Inside, Harry threw his satchel on the passenger seat, then started the ignition. Regardless of the hot steering wheel, he roared out of the parking lot. He was waiting at the side of the road when Mr. Professional drove sedately out of the visitor lot.

And the first thing he did, as he fell in behind the man, was to call Daniel Boyd with the license plate number.

A block from campus, Harry remembered the class of third-year history students sitting in the air-conditioned lecture hall. Another five minutes, and they'd all be looking at each other, wondering what was up. Was this a get-out-of-jail free card?

Should they wait? Or should they go?

He felt twinges of guilt but didn't even consider turning back. Some things were more important than careers.

The man drove as conservatively as he dressed, stopping at yellow lights. Traveling not one mile above, or below, the speed limit. His BMW shone beneath the hot sun, as if he'd washed it only that morning. And he signaled every move he made.

All of which made it relatively easy for Harry, an amateur at tailing someone by car, to keep him in sight from his vantage point a couple of cars back.

Relatively easy for Harry to find out where the man was going. When he pulled into the parking lot of the church Laura's parents regularly attended, Harry's gut filled with lead.

And the world came crashing in on him. Falling into place with a logic that left horrifying possibilities.

"Boyd." The detective picked up their private line in the middle of the first ring.

"I'm at Laura's parents' church. Follow me on this,"

he said, staring sightlessly at the blacktop, aware of the numbness spreading through him. "Tell me if I'm crazy. These people, her parents, their church friends, are as conservative as they come. To the point of spending millions of dollars to convert others to their way of thinking…"

"Other groups do that, too. Political groups. Religious ones."

"I know." Harry tapped the steering wheel, his jaw tight. "That politician, George Moss, you've heard of him?"

"Who hasn't?" Boyd's voice was gravelly. The man probably needed sleep. "Return to family values. He instills fear with the idea that there's not enough to go around—close the borders, close the doors, keep the people like Moss and his kind in and everyone else out."

"I don't know if Laura's parents are working on his campaign or not, but it wouldn't surprise me. They're full-fledged supporters."

"Okay." He seemed to be asking where Harry was going with all this.

"White supremacists," Harry continued, traversing again the horrifying road he'd just gone down alone. "Guys like the Ivory Nation brotherhood. They shroud themselves with a Christian identity."

"I get that. I'm not sure where any of this leads, though."

"Laura's mother, Sharon Clark, knew that the vials of semen I'd left at the fertility clinic had been destroyed even before Laura."

"How?" Boyd sounded a little more awake.

"Grace Martin, the manager of the clinic, goes to Sharon's church. That's how we came to choose that particular clinic. It was recommended by Laura's mom." He paused. "Grace Martin is David Jefferson's boss."

"I know who she is. I spoke to her during my initial investigation of Jefferson. She gave a glowing review of his work and his character. Always early, stays late, impeccable accuracy and cleanliness, respectful."

Harry couldn't stand to hear praise of any kind for the man who'd brutalized his wife.

"My in-laws never approved of my marriage to their daughter," he went on, needing to get to the end, to see if Daniel Boyd was there with him. If things were starting to make sense. "They really seem to believe I'm preventing Laura from a life of eternal paradise. The thought of us having a child together, a grandchild who'd confirm Laura's sin in loving a black man—well, that could've made them desperate enough to do whatever it took to *save* her." He didn't conceal his sarcasm.

"We're talking rape here, Kendall."

With sweat pouring down the back of his neck, soaking his polo shirt, Harry sat at the curb that bordered the church parking lot.

Was he actually thinking Laura's parents could be behind this? Could he really believe they'd arranged the horrific rape of their own daughter?

"Why would they recommend the clinic when they were so clearly against us having a child?" he asked slowly.

"Better the devil you know…" Boyd sounded as exhausted as Harry felt.

But Harry felt more than tired; he felt sick. How could he possibly be having these thoughts about his in-laws? They were good people. Honest—to the point of revealing their views about Harry's marriage to their daughter. But they'd always been cordial to him.

"So what about the kid you saw at the frat house?" Daniel broke in. "And this other guy—the well-to-do guy you just followed?"

"I have no idea."

"You were pretty sure the rapes were tied to the frat house. You're saying now you've changed your mind?"

Shaking his head, frustration gnawing at him, Harry finally said, "No. I just don't know how it all ties in."

"Could be that Jefferson's ties to the fraternity house, or anything going on there, have nothing to do with the attack on you and Laura."

"Maybe. Except I see the young guy cutting through yards near the frat house, then I see him with a man who's obviously a visitor to the campus. A man who happens to drive to her parents' church."

"And Jefferson, whose voice you heard at the frat house, works at the fertility clinic you and Laura went to—"

"And his boss is a member of this church," Harry added.

"I'll talk to Jefferson again," Boyd said. "See if I can get anything out of him. In the meantime, we need to find this mysterious kid. I'll do another run on his picture. And pass it along to the guys on the campus beat. You stick close to the frat house and if you see him again, don't lose him. Call me immediately."

Half an hour later, still sick to his stomach as he looked at the black car that hadn't moved, Harry put his own car in gear and drove away.

Laura postponed her plans to get out of her parents' house that week. The first part of the plan, to present Harry with the ultimatum that if she couldn't move back home, she'd get her own apartment, didn't seem like such a great idea anymore.

She was having a hard enough time speaking with him every day and not telling him about the note, and she knew that if she saw him, she wouldn't be able to keep her promise to Detective Miller.

It wasn't that she was afraid of Harry. After all, if he'd left that note—and she didn't really believe he had—he'd done it for one reason and one reason only. To protect her.

After Monday, and the possibility that the note could've come from a rapist who had access to Dr. Barnes's files, she wasn't quite as ready to live in an apartment all alone—no matter how secure it might be.

She'd been waiting to get a call back from Detective Miller and was finding it harder and harder to be patient. How long could it take to test a sample of paper for fingerprints or other defining marks?

"Hey, you want some chicken salad and crackers for lunch?" Kelly came upon her in the back garden just as Laura was finishing some planting on Thursday morning.

"At your place?" she asked her friend.

"Yeah, I have something I need to talk to you about."

Kelly looked concerned. Worried. And with fear striking her heart anew, Laura walked to Kelly's vehicle.

Sitting at his desk in his downtown law office, George Moss uncovered the salad his wife had packed him for lunch, then picked up the sealed envelope that had been delivered.

They were the newest polls—which, as a favor, from the president of the polling company, he was seeing before they were published.

And ten minutes later, his salad sat untouched as he hung up the phone, a gleam in his eyes and a smile on his face.

His lead in the polls was so great, his most serious contender for the nomination, had just dropped out of the race.

She was six weeks pregnant and could hardly eat a bite. Sitting with Kelly at her table, Laura remembered back to the day she'd found out about the baby. She didn't feel any different now than she had then.

Would it be this way until the end? For the next seven and a half months was she going to feel disconnected from herself? Out of control? Frightened? Confused? Resenting this pregnancy yet accepting it? In love with something she hated?

"Have you contacted an adoption agency yet?" As close as they'd grown over the past weeks, she wasn't surprised that Kelly had known what she was thinking about.

"No." Laura shook her head, wondering what Kelly had to tell her.

It had to do with Harry. Somehow she knew that.

"I haven't decided what I'm going to do," she said, nibbling a cracker. She had to eat. The baby needed sustenance even if she wasn't hungry. "Crazy as it sounds, I'm not sure, after all these years of yearning for a baby, that I can just give it away. Its beginnings were ugly—but it's also mine." She shrugged helplessly. "This baby can't be blamed for the horror of its conception."

Kelly's smile was filled with empathy. "I understand, Laura."

She sounded so sure that Laura had to ask. "You haven't ever been pregnant, have you?"

Saying nothing, Kelly dropped her cracker.

"You have."

The younger woman nodded. "Once."

"What happened?"

"I had an abortion."

She should've been shocked. Had been raised to believe that killing an unborn baby was a grievous sin.

But all she felt was an outpouring of compassion for her friend who'd obviously been hurt so much. And who still hurt.

They talked about Kelly's pregnancy for another minute or two, about the father of the baby—a college kid who'd taken her to the clinic to end the life of their child, paid for the procedure, and then dumped her. Kelly had made one unfortunate choice after another— all of which she was still paying for.

On the inside, where it didn't show.

They finished the crackers with half the chicken left

over. And then Kelly's gaze met hers and Laura knew her time was up.

"What's he done now?" she asked abruptly, wanting to get this over with, needing to be in control of *something*.

Kelly's hand covered hers and, instinctively, Laura held on.

"Listen, I'm just going to say it straight," she said. She took a deep breath. "I'm sure there's a reasonable explanation and everything will be just fine."

Oh, God, it was going to be bad.

"I went up to his office to talk to him on Monday," Kelly said. "I should've told you I was going, but I didn't want you to tell me no. I'm on campus every day and he's there and I'm concerned about you two. You're pregnant and losing weight. You've got shadows under your eyes, and worse, *in* your eyes. You're worrying yourself to death. You need him. I was going to offer to help you guys find a way to see each other."

The gesture brought tears to Laura's eyes.

"So what happened when you went to his office?"

"The door was open, but I heard voices, so knocked anyway. They didn't hear me."

"They?"

"There was a woman with him. A black woman, about my age. Maybe a little younger."

Laura didn't want to hear this.

"He was kissing her, Laura."

23

"Dr. Kendall? This is Denise."

"How'd it go?" he asked, holding the phone in one hand and his satchel in the other as he left his second class. He'd been waiting for the past hour to hear about Denise's meeting with Chelsea.

"You're not going to believe this, but the temp agency is in that same building on High Street."

"The one with the doctor's offices."

"Yeah."

"So maybe that's where they're all going?" Though why, he had no clue. What would a temp agency have to do with white supremacist drug-running fraternity brothers who had conservative church connections?

"Or Chelsea just saw the place on the way to the doctor's and needed a job."

Maybe. He wished he knew. The more he uncovered, the less he understood.

"Did you go in?"

"Yeah," she said, her voice a bit confused. "And get

this. I filled out the application Chelsea brought, and she took it in for me, as a favor, and they were thrilled and wanted me to do some testing down the hall—you know, words per minute and all that—which I did. I waited while they processed my test scores. The girl helping me thought the agency would be impressed. She screens all their applicants and knows their requirements. She sends me down to her boss, who's supposedly eager to meet with me, but when I get there, the lady looks shocked, like there's something about me she hadn't expected. And *then* she tells me they're happy to have me on the books but not to expect any work because they have more girls than jobs."

A couple of young men appeared from between two buildings. Harry watched, thinking he recognized one.

"They wanted you and then they didn't?" he asked Denise.

"Yeah."

No. He didn't know the kid. Or the girls walking toward him, either. Glancing back, he surveyed the distance he'd covered. There was no one.

"And it was *after* they saw you," he clarified, his mind racing.

"Yeah."

"You think it's because you're black?"

"What else could it be?"

"Well, whatever the issue is," he said, "this Chelsea obviously didn't know about it since she took you there."

"So whatever's going on, you're guessing she's not aware of it?"

"Either that, or the temp agency is nothing more than it seems and this girl just happens to work there."

"So we're back to thinking they're all going to the doctor's office?"

He shrugged. Maybe Daniel Boyd could figure this one out.

"You didn't recognize anyone else at the agency did you?" he asked instead. "See anyone we've seen at the frat house?"

"No," Denise said slowly. "But I went in early and there was no one else there."

Right. So it *could* be the temp agency the girls were going to. And even if it was, that might just mean one or other of them had passed on a legitimate job tip, as Chelsea had done with Denise. But that didn't mean they weren't also doing something else when they *weren't* working.

By the time they arrived back at work, Laura was numb.

"I'll see you tomorrow," she told Kelly as the other woman dropped her at her truck. Laura had already called in; she was taking the afternoon off.

"Are you sure you don't want me to come with you? I feel terrible, Laura. I wish I'd never gone there. I considered talking to Harry but it didn't seem right for me to do that."

Laura nodded. "It's okay," she lied. "I'm glad you told me."

"Just remember, Harry's under a lot of stress. And…he loves you."

Laura nodded again. She had to see her husband. To try to make some kind of sense out of a life that had gone completely wrong.

"Where are you?"

Harry glanced around the nearly deserted student union. "Having lunch," he said into the cell phone, his heart pounding since he'd recognized Laura's number on caller ID.

A phone call from his wife in the middle of the day wasn't good. Not these days.

"Where?"

Her cold, almost demanding tone threw him. He could find hardly any resemblance to the woman he loved. "The food court."

"Would you please stay there?"

"Yes." He was out of class for the day. He'd been thinking about his father-in-law. Knowing that higher-ranking members of the church had organizational meetings on Wednesday evenings, he'd parked outside the church after tae kwon do the night before. He'd seen Leonard Clark's car there, but not the BMW he'd followed earlier in the day.

Daniel Boyd had traced the BMW to a member of his in-laws' church. Richard Sammon. A prominent Tucson attorney with no record. Daniel was going to the man's downtown office that afternoon, intending to show him the picture they had of the unknown kid and ask who he was. He was also going to check out every establishment in the building on High Street.

He'd told Harry not to tip off his father-in-law at this

point. They agreed that, if her parents were somehow involved with this nightmare, Laura was probably safer with them than anywhere else.

Safer, but the less she knew, the better. Just in case she said anything to them.

And this afternoon, at Daniel Boyd's suggestion, Harry was calling the temporary agency to hire a young woman to computerize all his teaching files, although he had no intention of giving up his old manila folders. He was to have her fill out a form, including her social security number, presumably for college funding.

Once the girl was hired, Daniel would follow up on her social security number, access whatever private records he could hack his way into, and try to find some connection between her and any known member of the Ivory Nation.

Expecting a ten-minute wait—the time it would take Laura to get from the Botanical Gardens to the university—Harry nearly jumped out of his seat when he heard her voice behind him a moment later.

He thought she'd said his name. When he stood to face her, he wasn't sure she'd spoken at all. Her eyes were shadowed, closed to him, as she studied him. The experience was completely unfamiliar. Tragic.

"Are you having an affair?"

Harry gasped. *"What?"* Laura's look, her tone, her question, were surreal.

"Kelly came to your office on Monday and saw you kissing a young black woman."

He'd wanted to die many times over the past six weeks, but never as badly as he did right then.

Standing there in the almost deserted student union, he stared at the woman he loved, opened his mouth to speak—and couldn't come up with a single word.

"It's true, then." Her brows drew together, the first crack in this new, foreign demeanor, and Harry's heart tore yet again.

Reaching out to her, he intended to put his arm around her shoulders and guide her outside, someplace they could talk privately. His hand hung in mid-air instead, as she stepped away from him.

"We need to talk, Laura," Harry said, willing to do anything to take the pain out of Laura's eyes. To give her whatever she wanted, whenever she wanted it, for the rest of his life. "Will you please come to my office with me?"

"Is that where you take all your women, Harry?"

He deserved that. "Please?"

He thought she might refuse, but then she looked away and nodded.

The walk back was completely silent. Harry surveyed the surrounding area every step of the way to see if anyone was watching them. And while he stayed close enough to come to her aid if necessary, he was careful not to even brush the back of his hand against hers.

In his office, she declined to sit. And glanced at him pointedly when he closed the door.

"I'm not going to lie to you," Harry started in immediately, sinking into the chair behind his desk. "I let things get out of hand."

He hated to see the way her eyes just deadened when he said that.

"I'm not proud of myself," he continued. "I knew at the time I was making a mistake." How could he explain something to her that he didn't understand himself? "It wasn't a man-woman thing, Laura. Not really. I didn't have any sexual feelings for her."

"You can't very easily have sex without them, Harry." Her voice was dry, filled with sarcasm.

"We didn't have sex."

She drew back. "I asked if you were having an affair and you didn't say no." Coming from some women the statement might have sounded accusatory. From Laura, it spoke of confusion.

"We kissed," he said. "Just like Kelly said. Here in this office. On Monday. One kiss."

"And that was it?"

"Of course. I love you with all my heart, Laura. You know that. It's not ever going to change."

Her eyes filled with tears and Harry couldn't stay seated any longer. He went to her, pulling her into his arms, holding on—a drowning man who knows he's doomed, but grabs that last piece of driftwood anyway.

"Who was she?" Laura knew she should go. And she would. Soon. There were still so many things standing between her and Harry. His refusal to let her move home. His obsession with playing detective. The possibility of his having left that note in her truck.

White supremacists who wanted them apart.

The secrets and worries and threats that would never

be different. His black skin. Her white skin. And people who, for reasons of their own, weren't willing to let her and Harry live together in peace.

The baby she carried—and might keep, in spite of its parentage.

"Denise Marshall."

"The grad student you're always talking about?" Laura had never been jealous of the girl before. She didn't like the feeling now.

What Harry told her next depressed her even more. The valorous young woman was not only encouraging Harry in his quest, she'd joined it.

While Laura was hiding away at her parents' house. Pregnant with the enemy's child.

Leaving the office after his meeting with Laura, Harry checked in with Daniel and heard that a pair of size-eleven hiking boots of the same brand worn by David Jefferson and other Ivory Nation brothers, had been purchased a month before the rape. The clerk recalled that a young man had come in with Jefferson but paid cash for the boots. The clerk couldn't remember what the guy looked like, only that he was a little shorter than Jefferson.

But it was a start.

Harry set out for another night's work.

It didn't take Harry long to hire a college student from the temporary agency to work on the computer in his office on Friday morning. Boyd had installed recording devices, both voice and video, where they wouldn't be seen. Just in case.

Miller's call came just as Daniel finished. The detective was needed at the station. Not liking the expression on his face as he'd hurried out, Harry waited for the young woman to arrive and was completing his instructions to her when his own cell rang and he received a similar summons.

Daniel Boyd wanted him to come to the station immediately. His tone of voice said the news wasn't good. Harry left the young woman to her job, hoping she'd leave some trace of illegal doings in his office over the next few days, and drove down to meet Laura at the station.

"What do you mean Jefferson's been released?" Harry's chair crashed to the floor behind him as he stood, hands on the table, and leaned toward Miller. "How? Why?"

Laura could hear the hissing intake and release of Harry's breath, could see his arms shaking as they held his weight.

"What the hell's going on here?" he hollered, slamming the table. He paced the small room. Back and forth.

Laura watched him. And the detectives. Wondering what Robert Miller had learned about the anti-abortion threat. He'd never called her about it. Neither had Daniel Boyd.

Boyd's usually jaded eyes reminded her of the look she'd seen in her husband's eyes a time or two. Miller, on the other hand, acted as though this was all in a day's work.

· Which, to be fair, it had to be. He probably saw this kind of thing on a regular basis. And had to go home to his wife and kids and maintain an everyday life. A sense of normalcy.

He couldn't get caught up in the dramas he witnessed at work. The out-of-control emotions of victims. Or criminals.

"What happened?" she asked calmly, but with more volume than usual. She didn't feel calm at all.

"Jefferson's attorney moved to suppress the voice recognition identification."

"Why?" Harry yelled, turning around to face them, still breathing far too heavily.

Laura prayed he'd stay away from the table, beyond hitting distance of Robert Miller—the bearer of the news.

"One of those technicalities that give the defendant's rights precedence over the victim's."

"What the fuck does that mean?" Harry fumed.

"I walked Jefferson through the room while you were sitting there. A victim cannot see the defendant in custody before identification. It's prejudicial."

"That's bullshit! I didn't name him in a lineup. And I didn't *see* his voice."

Miller shrugged. He hadn't looked at Laura since the explanation began. Boyd remained uncharacteristically silent. He didn't seem well. Maybe he was coming down with something.

"Like I said," he muttered, "one of those technicalities. The law's the law and it all depends on how the judge calls it."

"You saw me there before you brought him in." Harry's voice held such barely contained anger she didn't even recognize it.

Miller, standing his ground on the other side of the table, shook his head. "Of course I didn't."

"You were in the hall when Detective Boyd opened the door…" Harry began.

Laura saw a silent exchange between Boyd and Harry and didn't understand it.

"You were looking straight at me," Harry insisted to Miller.

"From how far away?" Miller asked.

"Forty feet."

"I'd lost a contact lens that morning. Couldn't see squat if it was more than a few feet away. And when I saw Daniel, he told me you hadn't arrived yet."

"That was before I'd brought him up," Boyd said. "Listen, this whole thing is unfortunate and we look like fools here, but pointing fingers isn't going to do a damn thing for any of us." He turned to Laura and Harry. "Detective Miller and I offer our sincerest apologies to both of you."

"There was other evidence," Laura said, feeling hotter and hotter as she sat there. She wasn't safe. Not anywhere. The man who'd raped her had just walked out the station door—free to find her again anytime he chose. And the police were apologizing.

"All the other evidence is circumstantial," Miller explained. "It's not convincing enough to give the state a chance of winning."

"What is this, a game?" Harry boomed. "You talk

about winning! We're talking about our lives here, Detective!"

"There's such a thing as double jeopardy, Mr. Kendall," Detective Boyd said, still seated across from Laura. "If the state puts Jefferson on trial and loses, double jeopardy attaches and he can't be tried again. Dismissing the charges gives us a chance to collect more evidence, to build a stronger case, so that when the state goes to trial again, we'll get a conviction."

Which all made perfect sense. Except that it meant she had to walk out of there into a darkness worse than death. One fact had become very very clear. If David Jefferson wanted to find her, he would. And when he did, he'd do anything else he wanted to.

The justice system had shown the man he was invincible.

Tony Littleton was aware that, although he was Bobby Donahue's chosen one, the rest of the brothers in the Ivory Nation didn't respect him much. And he couldn't blame them. He was better with his mind than his body. He adored Luke, and the baby clung to him in meetings. Making him more of a woman than a man.

He'd just had his first lay in this, his nineteenth year.

And the shoelaces in his boots were still the staid, very telling black that had come with the boots.

But Bobby saw a man in him. And now he was finally going to become one. A man who didn't follow the brotherhood's code was weak.

One of the brethren had broken code. Acted on his own cognizance. But not Tony. He'd obeyed the orders of his immediate superior. Bobby would praise him for having done so. And now he'd show Bobby—his leader—that he wasn't weak. He would complete this job.

Hands shaking as he loaded the pistol, identical to one registered in another person's name, Tony ran the plan through his mind one more time. Take the target out with one shot. Plant the gun. Let the nigger take the fall.

He got hard thinking about it. Just like Bobby had said. He'd never steer Tony wrong.

And, after tonight, he'd be all man in Bobby Donahue's eyes.

24

"Thank God you're home." Thrusting her tongue in David's mouth, she kissed him deeply, grabbing his penis at the same time. "I missed you, baby. I was so afraid for you. They've never left a brother in for so long. What happened?"

"He turned on me."

She flew back, off his body, off the bed. "What do you mean? Turned on you? You'd be dead if he had!"

"I'm telling you, he denied me."

"Why'd they let you go then?"

"Things had already been set in motion. I had to tell my attorney about the tainted voice ID and it took time to get a motion through using the normal route."

"He's got a contract on you, then."

"Probably."

He didn't seem worried at all. She had to throw up. If he wasn't here to protect her…

To keep her in the loop…

How was she ever going to get her son?

* * *

"I visited Richard Sammon this afternoon. He claims he's never seen the mystery kid before in his life." Boyd spoke softly to Harry as they left the interrogation room. Miller was walking ahead of them with Laura.

His blood running cold, Harry hung back, keeping pace with the detective as Laura walked ahead. "He lied."

"It would seem so."

"Because he's involved."

"Probably."

Filled with an almost irrational urgency to get Laura to safety, Harry caught up with her. Jefferson could've waited outside the station when they'd let him go earlier, could be watching for them to emerge.

And if they managed to get away from the station undetected by Jefferson or his supremacist buddies, they couldn't go home. Or to Harry's office. Or the Gardens. Everyone would know how to find them at any of those places.

Miller would know.

Kelly wasn't safe. She was too close to Laura. At this point, the Nation would have people watching everyone they knew.

Ivory Nation members were clearly on to Denise, so he couldn't go to her.

And leaving town wasn't a safe option, either. The only way out of Tucson was over long, deserted highways through the desert.

Which left his in-laws. They might take drastic measures to save their daughter from what they saw as certain hell. From Harry. But they wouldn't allow her to be hurt if they could help it. They had what they wanted—with a white baby thrown in as a bonus.

Laura was their life.

With them she'd be safe. While he and Daniel Boyd figured out what they were going to do next.

"I'll follow you home if you like," Robert Miller said to Laura as he walked them to the door of the station. He'd completely ignored Harry since they'd left the interrogation room. A good move on his part, in Harry's estimation.

"No, thanks." Laura moved closer to Harry. "I'll be fine."

"You will be," Daniel Boyd said. "Jefferson isn't off the hook yet, and he knows it. All the state needs is a little more evidence. He's going to stay as far away from the two of you as he can."

"Bullshit," Harry said to both of them, managing to send Boyd a quick, knowing glance. "The man's a white supremacist, a hate-filled bastard who'd give his life for his insane cause in a heartbeat. He's not going to care about the cost to himself if he thinks he's working for the greater good."

Laura's hand slid into his. She was shaking. Harry cursed himself for not holding his tongue. He'd just scared the hell out of his wife.

Yet, under the circumstances, that wasn't all bad. They'd both have to be fully conscious every second of every day if they hoped to stay out of David Jefferson's clutches.

The hater had a personal grudge against them now.

* * *

"Leave your truck here."

Grabbing her arm, Harry didn't give Laura much of a choice. With more haste than kindness, he ushered her into the passenger seat of his car, hurrying around to climb in beside her. They were out of the parking lot before she'd even fully secured her belt.

Harry leaned over, opened the glove box, pulled out his pistol and left it on his seat.

Terrified—of everything but her husband—Laura stared out the window.

This was crazy. Insanity. She was a rape victim. Period.

So why did it feel as though they were running for their lives?

"Harry, you're scaring me. What's going on?"

Reaching over, he took her hand, squeezing it and then holding it in his on the console between them. "I need time to think. Nothing makes sense."

She swallowed. "Harry, I'm going to ask you something and I want a *yes* or *no* answer, okay? Then I'll explain and we can talk about it."

His jaw tight, he said, "Go ahead."

"Did you leave a note on the passenger seat of my truck on Monday?"

"No." His knuckles were white, the pulse in his neck more pronounced.

"It was there when I got off work," she said slowly, feeling heat, and then cold crawling up her body. "White typing paper, folded in a square. In capital, cut-out letters, it said *do not abort.*"

His silence was difficult to take, but she knew she deserved it. This was Harry. The other half of her. No matter how things looked, she should have trusted him. She *knew* this man, and yet she'd turned her back on him.

She spoke into the silence. "At first I thought it came from the second rapist, but the truck was locked and the door hadn't been jimmied. Miller said, based on the number of people who knew about the baby and those who had access to my truck, that it could be you. He said you might have done it to scare me into staying with my parents."

"And you believed him."

Not completely. She just hadn't *not* believed him.

"You've got a gun on the seat next to you, Harry," she said, as though that explained it all. It was only one of the many things he'd done over the past weeks that she would never have believed him capable of doing. "What happened that night…it changed us both."

Harry continued to make turns, to watch his mirrors. She had no idea where they were going. And didn't much care. Harry's car was a sanctuary at the moment, a place of safety.

A place to collect herself, to open her eyes. To think. To return to the woman she was—strong, intelligent, honest. A peacemaker, yet willing to take on the world for the right to live by her heart. Harry Kendall's lover. His wife.

"He sent the note to forensics," she said. "At least he said he was going to. I never heard back from him on it. I expected him to say something this morning, but he didn't."

"Could take a week or more, depending on how backed up they are in the lab."

That was more like the Harry she knew. Logical. Fair.

"He didn't think it came from the rapist, though, Harry. How could the guy have gotten in the car? And how could he have known about the baby?"

"He could have known from someone at the clinic. Supremacists are infiltrating all walks of life, Laura, spreading through this country like an epidemic, assisted by the fact that they're largely undetected. Ever since 9/11, this country has been ruled by fear. That fear is understandable, but it does crazy things to people."

He was right. Oh, God, he was so right.

"Everybody's afraid. Governors and politicians and lawyers and doctors, the supermarket check-out girl and the guy next door. They want to close the doors to keep themselves safe."

She'd missed this man so much. She hated what he was saying, but knew down to her very core, that he spoke the truth. He understood.

She understood something, too. Harry wasn't just talking about the other guy. He was telling her about himself.

"I don't think it's Barnes. Why would he care if I aborted a rapist's baby?" she asked quietly.

"It's a white baby," Harry told her what she already knew.

"But he almost seemed to encourage me to terminate the pregnancy."

He glanced at her, his eyes shadowed, tired. "I know.

Which is why I think our guy is from the clinic, like Jefferson, and accessed your records."

"But how would he get in my car?"

"Again, I have no idea. I'm not up on auto breaking and entering."

He made another turn.

"Where are we going?" she finally asked.

"You're going back to your parents' house. You'll be safe there."

"No, Harry. I want to be with you."

"I'll come over late tonight, honey, I promise. I need you, too. But we have to trick these guys into thinking that you're with your folks, not with me."

Harry's gun sat there on the seat, a symbol of the cold, hard, frightening place the world had become.

"Hey, you still at work?"

"Hello, Dan. It's only five o'clock. Of course I'm still here. What do you need?"

He knew what Jess meant. It was always about him. And his needs. It always had been.

Which was why she'd divorced him. He got that now.

"You know I love you, don't you, Jess? As much as I love anyone?"

"What's going on, Daniel?"

"Nothing." He thought about the rapist who'd gone free. The people he himself had failed. The woman on the other end of the line.

Whatever it took, he was going to get Jefferson.

"Don't bullshit me, Daniel. Not after all this time."

"No, really, Jess," he said, one hand on the wheel as

he took a forty-degree curve without slowing down. "I just realized it's been ages since I told you how I feel about you."

"Daniel Boyd, if you're out getting yourself killed, I'll never forgive you. Not ever. You get that?"

"Yeah."

He'd given up on forgiveness a long time ago.

Harry couldn't get the note in Laura's truck out of his mind. Or the fact that Boyd hadn't told him about it. Just as Boyd had told him not to tell anyone about their little agreement. Their partnership.

Too many secrets.

Not enough answers.

And a rapist was free tonight.

DO NOT ABORT. The words kept playing across his mind as he drove from Laura's parents' home across town to the university. So did the possibility that Daniel Boyd had thrown the voice ID. He said he'd told Miller before he brought Harry up that Harry wasn't in the room. But what if his timing had been a little off? What if, in actuality, he'd done that after having left Harry in the room with the two-way mirror.

His heart jumped painfully in his chest when his cell phone rang. Laura was on her way to a black-tie fundraiser with her parents. They'd told her about it when he'd dropped her off earlier, saying they'd bought her a ticket.

It was Denise.

"Denise, hi."

"I stopped in your office after five to check up on

the temp, like you asked," the younger woman said. "There was nothing of any use on either the tape recorder or the video.

"She had no visitors and made no phone calls, just sat at the computer all day," the girl reported. "You'd be getting your money's worth if you really wanted those files computerized. Over half the files are done already and there was nothing incriminating lying around or in the trash."

The bright sun reflecting off the cars in front of him made his head hurt. "So it was a total bust."

"I doubt it means anything to us, but I checked the Internet history on the computer she was using. There was a Web site I didn't recognize so I pulled it up."

"And?"

"Completely filling the screen was the photo of a young blond woman. A naked blond woman. She was sitting, facing the camera, her knees bent and her legs spread. She was licking her finger."

The girl was looking at Internet pornography? "You're sure she had no visitors?"

"He would've had to be invisible and silent."

"Okay, so we have a girl who's into porn."

"It's more than that." Denise paused and Harry waited. "The girl on the screen was your temp, Harry. I saw her this afternoon. And when I looked over the site, I recognized several of the other women from the pictures you took at the frat house."

"You're positive."

"Absolutely. They're running an Internet pornography site at the frat house, Harry."

"It's not my cup of tea, but it's also not illegal." So maybe he'd been wasting his time over there, after all.

Maybe Daniel Boyd knew that.

Maybe that was why Boyd had let him "help." To keep him occupied with a wild-goose chase.

"You ever been on one of those sites, Dr. Kendall?"

"No."

"I took that Internet security course last year, and they said these independent sites are a dime a dozen. They're not big moneymakers. The big money is in prostitution, mostly because it is illegal, and those porn sites are infamous for providing the hookup."

"So maybe that's where the temp agency comes in," Harry said, thinking out loud. "Men hire a temp from a legitimate agency and for a little extra they get to have sex with her, too."

"That possibility occurred to me, too."

Harry felt the adrenaline start to surge through his body as he started to believe that they were finally on to something real.

"I think I'll give that girl a call. See if she's busy tonight."

"Be careful, Dr. Kendall…"

Careful had disappeared from his vocabulary the night two fiends broke into his home and violated his wife. What a campus prostitution ring could possibly have to do with Laura's rape he had no idea, but maybe he'd get some answers tonight.

"Where are you going?" She might not even have known David was leaving the apartment if she hadn't come out of the bath when she had. He was supposed to join her there and she'd gotten tired of waiting.

Dressed in black, including the boots with the red laces, David had a hand on the doorknob.

"There's a fundraiser tonight. For Moss."

"And you're going dressed like that?"

"I stopped by the clinic today," he said, his gaze hard as he stared at her. "I had to know one way or the other if I'm out."

"And?"

"I am. I no longer have a job. But while I was there, I looked up a medical record on a hunch."

"And?"

"There's a woman. A white woman. I had sex with her six weeks ago. She's six weeks pregnant."

Other than during his jail time, he'd slept with her every night for almost a year—periods and all.

And he'd had other women as well? The idea shouldn't surprise her. Shouldn't hurt.

He was her jailor. Her rapist. How could she care?

"And?" She tried for as much dignity as she could manage standing there completely nude.

"She's going to be at the fundraiser."

His eyes took on a familiar gleam.

"No, David! You can't just take her from there."

"Why not? I took you, didn't I? Right from under the nose of the great Bobby Donahue."

"Only because he trusted you to kill me."

"The bitch might be carrying my son," David said. "I want what's mine."

Heart clutching with a fear so familiar she could

almost ignore it, she tried to think. Sex, the offer of a future child, wasn't going to serve her here. And then, as though God Himself had spoken to her—just as Bobby Donahue so often claimed had happened to him—she realized something.

"The fundraiser. For Moss, you said. Is Bobby going to be there?"

Eyes narrowed, Jefferson nodded.

The basis of Moss's entire campaign was family values. Her heart started to pound. *This was it.* The opportunity she'd been waiting for.

With a clarity she hadn't experienced in too many months to count, she followed the racing thoughts in her mind.

"Is it for families?" Moss would do something like that. Have a hundred-dollar-a-plate dinner and expect people to bring their children—and *pay* for their children. He'd use the funds to hire cameramen to catch cute moments for the late-night news.

"Yes."

She could hardly breathe. But she kept a straight face. Stayed calm.

Luke would be there.

"You're sure she's attending?"

"Her name's on the guest list."

"Then let me help you."

He paused, staring at her. "How?"

"This is a family gathering. You don't want to risk the lives of any of the little white boys who'll be there."

"Of course not."

"So you have to get this woman out of the ballroom."

They had to get her out because David would never get in.

"Of course. My name will be off the guest list," he said with heavy irony.

"That's where I come in."

The plan came to her as she spoke. But it was good. More importantly, Jefferson bought it.

After the longest year of her life, she was going to get her chance.

By bedtime tonight, her son would be safe.

25

"Why didn't you tell me this fundraiser was for George Moss?" Dressed in a black cocktail-length dress with cap sleeves and tailored bodice, a dress that was better suited to her mother than to her, Laura leaned closer to Sharon. Her mother was sitting on her right, between Laura and Len. Where she'd spent most of her life.

"Would you have come if I had?" Sharon whispered back, a smile on her face as she listened to Richard Sammon, a commodities attorney with a high-rise downtown office, hold forth on the vagaries of the stock market from across the table.

Of course she wouldn't, Laura answered silently, gluing a social smile on her face, too, encompassing Moss and his wife in her glance. Her parents had been invited to sit at the head table, with the guest of honor, much to Laura's disgust. There were still two empty seats, between Moss and Sammon. She'd heard Sammon tell Moss that two people called Bobby and

Luke were going to be late, that Bobby had been caught up in some business deal.

The good news was that Robert Miller, his wife and their oldest daughter were also at their table for twelve. They weren't close enough for Laura to be able to speak with any of them, but as the evening began— promptly at seven as the program claimed—she sat back, smiled at the very sweetly dressed Miller child and prepared to grit her teeth, thankful, at least, that she was safe.

She'd told David she had to check out the ladies' room. It was part of the plan. Get Laura Kendall to the bathroom, even if she had to find a way to spill something on the other woman's dress. And once there, she'd grab the woman, restrain her long enough to get her out to David's car. Dressed in the hotel's wait-staff uniform—compliments of a picked lock on a laundry room door—she dashed up a back flight of stairs to a pay phone in the elegantly appointed, marble-tiled lobby.

She knew the number by heart. If he still had the same one.

"Green."

"Is this Simon Green? Flagstaff, Arizona? Ex-FBI?"

"Who's calling?" As soon as she heard the guarded question, she knew it was him.

"You remember a bar called the Museum Club?" She'd worked there a year ago. Seemed more like a lifetime.

"Been there a time or two."

Glancing furtively around, she kept her voice low and her head bent. She wondered if Simon Green had ever talked to a ghost before.

"I helped you out once," she whispered.

"Go on."

"I need your help now."

"I'm listening."

She thought she heard a child's laughter in the background. And a woman's voice. And started to shake. She could do this. *Had* to do it.

She named the upscale Tucson resort where she was standing. "You know where it is?"

"Yes." Thank God for that.

"The prey you want is here tonight," she said. She was Luke's only hope. "Have someone here at 8:45 and I'll make certain you see something that'll stick in court." And she'd pray to God the cops got their timing right and saved Laura Kendall, too. She was planning to use David's escape route. To rush past him with the baby, forcing him to go inside to get his prey. If the police showed up just when everything was happening, Jefferson would be stopped. She had no interest in delivering the poor woman into that bastard's hands. But her priority was Luke—and escape.

"What do you get out of it?"

"My son. Whoever's doing your looking better not see me or the deal's off."

At least until after she had Luke stashed someplace where he could grow up safe.

After that Bobby's men could kill her if they needed to.

* * *

His legs were cramped, he was sweating like a pig, but otherwise, Tony Littleton felt no pain. Hidden in the bushes in front of Jefferson's apartment building, he was prepared to wait for as long as it took. He could see the big bamboo plant in the window. Jefferson would be back.

There was more than ten-thousand dollars at the base of that plant.

And when he arrived, Tony would be ready.

His finger on the trigger.

She watched the clock from the wings of the stage set up in the ballroom. David was out in the car waiting. Simon Green would be calling in his army. In a little over an hour, she'd be taking the ten or so steps to cross behind Laura Kendall's chair with a bowl of raspberry sauce in her hand.

Thank God for seating charts and place cards....

She saw that Luke's chair was still empty.

At seven-thirty, Moss stood behind the brightly lit podium in the cavernous room, and welcomed everyone to the evening's festivities.

"We've got some great news tonight," the impeccably dressed man said, his gaze taking in the entire room.

Laura missed whatever that great news was when a nice-looking young man, moving with a cougar's grace, approached their table with a toddler perched on his hip.

There was something about the combination of a tux and a toddler that spoke to Laura. As quietly as possible, the brown-haired man slid into his seat, settling the toddler in the booster seat that had appeared like magic from behind him and was placed in the chair to his left.

The little guy with big brown eyes didn't make a sound. He didn't reach for anything on the table, either, leaving Laura to wonder if he was sick. Those tiny hands were far too lifeless for a guy his size.

Pulling a sippy cup out of a black leather satchel, the missing Bobby—or so Laura presumed—set it on the table in front of the toddler, catching Laura's eye as he did so.

He smiled at her, and in spite of herself, she smiled back.

Daniel Boyd's phone rang before he made it out to his car as he left the station Friday evening.

Recognizing the Flagstaff number he picked up.

"Yeah."

"Nice talking to you, too, man." Simon Green's easy banter was loud in his ear.

Simon Green reminded him of failure. They'd never found the young woman who'd been suspected dead and then suddenly sighted in Tucson the year before.

She'd had Ivory Nation connections…

Daniel's blood singed his veins. "You know something."

It would be too much of coincidence otherwise. A call, on this day, from this man. A day he'd had to set another Ivory Nation member free.

"I know lots," Simon said, then quickly added, "She's there in town." He mentioned the hotel. "She

said if you get there by 8:45 she'll hand you Donahue.
But you have to let her go."

"She wanted for anything in Flag?"

"Not that I've heard."

"I don't know of any reason to hold her, either."
Neither one of them, of course, planned to look for any
such reason.

"She's planning to abduct her son from Donahue."

Shit. "The kid's there."

"Yeah. Get them out alive.

In his office, Harry dialed the number that Carrie,
the temp, had given him so he could tell her what time
he wanted her in the morning. Five minutes later, he
had a date, for the sum of two hundred dollars, to go
out with her the next evening. He reached for the phone
to call Daniel Boyd, to let the detective know his plans,
and then stopped. He remembered the two cops making
excuses for Jefferson's release. And telling his wife to
keep key information from him. The secret partnership. Boyd's claims that Jefferson was clean. The detective wasn't who he'd thought. Harry was on his own
again.

Turning to the computer, Harry quickly found the
Web site Denise had told him about. And went down a
list of names such as Pippy and Sunshine and Carly, all
with accompanying thumbnails of brightly painted perfectly sculpted female faces. Many of them he recognized from his hours of surveillance.

Nothing was as it seemed. *Nothing.* College students
working as prostitutes on the side? God-fearing church-

loving in-laws who'd hurt their daughter to save her? A cop gone bad. A society that wouldn't let him live in peace with the woman he loved.

Harry didn't want to accept any of it.

Bored before the speeches had even begun, Laura wished she could join some of the other guests in a glass of wine. Her parents would never approve, but at this point, their disapproval wouldn't have stopped her. The baby she was carrying did.

Bobby—both George Moss and Richard Sammon had called him that—was a charming, intelligent man. And a wonderfully attentive father. Laura could hardly keep her eyes off little Luke. She felt drawn to the child, with his elfin cheeks and faraway eyes. He looked, somehow, as though he knew secrets he wasn't telling her.

Or maybe it was just that the conversation around her involved things she couldn't care less about. Between the speeches there were brief intervals of chatter, and she found her attention drifting. Even Detective Miller—who was at their table at the specific request of her parents—was full of praise for Moss's policies.

It was 8:48 and so far they'd only made it through two speeches on the program.

"So what you have before you…" She tuned in to the elderly gentleman standing at the microphone, trying to remember who he was. His lengthy introduction had been more than twenty minutes before. And his was only the second name on the list.

"And I repeat…"

"Ah!" Laura jumped back—and up—as cool red gooey liquid streamed past her shoulder and over her left breast.

"I'm sorry! I'm so sorry," the young waitress exclaimed, a tipped-over bowl on the floor as she ducked to wipe at the mess she'd made. "Here, let me help you! Let me get you to the bathroom."

Chaos broke out as everyone at the table came to Laura's rescue. Bobby made it to her side first. With a wet wipe from his black leather satchel he began to sponge at her shoulder, in spite of Laura's protests.

"Oh, Mr. Donahue, you're prepared for anything!" Sharon Clark exclaimed in the self-deprecating tone of voice Laura hated.

"It's okay, really," she said, when the man's cloth moved lower. Turning, she looked for the young woman who'd offered to escort her to the bathroom. Not because she needed assistance, but because she didn't know where it was.

The girl was nowhere to be seen.

And five seconds later, another burst of frenzied activity broke out when someone noticed that little Luke Donahue was missing as well.

Leaving the pandemonium in the ballroom, Laura hurried out into the hall, searching for a bathroom. Her dress was soaked, sticking to her. And she smelled like raspberries.

"Right this way." An arm came around her shoulders.

Her heart froze. Her breath froze. She punched back with her elbows for all she was worth.

God, no.

She knew that voice.

No!

Harry. Harry!

She screamed, but no sound came out. Dug in her heels and fell out of her shoes as the arms around her, like bands of steel, pushed her along the carpeted floor. Stumbling, she fell to her knees and was lifted right off the ground and against a chest she'd felt once before.

"No!" Laura's throat burned with the force of the word. She clawed and kicked. Bit the hand at her shoulder. Squirmed so hard she pulled a muscle in her stomach. "No!" she screamed again, with only the vacant hallway to hear her.

A child was missing. No one had time for a thirty-one-year-old pregnant woman who was supposed to be on her way to the ladies' room.

Laura had no idea where he was taking her. Shivering, dizzy, sick to her stomach she sat hunched over the ropes tying her to the seat of the little sports car. She wasn't going to give in this time. Wasn't going to lie there while this man took things from her that didn't belong to him.

She'd die first.

Because this time around, she knew what came after the rape. And she couldn't go through that again.

Harry. Dear God, Harry.

With tears streaming down her cheeks, she hiccupped and prayed that her husband would never find out what happened to her that night.

* * *

Mass confusion abounded as Daniel reached the foyer of the ballroom complex in the hotel Simon Green had sent him to.

Waylaying a harried security agent, he demanded to know what was going on.

"A kid's missing. Three years old. Disappeared into thin air."

Luke Donahue. She'd succeeded. Good for her.

Catching a glimpse of Robert Miller on the opposite side of the room, seemingly organizing a search party, Daniel's gut started to kick into gear, telling him that something was very, very wrong. He knew Miller's politics. Didn't care about them one way or the other. But to have the man here tonight, when Bobby Donahue was down from Tucson with his son...

What about Donahue? Pushing his way through the crowd, Daniel found the Ivory Nation leader doubled over in a chair, surrounded by the well-known and wealthy of Tucson society. In the middle of them all, fawning over the man as though he were Adonis himself, was Sharon Clark.

And Daniel felt sick all over again. With frantic eyes he scanned the other women in the crowd, hoping to find Laura Kendall. She'd left a message, telling him she was going to be with her parents at a fundraiser that evening. She'd said she was afraid for Harry and asked Daniel to keep an eye on him.

She was nowhere to be seen.

And Harry Kendall suspected that her parents were somehow involved with the rape. The same people who were right now tending to the leader of Arizona's most powerful white supremacist organization.

All they needed now was for David Jefferson to show up.

"Mr. Clark." Daniel sought out her father. "Have you seen Laura?"

"She's in the ladies' room," Leonard said, his face pinched as he raised his voice to be heard over the chaos. At least David Jefferson was nowhere in evidence.

Daniel swerved through the masses of people swarming around the room, talking in frenzied groups. Accidentally tipping over a serving table filled with half-eaten desserts on his way, he was out in the hall, breaking into a run as he followed signs to the rest-rooms.

Calling out a warning, Daniel didn't even slow down as he entered the ladies' room, taking stock of the empty stalls in a matter of seconds and was back out the door, seeking any other restrooms in the vicinity.

Fifteen minutes later, with a pair of dress pumps in hand, he put a call into the precinct and went to track down his partner.

He had no proof, but Daniel knew, just as surely as he knew the sun would rise in the morning, that Laura Kendall had been abducted.

Finished in his office, thinking of his wife enjoying a five-star meal with her parents, Harry made his way over to the frat house. He couldn't lose a chance to spot the young man who was so mysteriously eluding identification.

He'd never seen him at the frat house on Friday nights. But there was always a possibility.

And doing something was better than sitting at home alone.

He had a lot of time to think, sitting there in the dark. To ponder his nineteen years of life. The things he believed in, what he'd accomplished. The strides he'd made in becoming the man he was born to be.

As always, his thoughts began to weave around the event that *was* life to him. His penis hard and sliding inside warm velvety softness. He'd only gone in twice, but he'd replayed the event a million times, until he lost track of the number of times he'd known the body of his first lover—Laura Kendall, not the imaginary Beth he'd invented for Bobby. Laura had taken him generously. Her body clasping his, pulling him in, pulling the orgasm out of him.

He'd have her again someday. God had promised him that.

How his hand found his way to his penis, Tony didn't know; he just saw it there, rubbing up and down, when suddenly the headlights came up the drive, shining on his jeans. He couldn't be seen from the bushes. He was sure of that.

But he could see.

And he recognized the sportscar that was David Jefferson's pride and joy.

Cocking the pistol, Tony took the heavy metal into his right hand, index finger on the trigger, and rubbed it against his hard length.

It would only be a few minutes now, and he'd be a man in every sense of the word.

Dragging air into her lungs with effort, each breath costing her precious energy, Laura focused on every turn, every landmark, every face she saw on the street as the rapist drove her through Tucson. He didn't speak to her. Didn't seem to know she was there at all.

Except for the hand he had between her legs. He'd pushed her dress up around her hips when he'd thrown her in the car.

They were in an apartment complex now. Pulling into a carport. She didn't kid herself. She knew what was about to happen. And planned to kill herself before this man could rape her again.

If she had to break her own neck, she'd find a way to do it. Harry would understand.

Because neither of them would survive the aftermath of another attack.

Neither of them had survived the first one.

She knew the car came to a stop more because she heard the gear going into park than because she felt the motion cease. She was too numb. Welcomed the numbness.

He came around to her side of the car. Untied the ropes. And laid a hand on her stomach, rubbing it slowly back and forth.

"A baby," he said, almost reverently, the gleam in his eye otherworldly as he stared at her belly. "A white baby."

His eyes changed, darkened. "*My* baby."

Laura began to cry.

He didn't seem to notice the tears falling down her cheeks. Didn't even look at her face. Picking her up, holding her body against him, he slid one hand beneath her bottom, claiming ownership.

She was going to fight. To die. But not yet. Right now she had to conserve her strength.

He took a step. And then another. She couldn't think about Harry anymore. Her dear husband was part of another life. Another time.

Her tears continued to fall, but she didn't really feel sad. She didn't feel anything. Except the need to be ready. To prepare. She wasn't going to be his prey again.

She was no one's prey.

Her body didn't matter anymore. She wouldn't have a baby for this man. The rocking motion of his body as he moved toward his destination, carrying her, infiltrated her consciousness. And receded. Again and again.

With his breathing growing more labored, she knew what was in store. What he was thinking. And wanted to kill him. Right there. With her own two hands. She, the ultimate peacemaker, the lover, wanted to murder another human being.

She could taste his blood. And needed more of it. All of it. Until there was nothing left inside him. No thought. No breath. No life.

He didn't speak. She was thankful for that. Grateful that she didn't have to hear that voice—the one that had kept Harry up all those nights.

The arm behind her back moved, his hand sliding forward to cup the side of her breast. The breast he'd bruised before. It had taken weeks for the mark to fade. The purple had changed to yellow and then a lighter tan as her body slowly healed.

The pain he'd caused hadn't faded at all.

He was heading for a set of stairs. Cement. With an iron rail. She couldn't make them out clearly in the dark, but they seemed to go on and on, up too far. Or maybe just far enough for a fall.

Her body tilted as he lifted his foot. She was going to move soon. Another step or two and she'd be gone. Long before he got to the door.

The shot rang out clearly in the night. A noise so loud she forgot to breathe. And barely heard the cry that exploded from her captor's chest. And then she was falling, just as she'd known she would. Except that the ground was closer than she'd expected. And the surface she fell on was warm and solid, while the little black cocktail dress soaked up the blood.

Daniel had an APB out within the hour. He'd plastered Laura's photo on every wire and computerized distribution tool he had at his disposal. And then, with a heart too heavy to carry around, he picked up his phone to call Harry Kendall.

Harry had the right to know what was going on.

And Daniel had the obligation to stand beside the man he'd failed and do his best to hold him up.

He'd been at the frat house for a couple of hours, filling up the midi storage card on his phone. Filling it with images that were going to serve no real purpose. He already had all the evidence he needed.

Unless the nerdy kid showed up. Finding that young man had become an obsession for him.

When his phone vibrated against his hip, Harry jumped. And felt the accelerated beat of his heart as he sat there alone in the darkness. He was avoiding Boyd's calls.

It was Denise.

"Get to the nearest TV and call me back," his grad student said the second he answered.

Within ten minutes Harry was sitting in his office, his light the only one on in the four-story building. He grabbed the control to the small television that sat on his desk and called Denise back.

"Channel 12," she said.

And then stayed on the phone with him as he watched a recap of the ten o'clock news.

"An APB is out on this man…"

Harry's blood ran cold when he saw his own photo flash up on the screen.

"U of A History professor Harry Kendall is wanted in the shooting death of a campus medical student who, just today, was released on a technicality in the suspected rape of Kendall's wife earlier this summer. A pistol matching the description of one registered to Kendall was recovered at the scene and detectives say Kendall's prints are on the barrel. The man is considered dangerous. Anyone who has seen this man or knows his whereabouts, please contact Detective Robert Miller, with the Tucson police…"

"Holy shit."

Harry fell forward against the desk, his head in his hands.

Daniel called the familiar number again, swearing with frustration when he got Kendall's voice mail. And then, when he'd used up every ounce of patience he had, he dialed the numbers again and gave the commands that would activate the emergency GPS locator on the other man's phone. He couldn't wait this one out.

Depending on where he was and what he knew, a few hours might make the difference between life and death for Harry Kendall.

With a mask over her eyes and her hands tied behind her, Laura walked for what seemed like miles, constantly aware of the gun barrel jabbing her in the back.

She had no idea how far she'd come or where she was going. She wasn't even sure they were near the campus anymore.

Campus always reminded her of Harry. She needed him with her. Now.

Her feet in the torn pantyhose were raw and bleeding.

And when she finally arrived—or was allowed to stop moving—in some kind of park, when the mask was removed and she was face-to-face with this new version of captor and terror, Laura gave a cry.

"You!"

"I knew you wanted me again," the young man said, grinning. "I knew you liked it."

He'd changed her tire in the grocery-store parking

lot. And Laura knew where else he'd been, too. On top of her in the bed she'd shared with Harry.

All these weeks they'd been searching for her rapist and he'd been there all along. Watching her. Waiting. Just like Harry had said.

With a long, drawn-out wail, Laura raised her leg and kneed him in the groin.

Harry heard footsteps in the hall. For a split second, he stood in his office like a trapped animal, watching the door, quivering inside. They might walk by.

But he knew they wouldn't.

There was an alcove under his desk. He could hide there.

And be unable to defend himself.

Or he could get his pistol out of the drawer, cock the trigger and wait.

"That's it, baby. Give me some of your passion."

Laura's captor grabbed her, hauling her up against his rock-hard penis. Where he should be doubled over in pain, this man was aroused.

"Let me feel you, love," the bastard crooned in a voice that was as much little boy as it was man. "Let me feel your passion."

He raised a hand to her breast, squeezing so hard it hurt. His lips were slightly open and Laura kneed him again. She stomped her foot on his insole. Bit the forearm reaching around her. Screamed out in the dark of the night.

And when he covered her lips with his, she wanted

to die. Her hands still tied behind her back, she tried to get away from the fumbling wet tongue. She reared back, gagging, just as he swooped forward, pushing against her, and she fell to the ground.

In the middle of the desert park he fell on top of her and she started to cry.

"Hold it right there." Harry stepped out from behind his office door, gun held steadily in front of him.

"Put that thing down, Harry." Daniel Boyd didn't even flinch as he stood there, facing a bullet.

Harry's hand didn't tremble. Nor did it lower. He would not be taken to jail, locked up like some animal in a cage, while a rapist and murderer ran free.

"Jefferson's dead, Harry," Boyd said, his voice loud in the silent office.

"I know."

"Put the gun down. I'm here to help you."

"Like you helped Laura?" Harry practically spat the words, moving closer, one step at a time. "Telling her not to tell me about the abortion threat?" Another step. "They got into her truck, God damn you! And you convinced her to keep that information from me!"

"Harry, I have no idea what you're talking about."

"And you! Playing along with that voice recognition crap when you knew all along it was tainted."

Two more steps and he'd have the hard steel barrel right between Boyd's eyes.

"Just a second, Harry," Boyd's voice rose with tension. As it should. This time Harry was calling the shots. "What are you talking about, abortion threat?"

"Don't fuck with me," Harry warned. He could see the red rimming the older man's eyes.

"God damn it, Harry! I'm not fucking with you. Listen to me. I'm here to help you, you asshole. They've got Laura. They killed Jefferson and they're going to be coming after you."

Harry didn't budge an inch.

"I know how they work," Boyd continued, more urgency in his voice. "They've framed you, and now they'll kill you. You go to your grave without ever having the chance to defend yourself, and Jefferson's real killer walks away scot-free. Case closed before it's ever really opened."

He faltered. Only for a second, but long enough for the seasoned detective to make a move. To take the gun from him, turn the tables and slap handcuffs on Harry's wrists. But it didn't happen. Boyd just stood there watching him. Waiting.

"Come on, Harry. Did you hear me? They have Laura. We've don't have any time to waste."

"What do you mean, they've got Laura? She's with her parents at…"

His voice drifted off as Boyd shook his head. And told him what he knew about what happened that night.

"All I've been able to piece together," he said, "is that somehow Jefferson got hold of her when she left the ballroom to go to the bathroom. He was killed outside his apartment. There was no mention of any woman with him, but there were footprints in the dust just beyond the staircase.

"About a size seven. No shoes. The heels Laura had

been wearing were found in the back hall off the ballroom foyer."

The blood drained from Harry's face. And his fingers. The pistol, still clamped on his hand, dropped to his side.

"Come on, man." Boyd's voice was commanding. "Don't fall apart on me now. This is showtime and that woman needs you. Now tell me about the threat. In the truck."

Somehow, despite the terror in his heart, Harry told Daniel Boyd everything he knew. And, as they talked about the photo lineup, the note in Laura's truck and several other aspects of the investigation Miller had handled, the truth became clear to both of them. Daniel had suspected it when he'd seen his partner in the ballroom.

"Miller's dirty."

And Laura trusted him.

"Hold it."

Laura heard the voice, recognized it. Thanked God for it. And began to sob in relief.

She couldn't see much in the darkness. Just a form coming toward them, arms outstretched, the silhouette of a gun in his hands.

In the middle of a horrific replay of the worst night of her life, Detective Miller had recued her.

Miracles did happen.

It was the last thought she had before the gun went off.

White supremacists were known to be bold, but even Daniel was surprised to discover that Robert Miller had called in his parameters—allowing him and Harry to drive straight to the park where, according to his call, he'd spotted a man and woman struggling. Ten minutes later, with his lights off, Daniel pulled up next to Miller's car and cut the engine. Gun in hand, he was out of the car instantly and on his way to the park, with Harry right behind him.

He'd made it as far as the edge of the clearing, unsure if the shapes in the distance were people or bushes, when the shot rang out.

"Laura!" Harry Kendall's cry was anguished. "Laura!" he cried out a second time and took off running, completely unprotected, into the open field. Without a second's thought, gun at the ready, Daniel took off after him.

"Laura!" Harry's voice carried out into the night.

"Harry?" The faint cry drifted across the field. "Harry!"

"Careful," Daniel grunted, running behind the younger man as he tore across the open field, Daniel at his heels.

"Laura! Hold on, honey. I'm coming."

Prepared to see the man fly into the air with the force of the shot he expected, Daniel stared into the night, looking for a target, knowing that the Kendalls' only hope was for him to take out the shooter before the shooter got them.

As he ran, drawing closer, he watched but nothing happened. There was no gunshot. Harry didn't fall. At least, not until he reached the prone body on the ground and fell down to his knees beside it.

"Laura. Oh, my, God, baby. Laura. Talk to me, honey. I love you so much. Talk to me."

"I love you, too, Harry." The words were surprisingly strong for someone Daniel had thought he'd find dead. "I think my arm's broken," she said, trembling as she lay there, half undressed, her gaze locked on her husband.

Ripping off his shirt, Harry placed it gently over her ripped bodice, running his hand through her hair, telling her everything was going to be okay, as Daniel, still looking for his partner, grabbed his radio to call for an ambulance.

Miller must have killed Jefferson. And been in the middle of raping Laura. But who'd shot the gun he'd heard? And—

"I've got him."

Jerking around, he saw Robert Miller come through the bushes.

And there, staggering in front of the detective, bleeding heavily from a chest wound, was the young man Daniel and Harry had been seeking.

"Meet Tony Littleton," Miller said, his voice harsh. "I don't think he's going to make it."

The detective didn't sound the least bit sympathetic as Daniel called for a second ambulance.

Laura and Harry heard as much of the story as they figured they'd ever know on the news Saturday night. Tony Littleton had died in a Tucson hospital earlier that day, but not before he'd given the police a full accounting of everything that had happened recently.

He'd named David Jefferson as the sole proprietor of the prostitution ring. It was being run, Littleton claimed, to finance Jefferson's medical training.

"Daniel said the Ivory Nation was running the ring," Harry told his wife, holding her against his chest, her plastered arm resting on his stomach. He didn't think he'd ever move from the couch in their living room. He had everything he wanted right there. In his arms. "The money, along with a substantial amount of support from members of your parent's church, was funding Moss's campaign."

"And none of that will ever get out and he's going to win and go to Washington," Laura finished for him.

They'd had a long talk with her parents that afternoon at the hospital. Laura's mother had been facing arrest because of the note she'd left in Laura's truck, hoping to save her from the sin of abortion. Sharon had used the spare key Laura had given her—and forgotten about. But Laura refused to press charges. Instead, Len had insisted his wife get counseling.

Bobby Donahue had been completely exonerated. While he'd had nothing to do with Laura's rape, according to Daniel, he'd certainly been the brains behind the porn and prostitution ring. Harry could only imagine what other crimes the supremacist leader had committed… That idea left a bitter taste in Harry's mouth. And a certain amount of fear in his chest. But he wasn't going to live his life focused on the bad in the world. If Donahue ever had the gall to come after either him or Laura, Harry would be ready for him. Somehow. Some way.

But Daniel Boyd said the leader of the white suprema-cist organization was far too smart to ever get anywhere near them. One thing about Bobby Donahue that had been proven time and again was that the man never put himself in a position where he might actually get caught.

Or have to pay.

"When Daniel called, did he say whether they found Amanda or her son?" Laura asked, her voice not sleepy so much as lethargic. Content. Her uninjured hand was moving slowly back and forth over Harry's shoulder and his neck, as though she couldn't stop touching him.

"Nope," he said now, his throat vibrating against her fingers. "I guess she's pretty street savvy. Daniel figures Bobby'll catch up with her eventually, but he hopes not. For the boy's sake, if nothing else."

"He was a cute kid," Laura said. "But not a happy one. I've never seen a more disciplined toddler in my life."

The mention of a child brought an uncomfortable pang to Harry's chest, but he let it pass through him. The future would bring what it would. With both of the men who'd attacked Laura dead, he was the only father that baby would ever know.

And because it was Laura's baby, he would love this son or daughter as fiercely as he loved her.

"You're going to have to forgive your mother, you know," Harry said as a commercial came on, just as Laura was thinking about her father. About the difference between the Bobby Donahues of the world and her father who, though equally rigid in some ways, would go to great lengths to offer a kindness to another human being.

"It's going to take a while to be able to trust her again," she said now.

"She left that note out of love, afraid you were going to do something you wouldn't be able to take back, something for which you'd pay in eternity."

"I know. But she had no right to push her beliefs on me."

"I think she understands that now."

Strangely enough, Laura did, too.

Harry's parents had called several times that day, offering to fly in if they were needed. Harry and Laura planned to take off the month of August and fly out to be with them, instead. Summer school would be over soon, and they needed the vacation. Time away.

Time together.

"Do you think Denise's run-in with the car was really an accident?"

"Who knows?" Harry's voice was tired but had lost all the desperate intensity with which he'd been driven these past six weeks. "I'm sure we'll never know."

The women involved in the porn and prostitute ring probably weren't facing charges, but the temporary agency had closed its doors for the last time.

Jerking upright, all lethargy gone, Laura started as a knock sounded at the front door.

Harry rose slowly and went to see who was there.

Daniel Boyd followed him back to the living room, declining the seat Harry offered him.

"I just came by to...uh—" The older man's voice trailed off, his discomfort obvious.

"Come by anytime," Harry interjected, standing beside him, hands in his pockets.

"No, I…" Boyd looked from one to the other, raising his head as he did so. "I want to thank you both."

"Thank us?" Laura asked, sitting up on the edge of the couch. "You saved our lives."

Technically, Miller had done that. And the ultra-conservative cop would continue to work side by side with Daniel Boyd. With one major difference, Harry had told her. Daniel Boyd was going to be watching every move his partner made and if Miller ever gave so much as a hint of impropriety, Daniel would see his hide nailed to the wall. While the other cop had arranged Jefferson's release—and been responsible for ensuring that Harry's fingerprints were on the pistol, using prints he'd lifted from a cup Harry had drunk from at the station earlier that day—neither of those things could be proven. Daniel knew they were done on the orders of Bobby Donahue. But that couldn't be proven, either. And when Miller had actually been able to prevent a crime, when Laura Kendall's life had been in danger, he'd done his job. He'd shot Tony regardless of their shared ties to Donahue. They'd never get any charges against him to stick. And at least this way, Daniel could keep an eye on him.

Daniel Boyd loosened his tie.

"I just wanted you to know that I asked Jess to marry me tonight." He glanced at Harry. "What you went through, never giving up, forging ahead even when everyone believed you were—"

"Nuts," Harry finished, and Laura cringed, in spite

of the smile on her husband's face. It was going to take a lifetime to deal with the pain created by the past six weeks. But it would be a good lifetime. A great one.

"Anyway," Boyd was saying. "I've wasted too much of my life paying for a past I couldn't control. Afraid to allow a future because I couldn't control it, either. But you two have shown me the strength of the human spirit—and, well…"

He frowned, clearly in uncomfortable territory.

"So what did she say?" Laura asked quietly, tears in her eyes as she watched the man who'd always hold a special place in her heart struggle with his own.

He'd taken care of Harry for her. She owed him.

"She said *yes*."

"Harry?"

"Hmm?"

"Could you do something for me?"

Head turning on the sofa cushion, he looked her straight in the eye. "Sure, babe, what?"

"Make love to me?"

He didn't move. Didn't say a word.

"Please?"

"I…"

"Harry Kendall, make love to me, please." She sounded fierce—until the note of pleading entered her voice.

Her husband, as understanding as always, took pity on her and ever so gently rolled her underneath him on the couch.

She might change her mind. When he got right down

to it, she might freeze up. But if she did, they'd try again tomorrow night. And the night after that.

That was just how she and Harry were.

Epilogue

The baby took a long time coming. Eighteen hours and forty-three minutes. But when he finally presented himself, a squalling, wiry-haired seven-pound boy, his parents and a smiling godmother named Kelly acted as though they'd just seen God.

And maybe, in that dark-skinned boy with his mother's blue eyes, they had.

New York Times
bestselling author

HEATHER GRAHAM

THE SÉANCE

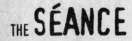

"An incredible storyteller."
—*Los Angeles Daily News*

A chill falls over Christina Hardy's housewarming party when talk turns to a recent murder that has all the hallmarks of the so-called Interstate Killer murders from fifteen years before. To lighten the mood, the guests drag out an old Ouija board for a little spooky fun…and to conjure the spirit of Beau Kidd, the chief suspect in the original case.

Kidd seeks Christina's help: The latest killing isn't a copycat crime, and he wants his name cleared. The Interstate Killer is still out there, and Christina's life is hanging in the balance between this world and the next.

MEET THE
DEADLY SEVEN

Seven titles from bestselling authors and new voices that will chill and terrorize you with their tales of murder, conspiracy and suspense.

JUNE

SEPTEMBER

JULY

JUNE

JULY

AUGUST

NOVEMBER

New York Times Bestselling Author

KATHLEEN EAGLE

**THE TERRIFIED EYES IN THE MIDDLE OF THE
HIGHWAY BELONGED TO A WOMAN—BATTERED,
BRUISED AND BARELY CONSCIOUS.**

Nick Red Shield swerved his pickup and empty horse trailer to
avoid her, but neither he nor the mysterious Lauren Davis could
avoid the collision of their lives....

Despite being more comfortable with horses than people, Nick's
drawn to the secretive runaway. But even in the safe haven of
his South Dakota ranch, the danger shadowing Lauren's life will
compel her to new acts of desperation to save her young son and
force Nick to confront demons bent on destroying them both.

RIDE A PAINTED PONY

"Kathleen Eagle is a national treasure."
—*New York Times* bestselling author
Susan Elizabeth Phillips

*Available the first week of
October 2007 wherever
paperbacks are sold!*

MIRA®

REQUEST YOUR
FREE BOOKS!

2 FREE NOVELS
FROM THE ROMANCE/SUSPENSE
COLLECTION PLUS 2 FREE GIFTS!

YES! Please send me 2 FREE novels from the Romance/Suspense Collection and my 2 FREE gifts. After receiving them, if I don't wish to receive any more books, I can return the shipping statement marked "cancel." If I don't cancel, I will receive 4 brand-new novels every month and be billed just $5.49 per book in the U.S., or $5.99 per book in Canada, plus 25¢ shipping and handling per book plus applicable taxes, if any*. That's a savings of at least 20% off the cover price! I understand that accepting the 2 free books and gifts places me under no obligation to buy anything. I can always return a shipment and cancel at any time. Even if I never buy another book from the Reader Service, the two free books and gifts are mine to keep forever.

185 MDN EF5Y   385 MDN EF6C

Name   (PLEASE PRINT)

Address   Apt. #

City   State/Prov.   Zip/Postal Code

Signature (if under 18, a parent or guardian must sign)

Mail to **The Reader Service:**
IN U.S.A.: P.O. Box 1867, Buffalo, NY 14240-1867
IN CANADA: P.O. Box 609, Fort Erie, Ontario L2A 5X3

Not valid to current subscribers to the Romance Collection,
the Suspense Collection or the Romance/Suspense Collection.

Want to try two free books from another line?
Call 1-800-873-8635 or visit www.morefreebooks.com.

* Terms and prices subject to change without notice. NY residents add applicable sales tax. Canadian residents will be charged applicable provincial taxes and GST. This offer is limited to one order per household. All orders subject to approval. Credit or debit balances in a customer's account(s) may be offset by any other outstanding balance owed by or to the customer. Please allow 4 to 6 weeks for delivery.

Your Privacy: Harlequin is committed to protecting your privacy. Our Privacy Policy is available online at www.eHarlequin.com or upon request from the Reader Service. From time to time we make our lists of customers available to reputable firms who may have a product or service of interest to you. If you would prefer we not share your name and address, please check here. ☐

TARA
TAYLOR
QUINN

32308 IN PLAIN SIGHT ___ $6.99 U.S. ___ $8.50 CAN.

(limited quantities available)

TOTAL AMOUNT	$ _____
POSTAGE & HANDLING	$ _____

($1.00 FOR 1 BOOK, 50¢ for each additional)

APPLICABLE TAXES*	$ _____
TOTAL PAYABLE	$ _____

(check or money order—please do not send cash)

To order, complete this form and send it, along with a check or money order for the total above, payable to MIRA Books, to: **In the U.S.:** 3010 Walden Avenue, P.O. Box 9077, Buffalo, NY 14269-9077; **In Canada:** P.O. Box 636, Fort Erie, Ontario, L2A 5X3.

Name: _____

Address: _____ City: _____

State/Prov.: _____ Zip/Postal Code: _____

Account Number (if applicable): _____

075 CSAS

*New York residents remit applicable sales taxes.
*Canadian residents remit applicable GST and provincial taxes.

MIRA®

www.MIRABooks.com

MTTQ1007BL